The fat sput's grin widened as he reached down, slowly, and parted the lapels of his threadbare travelling coat. Twin gun belts with pearl-handled heaters hung low across his hips.

"Enough formalities, duskie," he said. "I'm gonna ask you one last time: Are you Pike?"

Poole hawked and spat bloody sputum into the weeds.

"No."

Fedora swore, and he raised his hands, his fingers waggling as they traced comet-tails of lethal enchantment across the naked air. The skinny roughneck was a low-level jinxer. The worst he could do was hex a grown man to sleep. Poole inhaled as that cold lash of stunning magic lit a sunburst of pleasure in his guts.

Been too long.

Then he stooped, grasped the handle of the iron slop bucket he kept next to the front door, and heaved it across the yard. There came the satisfying crunch of bone as the bucket shattered Fedora's nose, followed directly by his high-pitched wail.

"Oowww! By dose...!"

The skinny roughneck spewed like a gutted hog while he hopped up and down amidst the shining shards of his thwarted hex.

"The bastard boke by dose!"

-From "Across The Black Plains."

13

A Collection of Horror
& Weird Fiction

by MICHAEL BOATMAN

Acknowledgments

"The Last American President" was first published in *Red Scream* magazine in 2005.

"Folds" was first published in the collection, *God Laughs When You Die...Mean Little Stories From The Wrong Side of the Tracks.* 2007

"The Flinch" first appeared in *Dark Delicacies III: Haunted.* 2009.

"Across the Black Plains" is original to this collection. 2015

"Manny Miracle is Alive and Well and Dying in the 29th Dimension!" was first published in *Lords of Justice,* 2008

"Our Kind of People," first appeared in *Dark Dreams II.* 2008

"Hadley Shimmerhorn: American Icon" first appeared in *Whispers in the Night.* 2007

"Born Again" was first published in Horrorworld's anthology, *Eulogies II: Tales From The Cellar.* 2013.

"Jimmy Sticks and the Outlaw Critter of Doom" was originally published in *Sick Things: An Anthology of Extreme Creature Horror.* 2010

"The Greenhouse" first appeared at Horrorworld's website. 2009.

"Christmastime in Zombietown" is original to this volume. 2016.

"Survivor: Monster Island 2025" first appeared in the Australian anthology, *DAIKAJU 2: Revenge of the Giant Monsters.* 2007.

"A Father's Work" first appeared in *Weird Tales #347.* 2007

CONTENTS

THE FLINCH

Sonny Troubadour was waiting to cash what passed for his paycheck when Scrape Rifkin's Cadillac pounded up to the curb and disgorged three hundred pounds of human sewage.

Sonny's guts convulsed as he watched the rest of his day slide down the toilet.

Just what I goddamn need, he thought.

Sonny pocketed his check and cracked his knuckles.

The chronically discouraged patrons of the WINDY CITY CASH-RITE CURRENCY EXCHANGE dropped to the floor as Norman Morris, AKA *Nomo*, and L'Dondrell Witherspoon, AKA *O-gazm*, burst into their midst waving firearms and bad intentions.

"That's right," Nomo said. "I want every one of you ugly bastards to lick this dirty-ass linoleum. Keep your asses horizontal and I won't have to shoot nobody today."

Sonny remained vertical. Nomo noticed.

"You got a problem with yo knees, motherfucker?"

Sonny shrugged. "Knees are fine," he said. "Just not goin' down today."

Nomo's brow crinkled. "You ain't *what?*" he said.

"What did he say?" O-gazm said.

"Big man say he ain't gon' *eat* no linoleum today," Nomo said.

O-gazm gaped.

"Watch the heifer," Nomo said, pointing to the manager, a big black blonde who peered out from behind her bulletproof plastic window. "If she moves… kill somebody."

Nomo pointed his Sig Sauer 9mm at Sonny's forehead.

"Look like we got us a bad man here," he said.

Sonny stared down the barrel of Nomo's gun.

No kind'a life for a man anyhow, he thought.

"He don't look so bad," O-gazm said.

Nomo's gold teeth bounced pellets of ghetto sunlight off Sonny's retinas. Notorious for spending other people's money on his smile, Nomo sported the kind of dental retrofit that makes racist South African gold exporters sing "God Bless America."

"Who you supposed to be?" he said. "Black Superman?"

"No," Sonny said. "But if you don't shoot me in the next ten seconds I'm gonna take that gun and whip your ass with it."

"Lord have mercy," the manager moaned.

Nomo shook his head as if he wasn't sure he'd heard right. His gaze flicked over Sonny's shoulder to where The Scrape's SUV sat rumbling at the curb.

"Five seconds," Sonny said.

"I'm gonna—" Nomo stuttered. The tip of his tongue poked out of the corner of his mouth, moistened his lips and darted back into its golden cave. "I'm gonna—"

Then Sonny rushed him.

Nomo fired high and wide over Sonny's left shoulder, blasting a hole through the front window and setting off the burglar alarm. Then Sonny bitch-slapped the 9mm out of his hand.

"Hey! Hey, man—" Nomo said.

And that was *all* he said, because his mouth was abruptly filled with Sonny's fist.

"Yo! Yo! Yo!" O-gazm said.

Sonny grabbed Nomo by the collar and swung him around in a wide, staggering circle. The barrel of O-gazm's Saturday night special jerked back and forth.

"Stand still, goddammit!" he said.

Sonny wound up like an Olympic shotputter and launched Nomo across the room. Nomo slammed into O-gazm and they both went down in a flurry of flailing limbs.

Sonny bent and picked up Nomo's gun.

Sensing the ass-mangling trucking their way, the would-be bandits rose to the challenge, each according to his gifts: Nomo assumed a classic "Crane style" kung fu pose while O-gazm pissed his pants. Fifteen seconds later they resembled a half-assed reproduction of a lesser-known Picasso pencil sketch.

Sonny hauled the brigands outside and speed-plowed his right foot, size 16 ½, up their backsides. Nomo and O-gazm hit the Cadillac and crumpled, having been literally kicked to the curb. A second later, the street-side back door opened and The Scrape stepped out.

"Jesus," Sonny said. "You look like shit."

The Scrape looked—*squeezed*—like a half-eaten Florida grapefruit with its innards scooped out, leaving behind an empty bit of skin and a whiff of rotten produce.

I'm looking at the rind, Sonny thought. *Man's been sucked dry.*

Looking at The Scrape made Sonny's head hurt.

The Scrape squinted up at the sun like a groundhog that was shaky on the terms of its contract. Then he pulled a pair of designer shades out of the pocket of his imitation tiger-skin jacket.

"Fuck you," he said. "You look like you could use some scratch, brah. You want a job?"

Sonny scowled. But then he remembered the daily spine-grind that was his post office gig, surrounded by gibbering *sistahs* who treated him like an adopted teddy bear one minute and a complete chowderhead the next, all under the watchful eye of his supervisor, *Bobbi with an I.*

Bobbi with an I was a Jamaican ballet instructor moonlighting with the USPS until Baryshnikov died. The day before, he'd invited Sonny up to his place in Boy's Town for "cocktails and career counseling." Sonny was beginning to have serious questions about Bobbi with an I.

Finally, Sonny remembered the disconnect notices piling up in his kitchen trash bin. His car, a brown Ford Fiesta with a death wish, was squatting in an impound lot on Randolph Street, banked for a D.U.I. he'd picked up a week earlier.

"Yeah," Sonny said.

"What do you need?"

By the time he was fifteen, Tommy "The Scrape" Rifkin had amassed a small fortune selling black market ordinance. By his twenty-first birthday, he'd taken over the local crack/ecstasy/crystal meth trade, all the while managing to evade select representatives of Chicago's Finest.

This talent for skullduggery—plus an obsession with all things NASCAR that brought new meaning to the word *autoerotic*—had secured Rifkin's induction into the South Chicago White Trash Hall of Fame.

The Scrape's nasal whine complimented his lair: half trailer park chic, half ghetto fabulous. A black leather La-Z-boy sat between a framed poster of Malcolm X and a life-sized stand-up of Dale Earnhardt, Jr.

"I need you to find my girl and bring her back," Rifkin said. "It's worth five large if you bring her back."

Rifkin swiped at his forehead with a paper towel while Sonny picked his jaw up off the table.

Five large, he thought, trying not to drool.

"Yo," Rifkin said. "You was almost the champ, right?"

Sonny tensed: People still recognized him three or four times a day and it chapped his ass.

"Yeah," Rifkin said. "I saw your style back at the *Cash-Right*. You was a *contender*, bro. Don King called your right cross '...an extinction-level cosmic smackdown from the Devil Hisself.' "

"That was a long time ago," Sonny said.

"Bro, I remember the Champ chewin' on your ear like it was yesterday," Rifkin said. "Vegas oh-six, right? Dude, that shit was disgusting."

"Five years ago," Sonny said. "Past is past."

It was during Sonny's last shot at the Title that the reigning champ, a semi-human piledriver named Baron Flake, laid him low with a left-handed uppercut to the occipital that detached his right cornea. Sonny woke up to find Flake gnawing on his left earlobe, his demolished eye spitting blood, while faerie lights popped and fizzled along his optic nerve like a paparazzi assault from Hell.

The hospital stay sucked and blew at the same time.

Afterward, Sonny attempted a comeback, but every time he heard the bell clang he would rush to the side and puke over the ropes. Finally, Sonny's trainer, the Inimitable Sharkey Washington, took him aside.

"My three-legged Pekinese got a better shot at a Title bout than you do, boy," Sharkey growled. "It's over."

Then Sharkey, who was the closest thing to a father that Sonny would ever know, wiped his protégé's second-hand breakfast off his polyester warm-ups and dropped dead from congestive heart failure.

"Ahem," Rifkin said. "Yo, Troub, you with me?"

Sonny shoved his memories aside to consider the matter at hand: Rifkin looked wobbly as Commander-in-Thief of this shitty little outfit. His focus fluttered around the room like a fruit bat on steroids.

Why won't he look me in the eye? Sonny wondered.

Rifkin noticed Sonny noticing him and—*flinched.* Nomo and O-gazm grumbled. Post pistol-whipping, the brigands looked surlier than ever.

Better close the deal now, Son—Sharkey advised from the Great Beyond—*'fore somebody separates this fool from his pointy little head.*

But Sonny was curious.

"Why can't you go and get her yourself?" he said.

"Mooother—*fucker,*" Nomo hissed.

O-gazm spat on the floor.

Rifkin *flinched.*

"Yo, Black Superman, you ask a lotta dumb questions," Nomo said.

"Sit your stupid ass down, Mo," Rifkin said.

Nomo backed down. The Scrape peeled another paper towel and went to town on himself. Sonny winced

Sounds like sandpaper scratchin' at dead wood.

"You wouldn't understand," Rifkin said.

Sonny agreed and decided that he was officially ready to get away from these people.

"Where was the last place you saw her?" he said.

Rifkin shook his head. "She stole something from me," he insisted. "Two weeks ago. I need it back."

"She s'posed to be dancin' around the titty bars in the Loop," Nomo said.

"What's her name?" Sonny said.

"Her name is Harmony," Rifkin whispered.

"Harmony Tremontane."

Twenty-seven hours later, Sonny was standing in the main room of The Shakedown, an upscale gentleman's club off Rush Street, waiting for another hardbody to take her clothes off and trying not to puke.

Innards were never the same after that last bout, Sonny thought. His stomach rumbled in agreement. These days, a night spent partying with a pint of Jim Beam always preceded a morning spent clutching the ky-bowl with one hand and a bottle of Maalox with the other.

Seems you just about livin' on J.B. and Maalox, Son.

Sonny shook Sharkey's voice out of his head, but he was staring at the bar and his mouth was watering.

Focus, he reminded himself.

The dancer on stage swept up her cash and ran off to a smattering of polite applause.

"This next young lady joins us after a whirlwind national tour of *O, Calcutta!*" the announcer said.

You gotta be kiddin', Sonny thought.

"Men, lets get it up for—Harmony Tremontane!"

Sonny's focus snapped toward the stage.

The music started. The red curtain parted. Sonny stopped breathing.

She was more than beautiful.

Earlier, Nomo told him that The Scrape's woman was a slag; skinny, with faux-luscious breasts that looked ludicrous on her shriveled frame. But *this* Harmony Tremontane was tall, with lithe brown legs that swept her across the stage with the muscular grace of a stalking panther. Her skin shone, caramel infused with powdered diamonds. Her thighs were full but taut, her face oval shaped, with shadow-limned eyes that flashed the color of heated honey. A bristling red-gold Afro framed her face like a halo made of sunfire. Her teeth were straight, so white they were nearly luminous in the darkened night club, her lips generous and painted a glistening candy-apple red. Any of these features was enough to stir Sonny's procreative juices, but it was Harmony's feet that turned the flame on 'High' and melted Sonny's hotplate.

Sonny liked nice feet. He'd kicked Vegas showgirls out of his bed for the barest hint of hammertoe. He'd dumped goddesses for the crime of a bunion. For Sonny, a woman's feet revealed critical elements of character. On this point, Sharkey had vociferously agreed.

Woman with a good foot means she got a good heart, Son, he'd often said. Sharkey had subsequently married several woman-shaped vipers with perfectly maintained feet. During one particularly eventful Thanksgiving dinner, Sharkey's third wife had actually attempted to stab Sonny with an electric meat thermometer. Ever the optimist (at least when it came to love) Sonny held hope, deep in his heart of hearts, that things might turn out differently for him.

Harmony's feet gave Sonny reason to keep hope alive.

They were spare and well arched, firmly ankled and buoyed up by prominent Achilles tendons, exactly the way Sonny liked. Her toes were straight, democratic, and free of deformation, her toenails christened the same heart-stopping crimson as her lips. Each perfect foot was ensconced within clear plastic-heeled "Come Fuck Me" pumps specifically designed to overflex the muscles of the calves and buttocks in a manner of which the Marquis de Sade would have approved.

"I'll be—*damned*," Sonny whispered.

If anyone could steal something from a freak like The Scrape and survive, it would be a girl with feet like those.

"Yep, that's her," one of the bouncers volunteered. "Harmony Tree-mon-*taaane*."

The bouncer was wearing a black t-shirt with the words "Does Not Play Well With Others" emblazoned across his seventy-five-inch chest.

"I heard she did pornos out in LA LA Land before she blew into Chi," the bouncer chortled. "Very talented. You feel me, Troub?"

The bouncer held up a hand in a "high-five" gesture, but Sonny was in no mood for camaraderie. Besides, he advocated rough disemboweling for anyone over thirty who didn't have time to say "Chicago."

"But ain't nobody gettin' within a mile of that tonight," the bouncer said. "She's with Block Tokomatsu."

High-Five pointed a sausage-thick finger toward a table near the stage. Seated at the table were five of the biggest human beings Sonny had ever seen.

Block Tokomatsu was a half-Japanese, half-Samoan gangster up from Milwaukee. He'd done a stretch out at Marion State Correctional on a murder-two conviction, plus stints here and there for all manner of anti-social activities.

Block Tokomatsu regularly beat the melanin out of *scores* of brothers for light exercise. He doled out ass-whippings the way the pope dispensed benedictions at Christmas: He was the Supreme Pontiff of the Righteous Beatdown.

"Hey, Black Superman."

Sonny turned to find Nomo lingering like a bad fart.

"That's the homely bitch right there."

Homely? Sonny thought. *Who's he looking at?*

"Hold on a minute," Sonny cautioned. But Nomo whipped out his wireless and pushed *Send*.

"Yo, she's here," he said. "At The Shakedown."

Nomo nodded—twice, and disconnected. He glared at Sonny with reefer-enriched rancor.

"Scrape say you better do yo' job," he said. "Else I'm gonna handle you like I *should 'a* handled you back at the currency S'change."

Do it, the Troub urged in Sonny's mind. *Just reach over and pop that neck like a chicken bone.*

Sonny savored the fantasy for a moment and decided it wasn't worth the shit-storm that would follow. He needed to be done with this crew like nobody's business, but there was still the matter of five-large plus expenses to collect before he could call it a night.

"I'll get her," he rumbled, certain that this was all going to end badly. "And the word is *Ex*-change you idiot."

While Nomo tried to figure out if he'd just been insulted, Sonny advanced toward the black leather hillock that was Block Tokomatsu's back.

Let's do this.

James Brown was extolling the virtues of being both Black *and* Proud via the state-of-the art sound system. The DJ worked two turntables with one hand and a hard drive with the other, a digital rain dance that filled The Shakedown with hip-hop thunder. Relentless rhythm jiggled Sonny's organs as he sat at a table behind Tokomatsu and his cronies.

How the hell am I supposed to get her past all those big Samoans? he wondered.

A bevy of the prettiest dancers adorned the Block's table, laughing too loudly, casting fox-eyed glances in the Block's direction even while they flirted with his lieutenants.

Tokomatsu looked oblivious to the cold war of sexual innuendo being waged around him. He tracked Harmony's every move, his eyes flickering between her and the main entrance the way a nervous pimp guards a hooker with her original teeth.

What have you gotten yourself into? Sonny thought.

Harmony finished her number—six feet up the "fireman's pole," her legs spread wide, flawless toes peaked in an exquisite dancer's "point." She slid to the floor, gathered up her cash, and vanished behind the red curtain. The lights changed and the mostly male audience erupted into a barnyard cacophony.

A flash of silver drew Sonny's focus to the waistline of one of the Block's lieutenants. A quick glance around the Samoans' table confirmed the sinking sensation in his gut.

They're all strapped, he thought.

Brute force was not going to get him around the Block.

Gotta think, boy, Sharkey might have said. *Can't punch your way outta every fight.*

Sonny gritted his teeth and closed his eyes.

Sixty seconds later he borrowed a pen from a passing loser, scribbled a note on a cocktail napkin, and handed it to one of the uglier waitresses along with a twenty for her troubles.

Two songs died before the waitress returned and Sonny learned that his night was about to get a lot more complicated:

Dear Shithead,

Do the world a favor. Blow your goddamn head off.
H.

Gotta do this the hard way then, Sonny thought.
You don't "gotta" do anything, Sharkey said.
Sonny waved the ugly waitress over again.
"J.B. *straight,*" he said. "Make it a double."
The waitress nodded and waddled off.

A few minutes later, Sonny was staring at a tall glass of the straight medicine, and marveling at how the overhead disco lights made the ice cubes twinkle.

"Merry Christmas," he said, even though it was July.

He emptied the glass and gestured a cute little Korean import over.

"Buy me a drink?" the stripper said.

"Private dance," Sonny rumbled. He got to his feet and the stripper's eyes brightened.

"Ooohh, you're a *big* one," she said. Then she smiled, straightened Sonny's collar, and led him into the back room.

Red light and naked women were everywhere.

In the corner to Sonny's right, two strippers were dancing for a man and his date, a tall redhead with no lips.

"Like redheads," Sonny said. Meanwhile, the animal crouching behind his eyes stood up and tugged on the bars of its cage.

Wish Flake was here now, he thought, recalling the human piledriver and his unholy uppercut: the red thunderflash that blew out the last candle on Sonny Troubadour's cake.

Feed him his own damn ear he was here right now.

Sonny sat on a red velvet chair and the stripper started to gyrate. "My name's Douglas," she said. "Twenty dollars for one dance?"

"Okay," Sonny said.

He reached into his wallet and gave over.

Then Harmony glided past his cubicle.

Sonny shoved Douglas out of the way and stood up.

"Hey, Hercules, no rough stuff!" she chirped.

"Sorry, Doug," Sonny said over his shoulder.

He crossed the room in four strides and headed Harmony off at the bathroom door. She almost bumped into him before she looked up.

"Well?" she said.

Sonny grabbed her around the waist, swung her over his left shoulder, turned, and froze. About two dozen fake fornicators frolicked between him and the door.

"Move!" Sonny bellowed.

Strippers and suckers scattered like roaches.

One girl screamed, then they all chimed in. High-Five, the bouncer from the front, appeared and blocked Sonny's path.

"Freeze, asshole!"

Sonny uncorked a right cross that lifted High-Five out of his shoes and put his lights out before his ass hit the cheesy red carpet.

The Troub was open for business.

Move, he commanded. *Move-move-move.*

Sonny kicked the exit door open and lunged into the alley. The woman hanging over his shoulder remained silent. She didn't struggle or scream.

Too scared, Sonny thought.

When Nomo saw Sonny chugging toward him, he dropped his cigarette and jumped into the driver's seat. Sonny threw open the back door, tossed Harmony inside, and dove in on top of her.

"Goddamn, Black Superman!" Nomo said. "You take yo' work serious!"

A hail of bullets peppered the right side of the Cadillac. Sonny whirled to see the Block and his lieutenants stampeding toward them, firing as they advanced.

"Drive!" he shouted.

Nomo jammed the accelerator and laid a smoking trail of burnt rubber across Rush Street. He blew through a red light and headed toward State Street.

"You're goin' the wrong way!" Sonny said. "Rifkin's place is on the west side!"

"Rifkin don't want Tokomatsu heatin' up his territory," Nomo shouted. "I'm takin' her to another spot!"

Sonny squinted as the headlight glare from the Block's black Mercedes shrank his pupils. Adrenaline burned the alcohol haze from the surface of his brain. The fighter's focus that once helped the Troub inflict brain damage on dozens of opponents cleared Sonny's head in an atavistic attempt to save his ass.

"You better drive like your nuts are on fire!" he said.

"Don't worry about my drivin'," Nomo hollered. "You just keep that skank in check!"

But Harmony was staring at the tenements whipping by, seemingly unfazed by her kidnapping. Nomo wrestled the Cadillac down the entrance ramp to a fuck-you chorus of blaring horns. While panicked drivers swerved and collided as Nomo shoehorned the Cadillac onto the expressway, Harmony studied her nails.

Nomo thumbed a red switch on the steering wheel and ignited the illegal afterburners in the Cadillac's engine. The ninety-second "burn" that followed punched Sonny into the leather seat cushions.

Nomo left the black Mercedes on the far side of a snarl of crushed metal and bleeding citizens dwindling in the distance.

"He's wrong, you know," Harmony said.

"What?" Sonny said.

Harmony smirked. "What's mine is mine."

Sonny winced. He shook his head at the bloom of pain that blossomed behind his right eye.

"You his woman?" Sonny said, trying to distract himself.

Harmony sucked her teeth. "I'm nobody's woman, fool."

"You ripped him off."

The girl's eyes flashed.

"I don't steal."

Sonny shrugged. One thing was certain: Once The Scrape had Harmony back in his camp, he'd never let her leave with her skeleton on the inside of her skin.

Harmony shifted, moved closer—Sonny was uncomfortably aware of the heat from her body—and *something*, a squiggle of quicksilver shimmered in the woman's eyes.

"*What's—*" Sonny said. "*Your eyes—*"

"You want some of this, fighter?" Harmony whispered.

She reached up behind her neck and undid the straps of her bikini top.

"Hey," Sonny said. "Hey now—"

Harmony let the top fall.

"You're the same as Rifkin," she said.

She'd been pretty a moment earlier, but the woman who faced Sonny now might have danced for kings instead of kingpins and dope slingers.

"Your eyes," Sonny said. "What are you doing?"

Harmony's smile became a scimitar gleaming in the dark. She slipped her right foot out of its plastic sheath and thrust it into Sonny's crotch.

Sudden, murderous desire ambushed Sonny's common sense. Enflamed, stupid with need, he reached for the stripper.

"What the hell are y'all *doin'* back there?" Nomo said.

Sonny's hand halted a hair's breadth from the stripper's thigh. Then something inside him flipped over and he puked onto the floor of The Scrape's Cadillac.

"Heeeyyy!" Nomo screeched. "Hey, motherfuckahhhh!"

"What—?" Sonny gasped. "What happened?"

The air inside the Cadillac was suddenly too dry to breathe. Sonny's vision doubled, then trebled: Harmony splitting into triplets as he watched.

Nomo screeched, "Rifkin gon' have my ass behind this, you big, dumb bastard!"

"Hush," Harmony snapped.

And something *happened*. Nomo shut his mouth and turned around. His head slumped forward onto the steering wheel.

"Hey," Sonny moaned, guts burning. "What's goin' on?"

Harmony was staring at him as if he'd just appeared out of thin air. Her clothing was completely intact.

"I—I—" Sonny stuttered.

He looked out of the window.

They were sitting in an abandoned grocery store parking lot, but Sonny didn't remember leaving the highway.

"Lady, who the hell are you?" he said.

Harmony's smile slashed a bright afterimage across Sonny's vision, like lightning gouging the spectral flesh of midnight skies.

"That's easy, Andrew," she said, though he'd never told her his real name. "I'm your dream date."

It was then that Sonny noticed two small crystal vials dangling from a leather string tied around the woman's neck. She fingered the vials as she spoke.

"Why don't we go someplace quiet?" she said. "I can show you what you've been dreaming about."

Sonny swallowed, cleared his throat.

"Skank," he said. "Parasite."

"Oh?"

"You're Rifkin's whore," Sonny snarled. "Or Tokomatsu's. Either way, from what I can see, you ain't worth the trouble."

Harmony laughed. The vials around her neck chimed. To Sonny, the chiming sounded like screams.

"We're not so different, you and me," she said.

Sonny shook his head, tried to clear his vision. Nomo slumped across the front seat like a marionette with its strings cut. The black walls of the Cadillac pressed closer, stifling Sonny in leather and chrome.

"You don't know anything about me," he said.

"I know you smell more like a distillery than a man," Harmony said. "But it's the smell of blood that made you what you are."

"Shut up."

"I know you sometimes wish that boy from New York had killed you dead, rather than made you into the thing I'm lookin' at now."

Harmony's fingers stroked crystalline peals of anguish from the vials, each note an accompaniment to the agony in Sonny's gut.

"You drink to kill the *despair*, but you can't," she said. "You was bigger than this. Once upon a time you held power in your hand, power that set you above other men. Then the world moved on, left you bleedin' in that ring, half-blind, too old and too stupid to get up."

"Stop," Sonny said.

Harmony leaned over and placed her left index finger on Sonny's knee. "I can change all that," she said. "I can take you to a place where the dead dance in fields of blood-red violets. Where the air is black with power and the earth is seeded with ashes."

Sonny shook his head. But he was standing at ringside and watching himself bleed.

"I— I don't want to *see*," he whispered.

"Oh, but you *do*," Harmony said. "I know *that*, too."

Sonny hovered, a dark Icarus, above the ghost world in her eyes. Then his wings took fire and he fell, burning, into its swirling atmosphere, captured by the gravity of her gaze.

"Let's go."

He had nothing left to lose.

"Don't touch me."

They were lying on Sonny's sofa in the living room of his one-bedroom apartment. The stripper stretched her leg over his chest and straddled him.

Some instinct warned him at the last instant and he tried to sit up. The woman set her hand at his throat and Sonny sensed the power to gut him tensed in her fingers.

"I *know* what you want," she said. "The smell of your dreams makes me want to puke.""

Harmony reached back and undid his belt. She yanked at his pants as she held him down. Sonny bucked, trying to throw her off. Her nails cut deeper into the flesh of his throat.

"We *are* alike," she breathed. "I'm a survivor, too."

The pupil of her right eye bulged outward, eclipsed both iris and sclera. In their place, a black orb shone wetly. There was a sound like the ripping of muscle, and a shock of red hair burst from her scalp.

Harmony clamped her fingers over Sonny's mouth, tore his flesh and mashed his scream against his teeth.

"Be still," she moaned.

The taste of blood filled Sonny with manic strength. He freed his right arm and struck her across the chin. Harmony brushed aside his attack, held him down as her face ran like heated wax.

"You want to be with me, fightin' man?" the thing whispered. "I've been alone for soooo long."

A white tongue the length of a man's arm slid out of Harmony's mouth and dove between Sonny's lips, filling his mouth with the taste of ashes. He gagged, grasped the thick stalk and bit down, trying to sever it.

Then something exploded in the hallway.

A high, bubbling scream pierced the red clouds in Sonny's mind. Pain beat back the shadows in his head. Harmony withdrew the tongue and spun toward the sound as the front door exploded off its hinges.

Nomo staggered through the doorway, clutching at the red hole in the center of his chest. Then he fell behind the sofa and The Scrape stepped into the room.

"Dude," Rifkin growled. "I'm gonna fuck… you… *up*."

Indeed, the shotgun he carried—a twelve-gauge Mossberg bullpup with a twenty-inch barrel and walnut pistol grip—testified to the whole congregation that Mama Rifkin's baby boy had come to set things straight.

But playing spine-tag with Teflon-jacketed armor-piercing mini-missiles was not on Harmony's "to do" list that night. She fixed Rifkin with a glare that would have given Siberia terminal freezer burn.

"Put that down, Thomas," she said.

Rifkin blinked, stumbled backward, and said, "Daahh."

Sonny noted the scraps of white powder clinging like fresh leprosy to Rifkin's sad mustache; The Scrape had apparently snorted enough coke to make Condoleezza Rice sing "The Dreidel Song" at a Nation of Islam celebrity fundraiser.

"Shut up!" Rifkin howled. He lifted the bullpup. "Me and Coco Chanel are callin' the shots, y'hear?"

Whatever magical influence Harmony normally wielded was gone, cock-blocked by redneck rage and third-rate Peruvian go-go powder.

"Baby," Rifkin moaned. "I'm gonna kill him, then myself, then you, then *myself* if you don't get off him right now."

Harmony got up, leaving Sonny exposed with a German tank ventilator aimed at his sack.

Sonny got to his feet.

"Yeah, punk," Rifkin crowed. "Ain't no dodgin' *this* smackdown. You feel me?"

Sonny nodded. "I feel you."

Rifkin smirked. "Damn right, you washed-up mother—"

Sonny charged.

At the same time, Harmony grabbed the bullpup by the barrel. Coco Chanel blasted a basketball-sized hole through the ceiling and scared the holy hell out of Mrs. Gupta-Sung-Jefferson, Sonny's landlady, who lived upstairs.

Then Harmony grew a third arm.

Sonny braked hard as the stripper clutched the shotgun with her right hand, Rifkin's throat in her left, and Rifkin's *balls* with a third hand that was attached to the arm that extended out of her lower back.

Sonny's headache reached down, pulled his lower lip over his head, and spiked it to the nape of his neck. His bad eye was transmitting a sight that a man fighting to stay sober should miss. Something like a cross between Beyoncé Knowles and Kali the Hindu Goddess of Destruction was giving Rifkin the nightmare "reach-around" of all time.

Sonny's left eye, however, still perceived Harmony as she'd been back at the Shakedown: somehow, luscious dancer and tongue-raping grief freak were one and the same.

"Please—give it back," Rifkin whispered.

Harmony dug her nails into Rifkin's throat. In seconds, stripper and slinger were covered in blood.

Harmony's tongue lashed out and double-wrapped itself around Rifkin's throat. Rifkin turned purple and Coco Chanel clattered to the floor. Harmony hoisted The Scrape over her head and body-slammed him hard enough to crack Sonny's synthetic wood floor. Then she shook him until his mullet sprinkled white flakes like a snowstorm over Minneapolis.

An evil sound issued from Rifkin's backbone—

Crack!

—and his foot shot out and kicked the shotgun across the room. Coco Chanel slid to a halt at Sonny's feet.

Harmony dropped Rifkin while Sonny retrieved the shotgun. And before even *he* understood that he'd made his choice, she pounced, her face melting as she came for him.

Coco Chanel coughed and punched Harmony in the throat. The stripper struck the far wall and stuck. Sonny had five seconds to realize that he had not been dismembered, then Harmony slithered up the wall and disappeared in a patch of shadow near the ceiling.

Then the lights went out.

"Shit—"Sonny hissed.

He spun, trying to separate the woman from the shadows over his head. Then, *sound*, a sensation like a million fire ants strip-mining his bones, filled the air. Something in Sonny's head ripped open and blood filled his bad eye. He screamed and dropped Coco Chanel.

The hag-thing dropped out of the shadows and landed on his back. Sonny windmilled around the room, smashed into the walls, knocked over furniture trying to dislodge her.

"One way or another, fightin' man," she hissed.

Pain detonated against Sonny's spine as her tongue pierced the skin at the base of his skull. The tongue burrowed, widening the tear in his flesh.

Gotta stop her, boy, Sharkey shouted. Sonny felt the tongue shudder, a sandpaper rasp against his backbone.

"Stop her, booyyy," Harmony said.

Sonny dropped to his knees.

The shotgun lay a few feet away. Sonny reached for it and fell on his face. The thing on his back plunged its proboscis deeper.

Sleep, the Troub thought. *Be nice to just lay down.*

Don't be stupid, Sharkey argued. *You lay down now and whatever's left to get up, it won't be Sonny Troubadour.*

And because he knew Sharkey was right, Sonny stretched out his right hand, his joints creaking, and reached for the gun. Something in his shoulder popped and gave way: Sonny stretched further, touched cool wood… and snagged it.

He rammed Coco Chanel up and over his left shoulder, felt the barrel penetrate soft flesh a second before he pulled the trigger. Then Coco Chanel spat thunder and hag-slapped Harmony across the room.

Sonny leapt to his feet, his breath a dry heave, his bad eye sifting the darkness. Harmony lay against the doorjamb, her face a ruin. Her stiletto heels gouged twin ruts into the floor as she pushed herself halfway up. Then she uttered a thick grunt and the back of her head dragged a red arc down the wall.

The lights flickered back on a second later.

Sonny touched the wound on the back of his neck and winced. Then he went to check on Rifkin.

Sonny had seen *dead* before but The Scrape made Latin look lively. He looked like a man who'd slipped in a puddle of discount tomato paste, suffered a heart attack and shat himself before dying from terminal embarrassment.

Sonny watched the last of his five-thousand-plus expenses soak into the floorboards of the apartment he could no longer afford.

Then The Scrape sat up.

"That hurt, you bitch!" he hollered.

Sonny joined in. The two of them screamed like Billy Graham and Charlton Heston at a prison gangbang.

"Dude, you're freakin' me out!" Rifkin said.

Sonny shut his trap.

"Vials," Rifkin said.

"Huh?" Sonny said back.

"Crystal vials. You didn't blow them up, did you?"

Harmony slumped against the wall like a blow-up doll whose glory days had come and gone. A single vial lay nestled in the petrified valley of counterfeit cleavage rapidly deflating beneath her bloody halter top.

Sonny heard that tiny scream again, clearer this time.

It was coming from *inside* the vial.

"Well?" The Scrape said. "What's the deal, bro?"

"One of 'em is gone," Sonny said. "The other one is—"

"Shit! Shit! SHIT!"

Rifkin banged his fist on the floor, each expletive provoking a mushy *pop* from his backbone. Then his spine gave way with a soggy lurch and his torso compacted a full two inches: Rifkin folded like an all-black revival of *Oklahoma* and slammed face-first into the floor.

Sonny's guts did the Hokey Pokey and he let fly for the second time that night.

Outside, car doors slammed. The police probably wouldn't bother to show up till sometime in the early A.G. (After Gentrification) however, so no one was worried about *them* getting in the way.

Rifkin pushed himself up onto his knuckles and glared at Sonny from a vast puddle of blood.

"Bring that shit over here, goddammit," he snapped.

Then one of his hands slipped and he fell on his face.

Sonny heard the *crack* but he didn't believe it.

"Owww!" Rifkin screamed. "By dose!"

Sonny wiped his chin and zipped up his pants.

"You're pathetic," he said.

"Hey!" The Scrape shouted at the floor. "I'm dot bayin' you to backdalk me, dickwad!"

"Keep your damn money, man," Sonny said. "Just pull yourself together and get out."

Rifkin snorted. "Hey, genius, I'd love to, but she broke by friggin' deck and I can'd ged up!"

"Sounds like a personal problem," Sonny said.

Rifkin screamed. The light bulb over Sonny's head flickered.

"Alright *look*," The Scrape snapped. "There's half a million dollars *cash* in by trunk. Gib me the vial and it's yours."

Sonny's brow furrowed. "What's in it?"

Rifkin rolled over and spoke to the ceiling.

"Harmony feeds off the real part of a man, the part that *means* you. She keeps it stashed in those vials."

Some kinda fucked-up testosterone vampire, Sharkey grunted. *Like my first wife.*

"She told me that without my essence I'm doomed to wander the Earth forever," Rifkin said. "Like the living dead, or the Wandering Hebrew or some shit like that."

Man gave you a second chance, Son, Sharkey opined.

Sonny cursed the day he let Sharkey lift him out of the gutter. Then he tossed the vial to Rifkin, who thumbed it open and inhaled its contents.

"Mmmm," he murmured. "Guess one's as good as another. Right, Troub?"

A second later, however, Rifkin shot to his feet, clutched his head, and painted the air with a fusillade of the finest Japanese profanity since Emperor Hirohito woke up on that fateful morning in 1945 and read in the *Tokyo Sun* that his monthly golf trip to Hiroshima had been postponed.

The Scrape made a sound like a yellow cat being strategically peeled. Then Mrs. Rifkin's gift to the dope trade fell dead to the floor.

Something flitted at the edge of Sonny's vision. He whirled, Coco Chanel at the ready.

Harmony's body was gone. The rump-shaker from Planet X had returned to the Great Beyond.

When Sonny stepped onto the sidewalk he was greeted by one half of the Samoan National Sumo Wrestling Team. Tokomatsu's men were pointing enough firepower to repel the French Navy at Sonny's Afro.

Tokomatsu stepped forward, his left hand raised.

"She dead?" he said.

"Don't know," Sonny said.

"Mmmmph," Tokomatsu grunted. "Rifkin dead?"

"Yup," Sonny said.

The Samoans observed a moment of silence. Then Tokomatsu hawked and spat on the sidewalk.

"Well, that's *somethin',*" he said.

Sonny noted that Tokomatsu avoided making eye contact. Testing a theory, he took a small step forward. Tokomatsu winced and took a step back.

The Samoans rumbled, and Sonny recalled that Rifkin had imbibed Tokomatsu's essence before he kicked.

"You *saw*," Tokomatsu whispered. "You saw what she was."

Sonny shook his head. "I don't know."

Tokomatsu considered his shoes. Then he shrugged.

"Yeah, brah," he said. "I don't think nobody knows."

And Sonny recognized the new thing in Tokomatsu's voice. It was the same thing he'd heard in Rifkin's voice the day before: the *Flinch*.

Tokomatsu glanced over his shoulder.

"I could kill you now," he said. "You know?"

Sonny nodded. "I know."

Tokomatsu nodded. "I could use an intrepid brother such as yourself on my team," he said. "You want a job?"

Sonny took a deep breath.

"Thanks," he said. "But I got some schemes working."

Tokomatsu shrugged. "Alright then."

The two men shook hands. Sonny even managed a smile.

"Alright then," he said.

But his gaze never wavered from the back of Rifkin's BMW, still idling at the curb.

HADLEY SHIMMERHORN: AMERICAN ICON

Nobody inside Deke's Valhalla Stop-n-Drop felt much like eating. They were too busy watching the walking dead people on the flat-screen television over the counter.

Hadley Shimmerhorn, who was nineteen years old and pretty enough to dream, was staring at the *Dukes of Hazard* clock over the door and quietly mouthing the words to "Ain't No Mountain High Enough." She favored "Mountain" as an audition piece because it demonstrated both her vocal range *and* her flare for drama.

Only twenty-five hours to go, she thought. Twenty-five hours until the producers of "America's favorite talent show" would learn that Hadley Shimmerhorn had what it took to become the next *American Icon.*

The sound of snapping bones snatched Hadley back into three-dimensional reality. She glanced up at the television, and for the first time in her nineteen years, horror silenced the angry blackbird in her head.

Onscreen, a dead man was eating Katie Cleric.

Cleric was the perky hostess of *Rise 'n Shine,* Hadley's favorite morning show. As the dead man rifled through Cleric's entrails, the camera zoomed in on the expression of startled wonder that had flash-frozen itself onto her face. Hadley could see flecks of blood between Cleric's perfect white teeth.

Cleric's co-host, a lovable black weatherman type, uttered a gobbling croak, stumbled, and crashed through the wall-sized window behind the stage. Two dozen deceased Midwesterners swarmed through the broken window, fell upon the lovable black weatherman, and tore him limb from limb.

Holy crap, Hadley thought. *It's really happening.*

Then the screen went black.

Emmet Pearson, the one-legged mailman, spoke first.

"What the fuck was that?"

Clovis Holyfield, the only female driver for National Cargo, grunted through a mouthful of tuna on rye, "They were rabid."

"Bullshit," Emmet snapped. "They was terrorists."

Clovis shook her head. "Those motherfuckers were crazier than a shithouse full of red monkeys."

Joe Swanson, the owner of Swanson Quality Used Cars and Trucks, reached over the counter and poked Ruby Ling. "Hey, Pocahontas," he said. "Any sign of my goddamn pancakes?"

Ruby Ling startled easily. She was quietly Chinese and didn't speak much English. She was also the only waitress who'd bothered to show up for work that morning. Her jaw hinged open as she rubbed the flesh on her arm where Swanson had poked her. Then she burst into tears.

"Why you always gotta be such a dick, Swanson?" Clovis said.

"Oh great," Swanson grumbled. "Black Butch speaks."

Swanson's dealership sat on the other side of Route 45, directly across from the Stop-n-Drop. Every morning at seven-thirty sharp, he dodged rush-hour traffic to come over and hassle the staff. Deke had done a commercial for Swanson, back when he was "Deacon Simmons," beloved quarterback for the Chicago Bears.

"That asshole would crawl through Hell wearin' gasoline panties just for cheap hash browns," Deke always said.

Friedrich Jackson raised his hand. "What's happening on the other channels?"

Hadley was pretty sure that Friedrich liked her, even though he was black and she was half-black and half-white.

Emmet fidgeted on his wooden leg and said, "Try CNN, dammit."

Nestor Mendoza, the grill man and most senior employee at the Stop-n-Drop, reached for the remote as Hadley eased around the cash register and stood behind Friedrich.

"—in downtown Chicago. I'm standing on the roof of the Burger World across the street from the *Rise and Shine* television studios, where this tragedy seems to have begun. We don't have much information, but this much is known: Katie Cleric and Ben Stoker, two of America's most popular on-camera personalities are dead: devoured, apparently, on live television."

"Oh, fer Christ's sake," Swanson grumbled.

"Saudi operatives," Emmet the mailman said. "Goddamn A-rabs are takin' terror to the next level."

Clovis made barking noises.

"Quiet, please," Mendoza said.

Hadley leaned forward and placed her hands lightly on Friedrich's shoulders. She felt him shiver at the contact.

"—where hundreds of these terrorists have descended on Michigan Avenue, attacking innocent shoppers, pulling people out of cars. Donnie, get a shot of the street."

The camera operator panned down to Michigan Avenue.

"Holyyy *shit*," Friedrich said. Then he flinched. "Sorry."

Hadley smiled. "No problem."

Chicago's premiere shopping drag was choked with screaming tourists. They were being run down and slaughtered by people like the one that ate Katie Cleric.

Some of the attackers moved with a stiff, jerky gait; they reminded Hadley of the time she'd gone to visit her grandpa Roosevelt after his seventh stroke. She'd found him doing the Lindy Hop with twelve other stroke victims as part of a rehabilitation program called *Swing Dancing for the Senior Spastic.*

A lot of the people on Michigan Avenue moved like grandpa's friends at the convalescent home. Many of them had been mutilated. Hadley saw one man with half a face fighting to drag a little old lady through a locked revolving door. When he couldn't get her through the door, the half-faced man sat on the old lady's chest and banged her head against the sidewalk until she stopped kicking.

But some of the attackers acted like normal people. The camera tracked one woman, a redhead wearing a black blazer and skirt with white sneakers. A smallish man wearing a pink suit ran toward the redhead with five stroke victims in hot pursuit. As pink-suit passed the redhead, she stuck out her right foot and tripped him.

The five strokers fell upon the pink-suited man. But as the redhead approached, the attackers pulled back. One of them was chewing the pink-suited man's toupee.

The redhead dragged pink-suit into an abandoned taxi and slammed the door. The taxi began to rock violently on its wheels. One of pink-suit's hands clutched the steering wheel and jerked it hard to the right. A second later, a jet of blood splattered the front windshield.

The seven people in the Stop-n-Drop stared at the screen. Then Ruby Ling vomited all over the *Dirty Harry* jukebox.

Mendoza thumbed the *Channel Scan* button on the remote.

"—movable slaughterhouse—"

Click.

"—people being devoured in broad daylight—"

Click.

"—shit shit shitting shit!"

Click.

"—walking corpses, although at this time that has not been confirmed."

"Freeze it," Hadley snapped.

"What's happening?" Friedrich whispered.

Hadley stared at the television, her heart thumping a heavy backbeat through her veins.

Because she *knew* what was happening.

Just like she knew what was going to happen next.

Mendoza thumbed up the volume.

"If you're just joining us: *Terror in the Streets.* America is under attack by what can only be described as *a ravaging army of cannibal terrorists.*"

"St. Theresa," Emmet the mailman whispered.

"—reports are flooding in claiming that these cannibals are the recently dead, returned to life. But those reports are being dismissed by authorities."

"*Rabies,*" Clovis snorted.

"Quiet, Butch," Emmet snapped.

"—earlier today, the president was airlifted to an undisclosed location following an attack at a corporate fundraiser in Houston. He was unavailable for comment. I repeat: this nation is under attack by an army—"

As the people in the Stop-n-Drop began to shout, Hadley walked over to the big picture window that faced the empty highway and looked out over the flat suburban landscape.

To the north, Chicago beckoned like a waiting wanton, her famous skyline visible even from Valhalla, thirty-five miles to the south. Hadley's eyes wandered over the landscaped greenery that extended into the horizon on every side: a verdant circle punctuated by little dots of white and gray, like the stone teeth of a gargoyle. She shuddered as the cold hand of irony made a fist around her heart.

I always knew this would happen.

Music burning in her head, Hadley spoke quietly.

"Everybody shut the fuck up."

Five pairs of eyes swiveled toward her.

"Friedrich," she said. "You and Oscar go get some boards, hammers, and nails; we'll need to cover the windows. Clovis, I'm gonna need the sat-telephone out of your rig."

"What the hell for?" Clovis said.

Hadley kept her voice level. *They didn't know.*

"The land lines are probably jammed already," she said.

"Without a way to communicate, we're ass-slammed."

Emmet and Clovis stared. Ruby Ling wiped her chin and belched softly. Friedrich stared at Hadley as if she'd just sprouted wings.

"What the hell is the Tragic Mulatto goin' on about?" Swanson said.

"Mr. Swanson, you'd better go get your people and bring them over here," Hadley said. "There's way too many windows in your store. Your employees are sitting ducks."

"Now wait one goddamn minute," Swanson said. "What makes you think the police can't handle this thing? They've probably got it under control already."

"Gee, you think?" Hadley snapped.

"Yes, *I think*," Swanson shot back. "Hell, this whole thing is probably some kind of publicity stunt. They said it started in a TV studio, for Christ's sake. There's no reason for us to fly off the handle here."

The scream from the kitchen stopped the argument.

"What the hell—" Mendoza said. "Eduardo?"

Mendoza went into the kitchen. "Eduardo, que paso?"

Hadley and the others went through the double doors.

The back door to the restaurant was wide open.

"Eduardo?" Mendoza said.

Eduardo screamed again: "Dios mio, ayuda me!"

"Parking lot," Emmet hissed.

Outside, Eduardo Corona, one of the busboys, was fighting with two dead men. One of the strokers, a black man with his hair in cornrows and a butcher knife stuck in his throat, grabbed Eduardo from behind. The other corpse, a bone-thin white man with a purple Mohawk, grabbed Eduardo's right hand and crammed it into his mouth. Eduardo shrieked. Then the black stroker bit him on the back of the neck. Eduardo's sneakers drummed on the cement like a man dancing on an electrified cattle grate, and his fingers came away in Mohawk's mouth.

Ruby Ling screamed, "They're killing him!"

But they were too late. As they watched, Mohawk darted in and bit off Eduardo's nose. A second later, Butcher-knife tore the busboy's throat out. Mendoza cursed and ran back into the Stop-n-Drop.

"My God," Clovis said. "Look."

The others turned.

Across the parking lot, a man was staring into the morning sun.

"Hey," Swanson said. "Hey, that's Pete Garrison!"

The sun-gazer's head turned toward them.

"Jesus Lord in Heaven," Emmet the mailman said.

The sun-gazer held out his arms and staggered toward the four humans.

"It's ol' Pete Garrison," Swanson drawled. "He owns the Dippin' Donuts over at the mall."

Hadley stared. Garrison's eyes gleamed with a thick, white glaze. His hair stuck up in wet, brown cowlicks all over his head. His lower jaw worked soundlessly, as if he were trying to chew something too big for his mouth.

A tatty green bathrobe hung off Garrison's shoulders. It flapped open on the right side, revealing a sagging belly and a nest of gray pubic hair. The left side was plastered to his body by a swath of dried blood that extended from his torso to his outer thigh.

"Hey, Pete," Swanson said. "Time to make the donuts?"

Swanson laughed. Garrison lurched.

"Pete, it's me, Joe Swanson."

"He's dead," Hadley said.

"*That man is not dead,*" Swanson hissed. "He's president of the PTA!"

Over by the dumpster, Eduardo's prayers had faded to a litany of startled gasps between bites as the strokers tore at him.

"I don't know, Joe," Emmet said. "He looks dead to me."

"Next person uses the 'D' word is gonna get knocked on his keester," Swanson snarled. "In case you geniuses hadn't noticed: He can't be dead. *He's walking around.*"

"He's walkin' around butt naked," Emmet mumbled.

Swanson scowled and turned as Garrison reached him.

"Listen, Pete," he began. "Tell these idiots you're as right as—"

Garrison grabbed Swanson, pulled him close, and bit a hunk out of his right cheek. Swanson screamed and went down, his face spouting red.

"Jesus!" he yelled. "Jesusgodshitjesus!"

Mohawk spat out Eduardo's knucklebones and stood up. At the same time, Mendoza flew out of the back door wearing his motorcycle jacket, clutching a meat cleaver in one hand and Deke's semi-automatic street-sweeper in the other.

As Garrison bent over to paw at Swanson, Mendoza reversed his grip on the assault weapon, swung it once around his head and caught Garrison across the forehead.

Crack.

Momentum lifted Garrison off his feet. He hit the cement and lay still.

Mendoza spun as Mohawk and Butcher-knife reached for him, swung the meat cleaver, and buried it in Butcher-knife's chest. The black corpse staggered backward five steps and sat down on its rump. Meanwhile, Mohawk grabbed Mendoza by the hairnet.

"Help me, you assholes!" Mendoza snarled.

He leant forward and flipped Mohawk over his shoulder. The stroker hit the asphalt, twisted, grabbed Mendoza by the collar, and dragged him down on top of him.

Mendoza dropped the shotgun.

Hadley moved without thinking.

She ran for the cleaver.

As the black corpse stood, Hadley grasped the handle of the meat cleaver and pulled. At the same time, she kicked out with her right foot and shoved Butcher-knife backward. The stroker stumbled and tripped over its own feet.

Mohawk was busily trying to bite Mendoza's arm but having difficulty chewing through the thick leather of his motorcycle jacket. Hadley swung the meat cleaver over her head and split Mohawk's Mohawk clean down the middle. The meat cleaver sank in up to the hilt. The skinny corpse shuddered and fell down.

Hadley was vaguely aware that Ruby Ling was screaming her name, but the music pounding through her veins muffled any other sound.

Ain't no mountain high enough, she thought.

A million miles away, something exploded. Ruby Ling screamed again. Then Hadley was grabbed from behind. She whirled and looked into the face of Pete Garrison.

As Garrison clutched at her, the left side of his bathrobe fell away. Hadley gasped at the foot-long trench of gnawed meat that gaped up at her from Garrison's torso.

Garrison opened his mouth.

"Eat this, shitbag."

A second later, there was another explosion and Garrison's face blew off. It flew over Hadley's right shoulder, sailed across the parking lot like one of those floppy Frisbees you could get for your Golden Retriever and stuck to the front window of the Payless shoe store.

Garrison dropped.

Clovis was standing there, her brown hands clutching the dual pistol grips of the smoking shotgun. She spat on the asphalt. Then she kicked Garrison in the nuts.

"I'm a Krispy Kreme girl m'self."

"I love two things in this world," Hadley said, later. "One of them is singing American R and B classics, preferably from the Motown catalog, circa nineteen sixty- four to nineteen sixty-nine."

Hadley spoke slowly. She wanted to make sure they all understood what she was going to tell them next.

"The other thing I love—is zombie movies."

"Zombies?" Emmet the mailman said.

Hadley nodded. "Romero was the first: the prophet of the

post-modern Living Dead genre. But there've been many others. I've seen them all. Trust me, people, we have a very bad situation on our hands."

They'd nailed up everything they could find over the front and side windows: three doors, two of the old wooden tables left over from before the last renovation, and the polished wood sides of the jukebox.

Mendoza was busily breaking down some wooden milk crates he'd scrounged out of the dumpster where they'd stashed Eduardo's body.

"It's not going to be enough, Oscar," Hadley said."

Mendoza looked at the front windows and nodded.

"I'm gonna find some more wood," he said.

Swanson sat alone in one of the booths. He kept his face to the wall, a cold compress pressed to his torn right cheek. Seeing Pete Garrison shot had taken something out of the normally rambunctious used car salesman.

But Hadley was worried about that bite.

She'd seen enough to know what happened to the victims of a zombie bite. So far, the phenomenon had behaved exactly as Romero had predicted, save for one critical point: Garrison was the only corpse from the parking lot attack who'd shuffled along in classic movie zombie fashion. Hadley was pretty sure she could outrun any stroker that moved like the ones from the Romero films.

But the black corpse with the butcher knife neckware had displayed only slightly less coordination than a normal human. And Hadley remembered the eerie speed with which the skinny corpse had attacked Mendoza.

It was so fast, she thought. *Faster than Mendoza.*

She'd heard the busboys telling stories about Mendoza's boxing days back in Mexico. He'd even fought professionally before his right lung collapsed during an exhibition bout.

What if all the others are like them? Hadley thought.

"We've got to get out of here," she said.

"Bullshit, "Emmet drawled. "I got one good leg, little girl. You expect me to run all over creation from those freaks?"

Swanson stood and stalked toward the counter. "He's right. Why not wait here until the police show up?"

"We can't call 'em, man," Clovis said. "Land lines are down, just like Songbird said. I can't raise a goddamn thing on my wireless; and the sat-phone is clogged with so much traffic I can't copy what anybody's sayin'."

"Riiight," Swanson said. "Bet you'd like to keep us locked up in here. Right, Butch? That way, you can paw all over the Tragic Mulatto whenever you want."

"What?" Clovis said. "What the hell are you babblin' about, Swanson?"

Swanson moved around the counter toward Clovis.

"Oh, I've *seen you*," he said. "Checking her out when you think no one's looking. You've been hot for her box since she started working here."

Hadley sensed something ugly crackle through the air.

"You guys—" she began.

"Swanson," Clovis interrupted. "That freak must have bitten you up your ass, 'cause that's obviously where you keep your brains."

Swanson's eyes narrowed. A purple vein popped out in his right temple as he spoke through clenched teeth.

"You dirty—black—*dyke*."

Clovis stood up just as Mendoza stepped in between them.

"Bring it on, Condoleezza," Swanson crowed. "I'll show you what a real man can do."

"Listen," Friedrich cried pointing at the television. "Everybody, listen!"

"—confirmed reports that the bodies of the recently dead are returning to life only to attack the living. This phenomenon is being reported in cities all over the world, and where the dead walk, murder and cannibalism soon follow. CBN News is warning everyone able to hear this broadcast: *Stay inside.*"

"Ahhh," Swanson said.

"—secure all doors and windows. Find a safe place to hide with your loved ones. *Do not answer the door for any reason.* Some of the recently dead are masquerading as policeman, door-to-door salesmen, and even Jehovah's Witnesses. *Some of these assassins are able to pass as ordinary human beings.* They are extremely dangerous. We have some disturbing footage to show you right now. We warn you: if any children are present, these images could prove distasteful."

"See?" Swanson said. "We're supposed to stay where we are."

"I have to agree, Had," Friedrich said. "I don't understand why you think we should leave."

Hadley reached up and turned off the television.

"Hey!" Emmet squawked.

"Has everyone forgotten where we are?" Hadley said. "We're right in the middle of *Valhalla, Illinois*."

"So?" Swanson said.

Hadley bit back the urge to stab the salesman in the neck.

"Mr. Swanson, there are seventeen cemeteries within a two-mile radius of where we're standing."

Emmet the mailman stood up as if someone had just goosed him with a cattle prod, and murmured, "Where the Midwest Comes to Say Goodbye."

"Everyone in this town either works at a cemetery or knows someone who does," Hadley said. "Route 45 runs past six funeral parlors, three hospitals, five retirement communities, and *nine different cemeteries*."

"Industry town," Emmet moaned. "Two thousand families clustered around seventeen boneyards—"

"I see your point," Friedrich said.

Just then, the front window exploded.

Deke Simmons and Mandy McCafferty staggered into the Stop-N-Drop.

When he was alive, Deke always called himself "one big bad son-of-a-bitch," but he also had a heart of gold. Six weeks earlier, Hadley had wandered into the Stop-n-Drop, needing to make a demo for *American Icon* but hard-up for extra cash. Deke had recognized her: a week earlier she'd sung the National Anthem at Deke Jr.'s Little League baseball game.

"Talent like yours might brighten up this dump, Songbird," Deke had said. And he offered her the cashier's job on the spot.

Someone had smashed Deke's face in and now he looked like an ebony Cabbage Patch Doll. His head shook back and forth, one eye bulging from his head like a man trying to pass the world's biggest kidney stone.

Mandy McCafferty also worked the early shift. She shuffled behind Deke, a big black frying pan dangling loosely in her right hand. Hadley saw several glittering yellow objects clinging to the gore clotted along the edge of the pan.

Those are Deke's gold teeth, she thought.

She'd heard the gossip about Deke and Mandy, had caught them loitering around Deke's *Roadwinder* Winnebago, parked out back, more than once.

Someone had torn big hunks out of Mandy's throat and the side of her neck. The top half of her yellow t-shirt was stiff with blood. From the waist down, Mandy was naked.

Emmet the mailman gobbled like a turkey. Then he turned and clunked toward the front door. Mandy spun and hurled the frying pan across the counter. The flying skillet struck the back of Emmet's skull and sent him sprawling. Mandy whined and lurched toward Emmet's body.

Deke headed straight for Hadley.

"Deke?" Hadley said. "Deke?"

Then Mendoza jumped on Deke's back.

Deke spun, his coal-black arms beating at Mendoza's face. Then Mendoza jammed a screwdriver into his ear. With a howl, Deke lifted the fry cook over his head and hurled him through the side window. Mendoza crashed through the glass and lay unmoving on the sidewalk.

Deke turned, Mendoza's screwdriver dangling from his mutilated right ear. The yellow handle bounced against his cheek.

"Holy jumping shit," Friedrich said.

Deke swiped at the screwdriver and howled like a dying Rottweiler forced to listen to Britney Spears's cover of "Doctor Feelgood."

Over in the corner, Swanson and Ruby Ling were making out against the jukebox. At least, it *looked like* they were making out. Swanson's face was buried in the crook between Ruby Ling's neck and shoulder, while Ruby Ling's hands clutched at the back of Swanson's head. Swanson pulled away, blood streaming down his chin, and Ruby Ling fell, gushing red violets, to the floor.

"Son of a bitch went over and never told anybody!" Hadley screamed.

"Finger—lickin'—*goooood,*" Swanson groaned.

Clovis shot Mandy in the face, blasted her back through the

broken window. Then Swanson tackled Friedrich.

"Help me!" Friedrich screamed.

Deke lunged at Hadley, forced her to retreat. Hadley aimed a half-hearted swipe at the ex-NFL star's hand and dodged around him.

Swanson was dragging the struggling Friedrich toward the restroom. Hadley ran toward them, knowing she was too late: Swanson was one of *them*.

One of the quick ones.

"Clovis!" she screamed.

Clovis was behind the counter rifling through the drawers and shelves. "Where the hell did Deke keep the goddamned ammo?" she screamed.

Swanson punched his hand through Friedrich's chest, ripped out something red and stuffed it into his mouth.

Hadley swung the meat cleaver up, intending to sever Swanson's head from his shoulders. But Swanson whirled and backhanded her across the face. Hadley flew across a nearby table, bounced off the vinyl seat of a nearby booth and slid out of sight. The meat cleaver landed a few feet away.

Two more zombies staggered in through the front window. At the same time, the kitchen door banged open and Eduardo stumbled, noseless and extinct, into the truck stop.

Clovis jumped onto the counter. Eduardo climbed up after her.

"Shit," Clovis hissed.

At the last moment, she turned and dove, reached out and grasped the blade of the big overhead ceiling fan. Eduardo grabbed Clovis's leg and bit down on one of her engineer's boots. Clovis kicked him in the face with the other foot, freed herself. She used the momentum to swing herself up and hooked her legs over the nearest fan blade. She hugged the ceiling fan, spinning lazy circles above outstretched zombie hands. Eduardo growled as he lunged for Clovis, fell off the end of the counter and hit the floor. Hadley heard bones snap.

"We gotta get to my truck!" Clovis screamed.

Swanson finished whatever he'd snatched out of Friedrich's chest. He turned and glared at Hadley.

"Low—low—prices," he moaned.

"Oh crap," Hadley yelped.

Swanson got to his feet.

"Move your ass, girl!" Clovis yelled.

But Hadley was wedged between the booth and the table post. Her right leg was bent backward at an awkward angle, her foot pinned beneath her in a kind of "hurdler's stretch."

"I'm stuck!"

Having decided to abandon his pursuit of the spinning Clovis, Eduardo dragged himself toward Hadley, his broken leg trailing dejectedly behind him.

Hadley's every move wedged her more tightly between the seat and the post. The other zombies, sensing easier prey, shuffled toward her. Swanson grabbed Hadley's right foot and pulled. Hadley cried out as her legs were pulled apart.

Then Swanson was grabbed from behind and hauled to his feet. Hadley was pulled forward even more, her foot gripped in Swanson's hand, until her back leg straightened out and she was able to slide out from beneath the table.

Deke had Swanson in a chokehold.

Swanson fought with a maniac's intensity, biting Deke's forearm, dragging long red runnels into the skin of Deke's neck and face with his fingernails. But Deke held on. He grabbed Swanson by the scruff of the neck, reared back with him and slammed his face into the table—

Bam! Bam! Bam! Bam! Bam!

—until Swanson stopped fighting and slid off the table.

Over near the jukebox, dead Ruby Ling sat up and giggled.

Hadley stood up.

Deke turned and glared at the other zombies. They stopped and regarded Deke with the air of conscientious students. And Hadley understood: Somehow, Deke had become one of the quick ones.

Hadley edged forward, her fingers reaching for the screwdriver sticking out of Deke's ear. Deke backed away.

"Nnooo," he moaned. "Helllpssss meee."

Hadley nodded, gratitude filling her eyes.

Clovis climbed down off of the ceiling fan.

"Hadley," she hissed. "I hear more of 'em comin'!"

"Moooorrree," Deke said. "Lotsss—more."

"We have to go, Deke," Hadley said.

Deke nodded slowly. Then he opened his mouth. Hadley tensed, ready to bolt.

"Sinnng."

Over by the front door, Emmet the mailman got to his feet, the back of his head leaking, and turned toward Clovis. Deke lifted a hand. Emmet whined, and stood still.

"Siiinnng," Deke said.

Hadley nodded.

" 'If you need me,' " she began. " 'Call me. No—no matter where you are. No matter how far—' "

More and more strokers were stumbling into the truck stop. But Deke held them. Hadley lifted her voice and sent the song out over the heads of her audience until her voice echoed up and down Route 45.

When she was done, Deke nodded. "Sonnngbirrrrd."

There were nearly fifty dead people moaning behind him.

"Hadley," Clovis hissed.

Deke faced the strokers who blocked the front window. The corpses shuffled and parted. Hadley and Clovis walked quickly through a gauntlet of the shuffling dead.

Hadley climbed up into the cab of Clovis's eighteen-wheeler. Behind her, Deke stood in the window shaking his head, the yellow screwdriver bouncing against his shoulder.

In the northern distance, black towers of smoke rose into the afternoon sky: Chicago was burning.

"Three million dreams," Hadley whispered.

"What?" Clovis said.

"Nothing," Hadley replied. "Better head south."

Clovis nodded. "Long as you keep singin'."

They thundered out onto the highway.

As they passed, the dead paused. But a terrible hunger tugged most of them toward the burning in the north, and they walked on.

Some of them cocked their heads to mark the passing of a newborn star.

BORN AGAIN

There were good days now. More days when Joshua Belton thought he could at least glimpse the possibility that he was free, that the Hard Man had left him for good. Sometimes an entire hour would pass without him once thinking about the children, and the things that had happened to them. Sometimes whole days would pass without him thinking of the blood and the tears, and the secret, creeping contentment he now despised. At those times he could even think about Brady and remember the good times. Like now. The sun was shining; it was pleasantly warm for late October, and he was just another father, sitting in the park watching the children play.

"I'm better," he whispered. "I've been redeemed."

"What did you say?"

The man with the tall redhead was standing over him, glaring down at him with the suspicion Joshua had come to know too well. That was alright too. He understood. He was one of them. After so many years spent looking in, like a wolf separated from a pasture by a fence too high to ever climb, he was on the inside.

One of the sheep.

Joshua winced. It had been a while since last he'd heard the Hard Man's voice, snarling at him in his dreams; roaring at him when he ignored its demands. But fifteen years ago, another voice had entered the echoing chamber inside his head. A powerful voice.

The voice that whispered and defeated the whirlwind.

It was the voice that had spoken from the torment of Golgotha and saved the world entire; The Voice, whose merest whisper could drown out the Hard Man's screams.

" 'It is finished.' "

"Sorry? Excuse me...but are you here with anyone?"

The redhead's father. Joshua opened his eyes to find him there, still glaring, expecting, no *demanding*, an answer. As if he had the right. Joshua took a deep breath and went to the special room that the Lord had prepared in his heart. He turned the key and let the light of salvation shine.

"Sorry," he said. "I was just enjoying the day. It's so stuffy at work. They keep the windows closed, even on really hot days. Herb...my boss...is trying to save on cooling costs. But it gets pretty uncomfortable when it's..."

The redhead's father flapped his hand as if to wave away the need to hear the rest of Joshua's statement. "It's just that...well some of the parents over there were wondering. This neighborhood is pretty self-contained; we all pretty much know each other and... well... nobody in our group seems to know *you*. And since you're not attached to any of the kids...we just thought..."

"I understand," Joshua said, standing. He wiped his hands on the cloth napkin Rose always provided in his lunch, and extended his right hand. "Josh Belton. I work at the radio station, over at the college. My family and I moved here from Illinois last year. My wife works at the hospital. She's an R.N."

Joshua could see the tension straining across the man's face, the overused smile, the one that never touches the eyes, beginning to fracture as he understood that Joshua was actually *engaging* him. Behind him, Joshua could see the other concerned parents, all women, watching their interaction like hawks watching a rabbit hutch. That was okay. They were smart to be concerned. No one understood that better than him.

"When I got the job—I'm an engineer—we understood that the Lord had opened a door for us. I usually eat lunch in the cafeteria. I can see this park from my table and it always looks so peaceful, with the kids playing and everything. I've been complaining *forever* to my wife about the stuffiness. She's been telling me to get out and see more of the town ever since we got here. Today I promised her I'd get some fresh air."

"I...uhmm...I see," the redhead's father said, shifting his weight uncomfortably from his left foot to his right and back again. Joshua suspected he had to force himself to keep from looking at his watch.

"See, Rose and I...we lost our son two years ago."

The redhead's father's façade cracked, just enough for Joshua to see the horrified parent underneath all that smugness.

"Oh my God," he said. "I'm... I'm so sorry for your loss."

"Thanks," Joshua said. "We left Moline—that's a few hours west of Chicago—Rosie...she's a travelling nurse...well she got a contract over at the hospital. And then those fools at the college actually gave me the best job I've ever had. The rest is history... as they say."

The redhead's father seemed to retract into himself. He'd come over with his chest stuck out and his fists clenched, as if he meant to batter Joshua with his suspicions. Now he looked confused. Vulnerable.

"This is the kind of place—the park I mean—the kind of place my Brady would have loved. The trees and the tall slides. He would have been all over that jungle gym. I called him my little monkey-boy."

The redhead was picking her nose—a habit Joshua despised. She had clearly grown bored with the conversation. Now she was tugging at her father's grip.

"Daaaddddyyyyy..."

"I *know*, sweetie. Just a second, ok? Sorry, Josh. How old was your son when he...?"

"Oh, Brady was nine. He was struck by a hit-and-run driver before the Lord called him Home. I guess the real reason I came here today was just to try to feel close to him again. You know?"

"Of course. Oh God, I can't even imagine what you and your wife must feel."

Joshua smiled. The smile felt genuine. He could feel the compassion for this man glowing like clean sunshine at the core of his soul. He could *feel* their connection.

"We have our daughter, Candace. She's fourteen. She's the reason we were able to go on. When you have kids, sometimes you have to pick yourself up and keep moving, you know? Just for them."

"I can't imagine."

"Well, we also had our faith," Joshua said. "Without the Lord's guidance we never would have made it through."

The redhead's father stepped closer and extended his right hand. Joshua accepted it. Gladly. At the same time, the redhead broke away and ran back to join the other kids on the playground.

"I'm sorry to have questioned you like that," the man said. "You enjoy your lunch. Not that you need my permission of course. I mean you've got every right to be here...just as much as anybody else. I mean..."

Then he did it. He actually glanced at his watch.

"Wow. I've got to get Shannon to our Daddy/Daughter class."

Joshua nodded and smiled, brimming with grace.

"No problem. I gotta get back to work myself. What was your name?"

"Oh. Sorry! Keith. Keith Alderson. Shannon, the redhead who's currently cruising for a major timeout, is mine."

"Oh, I know." Joshua nodded, easing into it now. He'd connected every kid in the park to a corresponding adult before he'd finished the first half of his tuna sandwich. "She's a real heartbreaker."

"Thanks. Well, Joshua, it was great talking to you. Maybe we'll see you again sometime."

Joshua grinned.

"You bet."

He was still feeling good when he walked through the front door of the quaint little two-story Colonial they'd rented for almost a year to the day of their arrival. He closed the door, shut out the wind and the bluster that had blown through town earlier that afternoon. Indeed, the euphoria he'd felt after defeating Satan in the park had nearly been overshadowed by the rumble of thunder. By the time he'd made it back to the radio station he was drenched. But even that wasn't enough to dampen his spirits. He'd surpassed this latest trial. He'd forced himself to walk into that park and face the Hard Man down, and he'd felt nothing. He was a blank slate. He was clean.

"Rosie? I'm home, babe."

Sausage, their two-year-old Schnauzer, barked furiously from the living room.

Probably needs to be let out of his kennel.

But why hadn't Rose or Candace taken him out? Other than Sausage's barking, the silence was odd. Rosie worked the night shift at St. John the Divine Presbyterian. She usually slept in the mornings, ran whatever errands she needed in the afternoons before coming back home to catch a quick nap before dinner. His wife of fifteen years still slept most of her days away even two years after Brady's death. She'd spent those first terrible months entombed in a kind of stunned grief, a black cloud that attended her waking moments like an invisible shroud. They'd come together in the wake of the accident that had robbed them of their greatest joy, but for a while, Joshua had walked along the edge of the abyss. That was when the visits to the parks and playgrounds had taken on a greater urgency. Because the Hard Man, what he thought of as his *old* self, had never spoken to him more clearly.

He'd rediscovered the Bible during his trial. At the urging of the prison chaplain, he'd taken up his own cross, truly borne its weight, and finally understood the dark power it wielded over him. In that very moment he'd accepted a new savior. He'd forsaken the Hard Man and been changed in the blinking of an eye. That resurrection had redeemed him. So much so that when he was acquitted it seemed that the Lord was leading him away from his old life, exchanging his devotion for a better one. He'd moved away, met Rose at his new church and married her. Candace had come along a year later, and Brady four years after that. It was all working as the chaplain had promised. He'd been born again.

He was so excited to tell Rose about his trip to the park that when he turned the corner into their living room, at first he didn't grasp what he was seeing. The room was dark, which was also strange. Rose hated to be in alone in the dark.

"Rose? What's going on around here?"

He reached for the wall switched and flipped it. Light pierced the darkness and illuminated the objects in the center of the room.

Rose...*his* Rose, was tied to one of the heavy dining room chairs they'd bought at Bed Bath & Beyond last year. Her face was streaked with mascara, her lipstick smeared, as if by rough hands, across her mouth and lower jaw. A sock, or some white cloth had been forced into her mouth and secured there with black duct tape, distorting her features even more.

Candace, their fourteen-year-old, was tied to the chair next to her. Her hands, feet, and mouth had been similarly bound, her lower face covered with duct tape. Both of them were crying; Candace's eyes, begging, pleading silently for him.

On the floor at Rose's feet, half-a-dozen open newspapers lay spread across the floor.

"Rosie? What is this? What...what...?"

"I imagine your wife must be thinking the questions anyone would be thinking at moments like this."

The shape that emerged from the shadows near the French doors coalesced and became a man. A man holding a gun.

"How are you, Mister Belton?"

Joshua stared, frozen, as the man stepped into the soft yellow light from the front hall. Keeping the gun trained on Joshua, he reached down and switched on the lamp at the table next to the chair which held Rose and his features flooded into clarity. He was old, maybe in his seventies. But his jawline was firm, his shoulders straight. He was tall, long-limbed, his head framed by a cap of snow-white hair. He was smiling. But no, that wasn't it. Half of his face was paralyzed, the right side as immobile as statuary.

"Sit down, Joshua."

"Who are you? What do you want?"

The shot, when it came, was a sharp bark, followed by the sound of breaking glass. Inches from Joshua's right hand, a vase shattered and fell to the floor in pieces. Joshua felt a burning lash across the back of his hand, and a sudden wetness, but the horror on Rose's face demanded his full attention.

"Just so you understand the way this is going to run," the old man said. "I'll give you an order and you'll do it. Every time you fail in this, I will destroy something you love. Do you understand, Mister Belton?"

Joshua nodded. The gun...the old man was holding the barrel next to Rose's head.

"Please...please don't hurt her."

"Sit down, Mister Belton. I won't tell you again."

Joshua sat down.

"Just so we're all on the same page, Josh...you should understand that I'm calling the shots. If you move before I tell you to, or try anything silly, I will shoot your wife...I'm sorry, dear. It's Rosemary, right?"

Rose nodded, her eyes bright. Her terror tore at something in Joshua's chest.

"Very good, Rosemary," the old man said. He reached into the front pocket of his tan windbreaker, then raised his left hand and showed Joshua a pair of handcuffs. "There'll be no need for any dramatics as long as we all behave ourselves."

Moving quickly, the old man ordered Joshua to raise his left hand, all the while keeping the gun trained on his face. With a practiced economy of motion, he hooked one handcuff around the armrest of the chair and snapped the other one shut around Joshua's wrist.

"Now, I'm going to undo the strip of tape around Mrs. Belton's mouth. It's quite easy. I can pull the tape with one hand. Your good lady has a question she'd like to ask you, and I want you to answer her. And a word of advice, Belton: I know the truth."

The old man pulled the tape away from Rose's mouth. She shook the last of it free, the thickest strip tearing a lock of hair from the side of her head with an audible rip.

"Who are you?"

Joshua shook his head, uncomprehending.

"What?"

"Answer truthfully, Belton," the old man warned. "Tell the truth or she dies."

"But...I don't know what's going on!"

The old man pivoted and fired into Sausage's cage. The dog fell to the floor of the kennel, dead. Candace screamed, the sound muffled beneath her half-mask of duct tape.

Someone will hear, Joshua thought. *Someone will come.*

But they'd selected the little house specifically with an eye toward privacy: It sat at the end of a long private driveway, set well back from Route 118, the rural highway that ran past their house on its way out of town. They'd often joked about it being their own piece of Heaven. The perfect little hideaway. The nearest neighbors were the Mayfields, nearly a quarter mile down the road. No one would hear. No matter how loudly they screamed.

The man with the gun spoke softly in the gloom.

"Ask him again, Mrs. Belton. I think you'll find him in a more truthful mood."

"Please don't hurt my daughter," Rose said. "Whatever he's done, she doesn't deserve this!"

The old man pointed the gun at Candace and fired. The shot,

though muffled, was still loud enough to evoke another scream from Rose.

But Candace was still alive, her eyes wide, stunned, but alive.

"I'm an excellent shot, missy. I earned high marks in the Marine Corps. Fought in Korea. You'll find that slug buried in the wall a few inches to the left of where your daughter is sitting. Now, Mrs. Belton, please ask your husband the question again. I promise you, I won't miss a second time."

Rose was crying, shaking her head, her dark hair obscuring most of her face. But Joshua could see her eyes glimmering through her dark strands. He could see the hatred building there.

"Who are you, you *bastard*?"

Joshua looked toward the door to his left. It led upstairs to the master bedroom and his office. If he could make it across the room, even dragging the chair behind him… It was only a matter of seven or eight steps…

"You'll never make it to the stairs," the old man said. "And even if you broke out of that chair and made it outside, you'd be leaving me here with these two lovely ladies. I know you're accustomed to abandoning injured women but I'll assure you that your escaping will end badly for them. "

Joshua nodded. "Okay. I understand. Please…"

"This doesn't have to get ugly, *Josh*," the old man said. "All I want is for you to answer a few simple questions. When I get what I came for I'll be on my way."

"Answer me, Josh," Rose hissed. "*Who are you?*"

"Stephen Campbell. My name is Stephen Campbell."

"Good," the old man said. "Now we're getting somewhere."

"Please let them go," Joshua said. "They didn't do anything."

"That may be true," the old man said. "Sometimes bad things happen to innocent people. Bad people do *unspeakable* things to innocent people for no reason at all. Isn't that also true, Stephen?"

Joshua nodded.

"Aloud, please."

"Yes! Bad things happen to innocent people."

"Good. We're cookin' with gas now, aren't we, Rose? You don't mind if I call you Rose do you?"

Rose glared at Joshua, her eyes shining.

"I can explain, Rose. I can explain everything."

"Who is Jessie Waverly?"

Joshua's eyes flicked toward Candace, who was staring at him now, shaking her head as if to beg him, *No. Don't let it be true.*

"Rose...don't..."

"Who is Jessie Waverly?"

"Rose...please don't listen to him."

"It's not me she's listening to, Campbell," the old man said. "It's you who's lived a lie all these years. You who's been holding back."

"Answer the question, Josh," Rose cried. "Answer or he'll kill us!"

"She's the last one."

"The last... *what?*"

"The last of my victims."

"Alright," the old man said. "Alright then."

Joshua speed-searched through his mental rolodex of alibis and excuses, built up over two lifetimes. But the betrayal in Rose's eyes held him in stasis. He couldn't think. And, trapped beneath the glaring illumination of her pain, he couldn't lie.

"So it's true? You hurt...you *raped* all those girls?"

"Rose, you have to listen to me..."

"Six girls?" Rose said, her voicing rising like the cry of an avenging angel. "Children? You *did* that?"

The newspaper clippings, some yellowed with age, lay scattered about Rose's feet. On one of them, he could even see his picture, the clip taken by an ambitious photographer the day he walked out of court a free man. The man had been insistent as Stephen Campbell was ushered into a waiting car by his attorney. As they'd moved through the press and the screaming mob, the photographer had slipped across the police barricade and thrust his camera toward Campbell's face. There he sat, one hand upraised as if warding off a blow, while his lawyer shoved the photographer away. The shot had been plastered all over the news later that day, along with headlines declaring the mistrial and subsequent dismissal of charges. Something about the way the detectives gathered evidence, the way the witnesses were led to identify him. The case against him was flimsy at best: Stephen Campbell wore gloves, used condoms and a mask when he committed his crimes. It was his voice that damned him, some of the girls claimed—a resonant baritone that all of them remembered.

An actor's voice. A preacher's voice.

"You disappeared after the trial,' the old man said. "I tracked you for years, kept up with you, waiting…dreaming about how I would make you understand. When you moved, I was able to follow you through the predator registration websites. An old friend in the Dayton Police Department provided me with the information I needed. Everyone understood that they'd screwed up, and so they were only too happy to help. But then you disappeared. I searched for you for five years, but I couldn't find you. You changed your name, forged documents…a whole new life."

"Why are you doing this?" Rose said. "He did what you wanted. Can't you let us go?"

The old man shook his head. He reached into the pocket of his jacket and produced a single cigarette. He raised a zippo lighter and flicked the wheel.

"I'm a little nervous, folks," he said. "I haven't smoked in thirty years. But since this is a special occasion I thought it appropriate. I hope you don't mind too much."

Joshua strained against the handcuff, but it held fast. Even now, as he struggled to find a way out, he was confident that if he could only draw Rose's attention he could assure her that he had changed; that Stephen Campbell died the day he walked out of prison. It was God's will. He had been born again. For her.

"You've built a beautiful life, Campbell. A family. A lovely home. It's almost perfect."

The old man exhaled a long streamer of smoke into the air, coughed, a wet rumble that built in the depths of his chest and rattled up through his throat.

"Excuse me," he said, clearing his throat. "That's one thing no one tells you about growing old; the things that happen to your body while time marches forward. No one tells you about the goddamned cruelty of it all."

"Please," Rose said. "We won't tell anyone. Just let us go."

"I'm afraid I can't do that, Rose. Not until I tell you exactly what my Jessica endured at your husband's hands."

He licked his thumb and forefinger, pinched out the lit cigarette, and shoved the remainder in his jacket pocket.

"While you were building this new life did you ever stop to consider what was happening to your victims, Campbell? The lives you ruined? Their families?"

The old man reached into his pocket and produced a single, wallet-sized photo. He held it up to allow Joshua to see it. But in the deepening gloom Joshua could see only a shape, a glimmer of blonde hair, a flash of faded colors—green, red...

"My granddaughter was sixteen years old—not much older than your girl is now—when you raped her. Up 'til then she'd been a straight-A student. She wanted to go to college and be a veterinarian. Can you imagine that? Sometimes she stayed up so late with her homework my wife and I worried about her. But she never wavered. Never *faltered*."

Moving slowly, Joshua pulled, straining, against the handcuff. And something deep in the body of the chair began to give way.

"After my daughter died bringing her into this world, Jessie was our only connection to her. Her dad abandoned her before she was born so it was just the three of us. But we were making do. Then you crawled through her bedroom window."

The old man studied the picture, his eyes focused on the small square of paper in his hand. Joshua felt the arm of the chair yield the slightest bit. In the quiet, the sound of wood splintering seemed as loud as a train whistle.

Be quiet. Be careful.

Hope flooded his veins with adrenaline and he remembered that the chair looked solid but was actually quite flimsy. He recalled lamenting the poor workmanship the day they bought it.

Someday, when we're in a better place, I'm gonna burn this cheap garbage.

It's fine, Josh.

You deserve better.

I've got better.

Now, the chair's cheap construction gave Joshua hope. The old man had cuffed his wrist to the chair's weakest point—the spot where the underside of the armrest met the post that had been glued into a hole in the seat. He pulled harder, and felt it give a little more.

"My wife, Hilda, we were married fifty years. When our

daughter died…Christ, it almost killed her. Then the doctor handed us our beautiful little girl. Jessie almost didn't make it; she was so small. But she came through. Hilda and I raised her, cared for her like she was our own little miracle. Like a promise from God."

The old man, still lost in his memories, had allowed the barrel of gun to drop toward the floor. He spoke softly, as if to an audience only he could see.

"When you did…what you did, it changed her. When they caught you, I promised her: now you'll understand. Now we'll get justice. And when you walked away…it was like you raped her all over her again. She slipped off the Honor Roll that same year. Stopped caring about school, grades… The drugs came next. She dropped out in the middle of her senior year. Started running around with a bad crowd, and got pregnant. She thought she could keep the baby. Hilda and I even offered to help her, on the condition that she go back and get her diploma. But she'd lost hope by then. Four years ago, she tried to end it. I found her in the bathroom with vomit all over her face. But she'd only killed the baby. After that, she took to the streets."

The old man looked up at Rose. "Do you understand what it is to mourn for a child who yet lives, Mrs. Belton? To wake up to a cop on your front step telling you your gift from God whores herself for heroin? Can you possibly understand what that feels like?"

"I'm sorry," Rose whispered. "I'm sorry for your family."

The old man smiled; a grimace. "Thank you. Yes, I think you must be a compassionate woman, Rose. I can't for the life of me imagine how you ended up here."

Joshua worked the armrest, using his forearm to push it back and forth inside the hole in the seat, carefully, moving in short jerks, trying to break the glue seal and rock it free.

"Jessie died six months ago of a heroin overdose. She left the women's shelter and prostituted herself to buy what she needed. Then she came home. Hilda and I were at our Bible study class. We'd kept her room for her, in the hope that she would come back to us. Only I think she was really returning to the place where she'd already died. April twenty-third: the anniversary of the day she met you, Campbell. Fifteen years to the very day. I'll never forget the sound Hilda made when I opened that bedroom door. I *can't* forget. Hilda died last month. Her doctor said it was her heart, but I know that she lost the will to live. That was when I decided to pay you a visit."

The old man's teeth bared in a feral snarl. Then he lunged across the room and struck Joshua across the face with the butt of his gun. Once. Twice. Three times. Joshua felt teeth shatter in his right jaw and his vision went white as a bomb-blast of agony detonated in his head.

When his vision cleared, he saw the old man place the barrel of the gun against the side of Candace's head.

"Do you understand, Campbell? Do you understand what you stole from me?"

"I understand!" Joshua gasped, fighting to stay conscious. "Brady...we lost...my son!"

"Yes," the old man said. "I know."

"Then you know," Joshua said. "You know how God can give you a second chance."

"A second chance."

"Yes! After Brady died...I met with our pastor. He told me that I could be delivered."

"Delivered?"

"Yes, that's right. I believed him. After my trial I knew I'd never make a life, never find peace. So I left."

Now he was speaking as much to Rose as he was to the old man, trying to explain, to help them understand the way things were.

"It was wrong to hurt those girls. Your Jessie. I...I know that. But I was forgiven. Rosie...*you* helped me understand that."

"A good woman of the church," The old man said. "Her faith helped transform your life."

"*God* transformed my life."

The old man seemed to consider Campbell's plea. Even through the pain in his face, his mouth, Joshua sensed this weakening of his captor's will: God was handing him an opportunity. The armrest creaked softly. He felt the wooden chair crack beneath his left hand.

"Are you...are you a believer?"

The old man started, as if jolted from his memories. "How's that?"

"A believer? You know...a Christian?"

The old man squinted, his eyes narrowed to thin slits. But he nodded. "Yes. Of course I am."

"You go to church, yes?"

"Hilda and I attended Holy Name Presbyterian, over in Brainerd," the old man said. "We'd worshipped there for nearly forty years."

"Good," Joshua said. Lights were flashing in his eyes. His tongue felt too thick for his mouth. But the old man wasn't shooting. He was *listening*. "Then you know the power of God's grace. How that power can change you into something better. You know what it means to forgive."

"I believe in redemption," the old man whispered. The gun dipped lower, the barrel aimed at the floor. "But I don't believe in you."

The old man looked down at Candace.

"I'm truly sorry you had to be a party to this, young lady. You look like a girl who might be going places. Smart. Pretty as a picture. So much like our Jessie. Isn't that right, Hill?"

Candace's eyebrows knitted, her mascara, which Rose had only recently allowed her to use, had left twin tracks along her cheeks.

"I'm Candace," she said, simply. "My name...it's Candace."

The thunder of the shot tore the air in the living room. Then Candace's head slumped forward. Joshua saw a gout of blood erupt from her temple and spatter the wall behind her.

Rose, *his* Rose, screamed; a wailing shriek, singeing the air with horror.

"Your girl's in a better place, Missus," the old man said, gently. "She's with my Jessie now, wrapped in the arms of our Savior. I believed your husband when he said you were a woman of faith. I think, in time, you'll come to understand what I mean."

The old man reached out with his empty left hand as if to touch Rose's hair. Rose screamed, gnashing her teeth even as she wept and raged. With something like sorrow in his eyes, the old man turned to Joshua.

"I expect we'll meet again, Campbell. A final reckoning, as they say in the movies. I suppose, now that we're members of the same club, that only makes sense."

The old man set the gun on the coffee table, and walked toward the French doors and opened them. He stood in the doorway, outlined in silver moonlight, a mere silhouette.

"He didn't die right away. Your boy. It took him a while. After I hit him, I circled the block, parked the car, and walked back. He lay there in the street, breathing, heavy-like. The people who came, they tried to help, but by then it was too late. One lady said she was a nurse. She held his hand while he died. He wasn't alone. Like my Jessie."

The old man hitched in a breath, as if stifling a sob.

"I wanted you to know that, Campbell. He wasn't alone."

Then he was gone.

It took him five minutes to break the chair. When he had freed himself, he stood up and faced Rose, seeing her with new eyes.

Old eyes, the voice in his head advised. *True eyes.*

"Call 911, Joshua!" Rose snarled. "She's still alive! Candace... *she's still alive!*"

Campbell looked and saw that Candace was moving, shuddering in her restraints. A slow runnel of blood leaked from the wound in her temple.

Right again, Rosie.

"Why are you just standing there? Call 911, Josh!"

Campbell took two steps toward Rose.

"No! Don't worry about me! Call the police! Call 911! She's alive!"

He wrapped his hands around Rose's throat and began to squeeze. It had been a while, years in fact. He'd strangled the others, too; throttled them until they lost consciousness. A few times he'd been tempted to finish the job just to know what it felt like, but something, some shred of compassion, had always stopped him short. Now, it felt familiar, like riding a bicycle. It felt *real*. Rose fought him, spitting and straining against the tape that bound her wrists and ankles, but in the end, she couldn't win. He watched the lights go out in her, watched the blood vessels in her eyes burst like blood-soaked fireworks until the whites turned red, then black. And when he'd made sure she was dead, he picked up the gun the old bastard had left on the coffee table and shot his daughter in the head.

He'd suffered too much; worked too hard to create his new life. There was no way Rose would let him move forward into that bright future now that she'd learned his secrets. He stood in the center of the living room where they'd danced and made love, and said his goodbyes. Then he went to bed. He had a long day ahead of him and he needed his sleep.

He waited until the next night to burn the house. That morning, he'd called in to work to tell them he wouldn't be in for a while. A family emergency out of town. He'd called in for Rose and told her supervisor that she'd gone to visit her ailing mother in Phoenix. He'd assured the woman that her prayers were appreciated and that he'd pass them along. After that he'd called Candace's school to tell them she'd gone with her mother. That would give him enough time to get out of town. He'd gone to the bank and closed out their life savings, withdrawing the money he'd need to make his way until he could begin again.

As he watched the flames engulf the immaculate little Colonial, he gripped the gym bag that contained the things he'd need on his journey: cash, about twenty thousand dollars in large and small bills. He'd left Campbell's passport and any other identifying documents to burn with the house. He wouldn't need them anymore. He'd created a new life for himself once before, after the acquittal. He could do it again. He checked the pistol the old man had left behind, and he wondered, briefly, if this moment had been destined for him all along, God's way of pointing him in the direction he should go. The old man had given him just enough information. He remembered the girl, Jessie, a petite blonde with freckles, whose nose was crooked from having been broken and badly reset. She'd cried silently, begging him not to hurt her family, promising not to tell, until he'd finished. He remembered watching the whites of her eyes turn first red, then black, as he choked her. He remembered the little house where they'd met—the immaculate Tudor situated in the center of Jessie's block. He knew the old man's church, had even attended a funeral there, a lifetime ago, with friends who'd ultimately abandoned him. The old man had given him just enough information to find him and send him to Hell.

He knew this was right—

God's will.

—could feel the *rightness* of it in his bones, and the ancient rage the old man's attack had resurrected in his soul. He would visit the old man, tie up those loose ends, and then head north, possibly into Canada. Yes, all the answers were laid out for him, shining before him like a road paved with gold; the way his mother had always insisted that the streets of Heaven were paved with gold. Yes. He would travel God's road until he found his new home. A new life. He was free.

Born again.

MANNY MIRACLE IS ALIVE AND WELL AND DYING IN THE 29TH DIMENSION!

"Death to all baby-killers!"

The Pro-Lifer hurled the screaming nurse over the side of the Gloria Bowers Family Planning Center. The screaming nurse soared high into the air, flipped over backward, and plummeted headfirst toward certain death nine stories below.

Sydney Carter, eleven years old and small for her age, shoved her way to the front of the screaming crowd. She had to see. *Had* to.

Because she knew *he* would be there.

The crowd below had gathered to witness the Pro-Lifer's latest "statement"; hundreds of bystanders, reporters, police and emergency rescue teams fought for the best view of the action. Glittering electronic eyes swiveled skyward, refocusing to capture the screaming nurse's last moments. The crowd roared with one voice.

Sydney held her breath.

And as it sometimes happened with Sydney, her secret talent captured the small details: the nurse's eyes wide with terror; her arms pinwheeling; white sneakers kicking like a woman swimming toward oblivion; a sudden flutter of motion, as if the air congealed around her for the briefest of moments.

Then she vanished.

The crowd gasped. The air above their heads was clear. No corpse lay, smashed beyond recognition, at the foot of the clinic. Sydney turned as the falling nurse's scream pierced the stunned silence from an entirely different direction. She looked up, her heart thundering in her chest.

Valiant was there.

The Far Traveler hovered twenty feet above the heads of the crowd, the screaming nurse clutched in his arms like a new bride. This close, his eyes blazed, the movements of his silver pupils leaving lighting-flash afterimages in the air.

He was even bigger than in Sydney's visions, tall as a mountain, with the shoulders of a demi-god. His skin was a luminous golden brown beneath thick, close-cropped hair as black as the space between the stars.

Even his uniform was famous, the shimmering golden one-piece that clung to his muscular frame had been spun from a fabric so exotic that it moved like skin and shone like polished mirror glass; the silver sunburst in the center of his chest plate burned with a light that could dazzle the innocent and the guilty.

But what Sydney noticed about Valiant was his hands. As he set the still-screaming nurse gently onto her feet, Sydney's talent allowed her to study the hands that had saved billions. They were large (Valiant was well over six feet tall), smooth, the nails immaculate, almost pristine. They looked like the hands of a man unaccustomed to hard, physical labor.

But Sydney knew that Valiant was anything but lazy. In the two years since he'd first appeared in Chicago, he'd saved the planet at least fifty times.

"She'll be fine," Valiant said to the crowd of National Guardsman, police officers, paramedics and reporters who surged toward them. "Please, give her some space."

Sydney rushed forward, and was immediately shoved to the ground by a horde of screaming teenagers.

"Valiant!" "Over here!" "Save me, baby!"

She winced as her knees and the heels of her hands scraped the concrete.

"Owww!" she cried. "Watch it, you jerks!"

Some dim aspect of Sydney's talent sent a thrill of anticipation rocketing up her spine, and she rolled out of the way a second before a yellow taxi smashed into the street a few feet from where she'd fallen. A moment later, the taxi exploded. The concussion blasted manhole covers into the air all along Michigan Avenue.

The Pro-Lifer stood at the intersection of Michigan and Randolph. He was holding the front end of a smashed limousine in his arms, crushing nearly a ton of steel between biceps the size of basketballs.

"Face me, fool!" he thundered. "Those who would defend the murder of innocents will be cleansed!"

Valiant faced the hordes of admirers that flocked in his wake. "Get away from me!" he shouted.

No one argued with him. The Pro-Lifer had been implicated in the destruction of nineteen family planning centers from New York to L.A. He'd pulled them down with his bare hands and burned the wreckage with his laser-vision blasts. More than a thousand people, mostly doctors, nurses, and even some patients, had been killed in the attacks. The crowd scattered like mice fleeing a raging wildfire.

The Pro-Lifer was even bigger than Valiant; nearly nine feet tall, he weighed more than a thousand pounds. Three years earlier, he'd destroyed a small skyscraper in Seattle, dragging the survivors from the rubble and trampling them beneath his steel-toed boots. Only Valiant had been able to rescue the two dozen survivors, using his powers to blast the Pro-Lifer miles through the Earth before plunging him into a molten river of lava beneath Mount St. Helens. Super-intense heat was the Pro-Lifer's only known weakness. Other than that, he was virtually unstoppable.

Valiant turned back just in time to take the full force of the truncated limousine as it struck him head on. The Pro-Lifer unleashed a laser-vision blast that instantly ignited the limousine, sending a flaming mass of molten metal and alien hero sailing across Michigan Avenue. Valiant and the burning limousine smashed through the window of an abandoned Dunkin' Donuts, through the back wall and out into the alley beyond. A moment later, the Dunkin' Donuts exploded in a howl of flame.

The Pro-Lifer flexed his armored shoulders, raised his fists above his head, and roared his manifesto.

"For the Unborn!"

Sydney clapped her hands to her ears. More windows shattered. Then the Pro-Lifer thundered toward the family planning center.

A disembodied voice spoke, seemingly from everywhere and nowhere at once.

"You're going to have to do better than that, Arnold."

The air around the clinic shimmered, as if the fabric of reality were being contorted by an unseen hand. For a moment, every human being within a mile of the center sagged beneath a sudden, unpleasant heaviness. Sydney staggered as her knees wobbled and her arms grew too heavy to lift. At the same time, she could barely contain her excitement. She'd read about Valiant's ability to manipulate gravity.

A moment later, the Far Traveler stepped out of the thin air, right in front of the Pro-Lifer.

"Give it up, Arnold," he said. "I've got a lot on my mind today."

The Pro-Lifer roared, lowered his head and charged. Valiant extended his right hand; his fingers spread wide, then clenched into a fist.

The heaviness that pulled Sydney toward the ground vanished. The Pro-Lifer stopped. His knees buckled as Valiant increased the gravity envelope around him by nearly a dozen times Earth normal.

The Pro-Lifer laughed.

"Learned a few things while I was burnin' in that Hell you sent me to," he snarled. "My power is a function of my will." He reached up and tapped the side of his iron-wrapped skull. "If I don't want to move, *nothin' on this Earth can move me.* And I got willpower I ain't even touched yet."

The Pro-Lifer chuckled. "I can do this all day, boy," he said. "How 'bout you?"

Valiant grimaced. The air around the Pro-Lifer seemed to thicken. It grew even denser, *hotter.* The Pro-Lifer's knees bowed outward a little more; the street beneath him groaned and fractured into a spider-web pattern of ruptured concrete. Behind him, a line of cars flattened as if smashed by the staff of Osiris.

The Pro-Lifer shook his head, flinging droplets of sweat all around.

"I can deflect your fancy powers, *amigo,*" he sneered. "What else ya got?"

Valiant's smile faded. To Sydney, he suddenly looked less like the shining hero she'd come to adore. To Sydney, whose special secret talent sometimes showed her little things that other people might miss, Valiant looked scared.

"You're right, Arnold," Valiant snarled. "I *don't* have time for this."

The Far Traveler unclenched his fist, and Sydney felt the air grow thin again, *cool* again. The Pro-Lifer stood erect, and shrugged, like a man throwing off a light cloak.

"I'm gonna exterminate a million baby-killers, boy," he rumbled. "And there ain't a blessed thing you can do 'bout it."

Valiant's grin returned. But this time it was cold, resigned, as if acknowledging some inescapable truth. "I know."

The Pro-Lifer screamed.

"What…what are you doing?"

Valiant took a step forward and lifted his left fist.

"I'm interfering with the nuclei of the atoms in your body, causing them to decay at an accelerated rate. You should be feeling pretty warm right now."

Indeed, from where she stood, Sydney could feel waves of intense heat emanating from the Pro-Lifer. The Pro-Lifer shook his head, funneling Valiant's power into the Earth below his feet. He took one thundering step forward.

"I'm…dealin' with it…*buttstain*," he grunted. "That…all you… got?"

" 'Fraid not," Valiant said. "When you interfere with the weak nuclear force, which is what I'm doing inside your body at this moment, you set off a radioactive chain reaction. As we speak, the cells in your kidneys, liver, lungs, and brain are becoming highly radioactive."

The Pro-Lifer stopped. Now his face was pouring sweat in great slopping sheets. "Wh…what's that you said?"

Valiant nodded. "You heard me. In a very real way, I'm giving you cancer and chemotherapy at the same time."

The Pro-Lifer screamed and clutched at his chest.

"You can't do this!" he howled.

Valiant nodded. "I *can* do this, Arnold. Like I said before: I don't have time for this. Right now I can call it all back. I can make you normal again. But you have to submit. Right here. Right now."

The Pro-Lifer fell to his knees. The heat baking off of him melted the wrecked cars a few feet away. His face had become a mass of suppurating boils.

"Late-stage radiation sickness, Arnold," Valiant said. "That's gotta hurt. Do you submit?"

The Pro-Lifer fell onto his face, his fists clutching at his stomach like a child that has eaten too much candy.

"It...HURTS!" he howled. Then... "I give! I give!"

Valiant nodded. A moment later, the Pro-Lifer, exhausted and panting, rose into the air, surrounded by the golden halo of Valiant's power. Sydney could see his boils fading as he rose, and knew that Valiant was as good as his word.

"Wait a minute!" the Pro-Lifer, restored now, howled. "Where are you sendin' me this time?"

Valiant gestured, and the golden nimbus shot straight up, carrying the Pro-Lifer into the sky at astounding speed. In moments it was gone.

"Valiant! What did you really do to him?"

The reporters peppered the cooling air with questions. Sydney noticed that all of them chose to shout from across the street. No one dared venture too close.

"The Pro-Lifer has been secured," Valiant said. "The dark matter servitors in my lunar base are placing him into a meta-containment unit as we speak."

"Was it really radiation sickness?"

"Was the public ever in danger?"

Valiant's shoulders slumped. He regarded the gathered media with a kind of sad resignation that Sydney had never seen before.

"I would never endanger the public," he said, as if stung by the idea. "I surrounded him with a bubble of focused dark matter. It's a million times more effective than lead shielding."

Sydney moved forward through the throng of admirers, trying to get his attention before he flew away.

Five little words.

If she could just whisper the message she'd divined from her Dream, she knew she could get his attention. As Valiant's golden boots lifted from the sidewalk, Sydney pushed her way through the throng

"Manny Miracle is alive and well!!"

Valiant never looked back. The Far Traveler sailed off and vanished behind the John Hancock Building.

But for just a moment...

Sydney shook her head. She thought she'd sensed Valiant slow down, his head turning in her direction by only the slightest amount.

You're being stupid, she thought.

But still…

The Far Traveler landed in the back yard of Miss Jackson's house, warping the rays of the setting sun away from him as he stepped onto the back porch, carefully, so as not to alert his foster brothers and sisters to his presence.

To an outside observer, he would have appeared as a blurred glob of motion, easily misperceived as a heat haze or optical illusion. Miss Jackson's back porch would appear perfectly normal, nothing out of place; certainly nothing to indicate that one of the most powerful superheroes in the world dwelled there.

Valiant reached for the doorknob.

"*Easy, V,*" Manny said from the Void. "*We can't afford another busted door.*"

"*I realize that, Manny,*" Valiant said. "*I'm five thousand Earth years old, you know. I've amassed a considerable store of data over that time.*"

"*Yo, you've forgotten most of what you knew,*" Manny said. "*And livin' on Earth ain't exactly a walk 'round the solar system.*"

Valiant let Manny's sarcasm pass. His host sounded tired. Even in his astral form, floating in the alternity, his psychic emanations were weak.

"*That's right, homeboy,*" Manny laughed. "*I ain't got a lotta energy left.*"

"*Don't joke about such things, Manuel.*"

"*Who's jokin'?*"

Valiant opened the back door and went inside. A quick infrared scan confirmed that the place was empty. It was Wednesday, which meant that Miss Jackson, Manny's foster grandmother, was still at church; his foster siblings, Hector, Damitra, and little Teresa still at their various afterschool activities.

"*Good,*" Manny sighed from the Void. "*Let me out.*"

Valiant walked into the bedroom Manny Milagro shared with Hector. He lay back on Manny's bed, which creaked dangerously beneath his weight. The Far Traveler's muscular legs dangled over the end of the small child's bed until his golden boot heels banged against the scarred wood floor.

"You look ridiculous," Manny chuckled.

"No more ridiculous than I feel," Valiant replied.

"Good rest, Manny."

"Far seeing," Manny replied.

Valiant closed his eyes.

Then he opened the shining door in his mind.

The tiny bedroom was flooded with light. Somewhere, a sound like the birthing cry of a newborn star pierced the veil that separates Here from There, Now from Then. The little bed's springs relaxed as Valiant's weight lessened.

Manny Milagro opened his eyes.

He looked around at the room where he'd spent the last five years, his perusal taking in the contents of the night table next to his bed: skin cream for his wrinkles and dry spots; suntan lotion to protect the dome of his rapidly balding head, not to mention the army of vitamins, heart medications and analgesics.

"You're a walkin', flyin' pharmaceutical rep, Milagro," he sighed.

His alarm watch went off. It was 3:30. Time for his meds.

Manny got up, ignoring the pain from his enflamed joints. His arthritis was screaming at him today; funny when he considered that it was Valiant who'd done all the heavy lifting. Since morning, they'd foiled three bank robberies, rescued two damsels in distress, towed a sinking ocean liner to safety, and finished off the day with the whole Pro-Lifer fiasco.

"I thought that went rather well," Valiant said from the Void. *"No loss of life, no excessive property damage."*

"I hope the servitors can handle him."

"Trust me," Valiant said. *"They've handled worse."*

"What do you think she meant?"

Valiant was silent for a moment. Then...

"I don't know," he said quietly. *"I've been thinking about her myself."*

Manny swallowed another pill. "She knew my name," he said. "Worse, she's put the two of us together somehow."

Valiant was silent, considering the possibilities.

"You think she's a shapeshifter?" Manny said. "Maybe one of the Gorgons?"

"We put the Gorgons into hypersleep," Valiant said. *"I would have detected their escape."*

Neither the boy nor the superhero spoke for a while. Finally, Manny winced, and reached for his pain pills.

"Not much time now," he said.

Valiant offered the little hum which signified agreement in his native language.

"Have you made the Choice?"

Manny shook his head, ignoring the pain that the movement wrung from the stiff joints in his lower back and neck. "You know damn well I haven't," he said.

"Don't swear, Manuel," Valiant hummed. *"Besides, I was thinking that perhaps the girl…"*

The front door opening interrupted him.

"Manny?" Miss Jackson called from the living room. "I'm home."

"Later," Manny whispered. "I'll be right there!"

But as he walked toward the living room, Manny's limbs felt leaden. His heart seemed to labor in his chest and his vision… flickered.

"Yes," Valiant said from the alternity. *"Later."*

But soon, they both knew, they would be forced to make a decision.

They'd just reached escape velocity when an emerald flare of energy flashed over the southern hemisphere.

"What the hell has she done?" Manny said from the Void.

"Swearing," Valiant sighed. *"I've got enough to worry about without listening to you backslide."*

"That power signature was huge, V. If she's killed anyone…"

"Focus, Manny."

Manny focused. He'd been joined with the Far Traveler long enough to recognize the alien hero's "no nonsense voice." They turned west and arrowed through the blackness of space, streaking toward the brilliant emerald flash.

Three minutes later, they faced "the problem." She was hovering over Australia, held aloft by a swirling green halo of telekinetic energy. And although she was one of the most evil beings on the planet, Lady Gaea had never looked more beautiful.

"I was beginning to think you weren't coming," Gaea said telepathically. "I've crippled gods for ignoring me."

Behind her, the space shuttle *Conquest* hovered, trapped within a prison of ice and stone, held prisoner by Gaea's will. The shuttle's cameras had filmed her as she snatched a meteor swarm out of orbit. Using her powers to reshape the meteors into a hollow globe, she'd then sealed the *Conquest* inside. The crew, if they were still alive, had only minutes to live. Gaea was using her telekinetic abilities to compact the globe, compressing it more and more by the hour.

She'd demanded a halt to all off-shore oil drilling in exchange for the safety of the *Conquest* and its crew.

"What's this all about, Gaea?" Valiant said. "You know they'll never stop drilling. So what do you really want?"

The self-styled Earth Avenger floated closer, her emerald gown flowing behind her in the photon stream generated by her powers. Lady Gaea was a super eco-terrorist. She considered herself the protector of a beleaguered planet, one abused by pollution, global warming and human overpopulation. She believed human kind to be an infection for which she was the cure.

"You *know* what I want," she said. "What I've always wanted."

"The destruction of the human race?"

Lady Gaea smiled and shook her head. Her long green dreadlocks streaming around her head like a cloud of serpents.

"That comes later. Right now, Traveller... I want you."

Lady Gaea raised her hands as arcs of emerald lightning danced between her fingertips.

"I hope you intend to defend yourself," she said. "I want to see you at your most glorious before you die!"

She launched the first volley, a massive lightning strike drawn from the life force of the planet below. As long as she remained within a hundred miles of the planet's atmosphere, she could control its energies. The lightning fried the space between the combatants as Lady Gaea drove her power against the Far Traveler.

Valiant erected a shield of electromagnetic force which absorbed Gaea's attack and converted the electrical surge into power; power that he could use. He raised his fists and sent a surge of cosmic energy raging toward Gaea.

The bolt struck her dead on, knocking her head over heels toward the Earth. Captured by the planet's gravity, Lady Gaea bounced across the thin layer of atmosphere like a burning stone skipping along the surface of a vast blue lake.

Valiant turned his focus to Gaea's sphere. It was the size of a small skyscraper: a prison of rock and "dirty" ice hovering at the edge of space.

"*Jeez,*" Manny said.

"*Indeed.*"

Behind them, Lady Gaea rose like a green moon. She waved her hands, and a lash of telekinetic energy grabbed meteor fragments as big as houses and thrust them toward Valiant.

The Far Traveler opened a small slit into Dimension 29 and funneled the rushing torrent of debris into it. Then he dropped into the slit and zipped it closed behind him.

"Where are you, my love?" Gaea broadcast to the suddenly empty space around her. She turned toward the *Conquest* and briefly touched the minds of the terrified crew still trapped inside.

Lady Gaea smiled.

Major Amanda Curley and the crew of the *Conquest* didn't have time to question the shining savior who'd come to their rescue. Curley watched and prayed, as the Far Traveler floated her people toward the glowing portal he'd opened up with a flash of his heat vision, or whatever it was these people used to save the day.

"Thank you," Major Curley said.

"Your people are safe," Valiant said. "Now it's your turn."

The Far Traveler raised his hands and...*wavered*. His hands began to tremble and his eyes widened in alarm. A second later, Major Curley was stunned by a blinding flash. When her vision cleared, she saw a dwarf, or something *like* a dwarf, hovering in the space where the Far Traveler had been.

Thin strands of wispy white hair covered the floating dwarf's head and the skin of its face resembled dried brown parchment. It was wearing blue jeans, a red, white and blue Chicago Cubs jersey... and what looked like an ancient pair of red Nikes.

"*Manny! You'll die up here! Wake up!*"

The dwarf's eyes snapped open, and Amanda Curley saw that it was really a boy—a boy hovering, unprotected, in the vacuum of space. When the strange boy saw Major Curley his eyes widened in sudden terror. Then the dwarf clapped its hands over its mouth and vanished.

"Sorry, V."

Valiant reappeared an instant later.

Outside, Lady Gaea rocketed toward the *Conquest,* carried forward by an emerald firestorm of destructive psychic power.

"Gotta stop it now, V," Manny whispered. *"So tired."*

Valiant shoved Major Curley through the glowing portal a second before Lady Gaea slammed into him, her momentum great enough to blast them both out of the shuttle and into space. Then the two of them plunged into the planet's atmosphere.

Caught in Gaea's grasp, Valiant smelled burning flesh and hair and realized that the smell was coming from him. He hadn't had time to erect a shield around himself before reentry. Gaea's telekinetic grip was too strong. He couldn't break free.

"This is all I've ever really wanted, my love," Lady Gaea screamed, clutching him tightly. Then she kissed him.

"Awww man," Manny said. *"I'm dying, but this is disgusting."*

Below them, the red and yellow sands of the Australian outback reared up, looming closer as they streaked toward the Earth. At ninety-thousand feet, Valiant clenched his right fist and they began to accelerate.

"What are you doing?" Gaea shouted over the howling wind. "I can't move!"

"I just multiplied our mass by a factor of two hundred," Valiant shouted. "We're now nearly as dense as the artificial satellite you created. Eighty thousand feet, Gaea! If we strike the Earth at this velocity we'll cause incalculable damage to the planet!"

"What?"

"Forty thousand feet!"

"You wouldn't dare!" Gaea shouted. "You're bluffing!"

"Think of the meteor strike that killed the dinosaurs, Gaea. This impact will make that one look like a slumber party. Fifteen thousand feet!"

Lady Gaea's eyes shifted toward the ground. The red desert was rising up quickly, filling the horizon, *becoming* the world.

"But...you're a hero!"

"I'm dying, Gaea!" Valiant shouted. "Look into my mind and you'll see I'm telling the truth!"

She did. She sensed Valiant's vast power, the life force that stretched millennia into the past; and she sensed the darkness seething where his memories should have been.

But the emotions she read, the pain and fear, were those of an adolescent boy—a boy that was somehow trapped in the shining form of a god.

"I don't...I'm not..."

"Five thousand feet, Gaea."

"But you're not what I..."

"Say goodbye, Gaea."

She released him. Confused, disoriented by what she'd seen in his mind, she let him go. Which was exactly what he'd intended.

Twelve feet from the ground, Valiant ripped open a portal and the two of them plummeted into Dimension 29. Lady Gaea screamed as that lifeless void filled her hyper-receptive telepathic mind and shut it down.

Manny, awake now, floated over to take a look.

"Dude," he said. "Up close she's even scarier than she looks on TV."

Valiant shrugged.

"She possesses a kind of crude beauty," he said. "Aesthetically, I find her an exceptional specimen of your race. If not for her sado-masochistic sexual delusions I might be tempted to..."

"Gettin' nauseous here, V."

"Sorry," Valiant said. "Are you alright, Manny?"

Manny shook his head. "Nearly time, V."

Valiant nodded. "But the Choice..."

"I'll *do* it," Manny snapped, rougher than he intended. "You just get us back to Chicago."

Three minutes later, Valiant opened an exit portal and stepped out onto the lawn of the North Lake Institute for Posthuman Studies.

A containment team scrambled out onto the lawn and took charge of Lady Gaea. She would awaken, mentally bruised, but essentially unharmed, interred in the "Cellar," the Institute's high-tech metahuman containment facility.

Valiant freed the Conquest's crew from their dark matter rescue pods and entrusted them to the police and technicians.

"Let's go home, V," Manny said. "I'm fadin' fast."

Valiant nodded and leaped into the sky.

The little girl from the family planning center was waiting for them back at Miss Jackson's house.

Valiant descended, invisible, into the back yard. Sydney, however, was staring at him as if he were standing in plain view.

"I can see you," she said quietly. "Weird."

Valiant turned, prepared to vault away.

"*Wait, V,*" Manny said. "*Let's see what she wants.*"

"I know you can't show yourself here," Sydney said. "I know you probably have some kind of secret identity or whatever. I get it."

She stood up and walked unerringly toward where he stood.

"I can feel you there. I don't know how that can be, but I just... just *know* things about you. Where you'll be, how you feel. I even know a little about how your powers work."

This took Manny by surprise. Since bonding with the Valiant force he'd striven to keep the nature of their powers a closely guarded secret. The less their enemies really understood about Valiant's abilities the better. Besides, Manny understood precious little about them himself.

"You control the four fundamental forces of the universe," she said. "Electromagnetism, gravity, the strong nuclear force, and the weak nuclear force."

She smiled, her voice trembling with a fearful excitement. "Which means you can do just about anything you want."

Manny chuckled to himself. "Anything" was a long way from what the Valiant force allowed him to do. For him, gravity and electromagnetism were the simplest of the fundamental forces to manipulate. He just seemed to have a facility for it.

The other Forces were a different story.

The strong nuclear force, which holds the nuclei of atoms together, was too unpredictable; it's potential for catastrophe too overwhelming. A significant cessation of the strong nuclear force would allow those nuclei to disintegrate, leading to the dissolution of reality.

The weak force was too subtle. It governs radioactive decay and could, if left unchecked, ignite a chain reaction that could overheat the Earth's core, leading to the destruction of the entire planet.

The strong and weak nuclear forces were more opaque to Manny's senses. When forced, he could access minor aspects of their potentials, but he would never be comfortable with them.

Even so, he was one of the most powerful "superhumans" on Earth—a class 8, ranking with Lady Gaea and the Elemental in power. But he wasn't omnipotent. He'd learned, all too recently, that even the Valiant power had limits.

"I need your help," Sydney said. "I need it really bad."

"We can't speak here," Valiant said. "I won't endanger my housemates and the woman who shares her life with us. Will you come with me?"

Sydney nodded and extended her hand.

Observing from the void, Manny was touched by the girl's display of trust. He'd fought a thousand villains who would have taken advantage of Sydney's innocence. He was sure she knew better. The faith shining in her eyes, however, communicated how she felt about Valiant. For her, he was now and would always be, a hero, incapable of harming an innocent little girl who adored him.

I'm not so sure 'bout that, Manny thought.

Valiant dropped the light-distorting field. For the briefest instant, the Far Traveler towered in full view, above the little girl. Sydney gasped, and took a step back despite herself. Valiant smiled. He'd only learned the trick of it recently. It had taken him nearly a year to understand exactly which facial muscles were involved.

"Are you afraid of heights?" he said.

Sydney laughed. Then, her eyes wide with wonder and a strange...*knowing*, she placed her hand in his.

They vanished.

The observation deck of the Lincoln Tower was empty. It had been closed down for repairs after a battle between Valiant and Pulsar demolished the top three floors of Chicago's Tallest Tower.

Valiant set them down gently on the roof.

Sydney sat down on one of the benches, next to the bronze statue of Abraham Lincoln, for whom the Tower was named.

"Now, young lady," Valiant rumbled. "I think you'd better tell me exactly what this is all about."

Sydney swallowed a thick lump in her throat. Now that they

were here, together in this place so familiar to her from the Dream, she didn't know where to begin.

"It's the dreams...my dreams."

Valiant frowned.

"She's a little freaked out by you, V," Manny said. *"Let me do the talking."*

Valiant nodded and allowed Manny to take over the interview. He'd only been on Earth for six years. In that time he'd memorized volumes on human history, psychology, and the inner workings of the human mind.

Human emotion, however, was another matter. Strange and fluid, it was a wild realm better left to one of their own to navigate. In the millennia since he'd left his home world to soar the cosmos, searching for the keys to his lost past, he'd encountered thousands of sentient races. But nowhere in the galaxy was sentience more convoluted, more unwieldy, as among the humans of Earth.

"What do you know about Manny Miracle?" Manny said, using Valiant's voice.

"He comes to me in dreams sometimes," Sydney said. "Valiant I mean. He wakes me up from a long sleep and we fly up here. We talk, but I'm not really speaking to Valiant, or not *just* Valiant, anyway. Somehow, someone else is with us, hovering around, like a ghost. I don't know anything about him except his name: Manny Miracle."

Valiant arched one black eyebrow. "You've dreamed of all this happening? You and me? Here? In this place?"

Sydney nodded her head, her eyes shining.

"Yup. Sometimes I know where you'll be before you even show up. Sometimes I even know what you're feeling. Guess that means I have powers too, huh?"

Valiant and Manny considered carefully before answering, "It would appear so."

"Maybe I'm a precog, like Trance," she said. "Or clairvoyant like Doctor Warlock!"

"Or maybe she's nuts like Lady Gaea."

"Quiet, Manny."

"I'm not nuts," Sydney said. "And I'm wide awake."

"You can hear Manny?"

"Yep," Sydney said proudly. "He buzzes. Like a little fly zipping around my head. It's kinda irritating. In my dream he doesn't say much. He just says the same thing over and over again, like a broken record."

"What does he say?" Valiant asked.

Sydney shrugged. "He tells me to be brave," she said. "That courage is all any hero needs to save the world."

Sydney shrugged "He does what my mom says I do. He repeats the same thing over and over again. Just like a broken record."

"*V,*" Manny said telepathically. "*What's happening?*"

"Somehow, we're like, mentally connected," Sydney answered smoothly. "And do you wanna know why?"

Valiant leaned forward. All of this was quite beyond even their shared experience, and he couldn't remember if anything like this had happened before. "Why?"

Sydney clasped her two fists together, as if she were shaking hands with herself.

"We're linked," she said. "Partners."

Valiant stared at her, uncomprehending for a moment.

"Don't you get it?" she chirped. "I'm your new sidekick!"

"*Oh Jesus,*" Manny moaned.

"Listen, Sydney," Manny said through Valiant. "We...I mean... *I* don't *need* a sidekick, especially not a little kid."

Sydney's face collapsed in on itself. The light in her eyes dimmed.

"I mean, if you dreamed about all this, didn't you know what my answer would be?"

"I don't see everything," Sydney said. "And sometimes I get the order of things all wrong."

Valiant stared at the little girl as she slumped dejectedly down onto the bench. She wiped at her eyes but failed to stop the fat teardrops that streaked her cheek.

"We're *supposed* to be partners," she said, as if chastising herself. "I *feel* it."

"Why is this so important to you, Sydney?"

When she looked up at him, her eyes were bright with tears.

"It's my sister," she said. "Her name's Tracy. She's..."

For a moment, her lips trembled. She looked away, as if ashamed of her tears. When she finally spoke, her voice was barely audible, even to Valiant's ears.

"She's sick," she said. "Like *really* sick."

Valiant froze. In the alternity, Manny sat up a little straighter.

"She has leukemia," Sydney went on. "She's only fifteen years old. Both my mom and my dad are doctors, but even they can't help her."

Sydney looked around as if searching the corners for eavesdroppers.

"Something's wrong with her blood," she said. "My mom just cries when the come home from the hospital. My dad looks scared all the time now. I'm scared too."

She looked Valiant in the eye then.

"After the dreams started, I watched a documentary about you on the All Heroes Channel. It said that you're an alien, that you can control radiation and chemical reactions."

A lightless abyss opened in Manny's mind. He was beginning to see where this was heading. Sydney looked away, her eyes taking in the sweep of the city more than a thousand feet below.

"I thought if I volunteered to be your sidekick, you'd use your powers to help fix Tracy."

Valiant stared at her for a moment. Then he stood up.

"I can't help your sister," he said.

"But why not?" Sydney shot back. "You can control radiation and chemical reactions right?"

"To a limited extent, but…"

"They use radiation and chemicals to help people with leukemia don't they?"

"I suppose so, Sydney. But…"

"You can try can't you? You can at least try!"

Valiant held up one hand. "It's not that I don't want to help," he said. "It's just… It's extremely complicated."

"Didn't you stop the Terror Gods when they turned Ireland into a vampire colony?"

"Yes, but…"

"You pushed one of Saturn's moons back into orbit after Lunatik stole it, didn't you?"

"A *small* moon yes, but…"

"You saved Karen Keen from the Red Mauler, even after he stole all your powers. Everyone *saw* you do it. *It was on TV!*"

"Sydney," Valiant said, grasping her shoulders, gently. "My powers don't work that way."

The Far Traveler sighed, and sat down.

"I have great power, yes, but I also have certain limitations. I can move a mountain, or even blow it apart. But I can't put it back together. Believe me, I've tried. See, I don't know how to *create* things."

Valiant shrugged again. Fists that had smashed battleships clenched and unclenched in his lap—infinitely powerful and utterly useless.

"I suppose I must have known, once, long ago," he said. "But the journey through space was exceedingly difficult. I lost my way. I had used nearly all my power just to make it to Earth, and when I arrived, there was very little of my former self left. I was as weak as a newborn baby."

Sydney's gaze seemed to see through him. Her sad eyes pierced him to his core.

"If I used my powers on your sister, I'd only make things worse. I could kill her, Sidney."

Sidney was silent for a long moment. The Far Traveler waited. Finally, she spoke.

"It's like I'm waiting for some stupid miracle to come along; hoping like maybe the doctors forgot somethin.'"

Sydney got up and walked to the guard rail. Her voice carried back to Valiant, carried on the wind, as she gazed out over the lights of the city.

"Sometimes I fall asleep hoping that I'll wake up and be somebody else; somebody whose big sister isn't sick. Sometimes I wish it really was just a stupid dream."

The pain in her voice reached across the space between them, leaving Valiant confused. He was unable to share her sadness, the feeling of outrage and dread that seemed to hover over her like a shroud.

But Sydney's sadness reached even further, across the vast abyss that separates worlds, into the alternity, where it settled in the heart of its only resident. That sadness found its echo in Manny Milagro's own dark spaces.

"You're a superhero," Sydney said quietly. "You don't know what it's like to live in fear."

"I want to show you something," Manny interjected. "Will you trust me just a bit more?"

Sidney studied his face, as if appraising its worth. Something in that calculating appraisal broke Manny's heart. Her faith in him was burning, ignited by his weakness.

"I trust you," she said.

"Manny...what are your doing?"

The Far Traveler stood up. "Stand back."

She did. He closed his eyes and opened the shining door. There was a flash of light and a distant rumbling in the Earth.

Manny Milagro stood facing Sydney.

"You're wrong, Sydney," he said. "I know what it's like to be afraid."

He was wearing his favorite Chicago Cubs jersey, jeans, and the "Go Cubbies!" baseball cap he'd gotten during his last stay at St. John's Children's Hospital. He liked the cap because it hid his baldness from those who would stare whenever he showed his face in public.

He was a full head shorter than Sydney although he was three years older; his eyes were bloodshot, their edges encrusted with a thick yellowish fluid, the buildup from his eye medication.

Sydney gaped, amazed. Then she said, "Manny Miracle."

"Milagro," he said. "It's Spanish."

Sydney stared at him some more. Her expression, part fascination, part revulsion, was familiar to him.

"What are you?" she said. "Are you an alien?"

Manny laughed. For the first time in a long while, he filled the air with the sound of his laughter.

"No," he said. "I was born in Brooklyn."

"You look..."

Manny smiled. "When I was nine years old I was diagnosed with a condition called Hutchinson-Gilford Progeria Syndrome. People call it 'rapid aging disease.' It wrinkles my skin, makes my hair fall out, destroys my joints, and my heart and slowly shuts down my vital organs. Most people with progeria only live to be about thirteen...years old. The doctors tell me that I'm something of an anomaly, because I'm still kickin'."

Manny smiled and spread his hands like a magician revealing his mysteries. "But not for much longer."

Sydney's jaw dropped open. She peered at Manny, like a scientist studying a rare, but diminutive insect.

"You're just a kid."

"Yep."

"How old are you?"

"Fourteen."

Sydney's silent appraisal continued long enough for Manny to grow uncomfortable. Finally she delivered her verdict.

"Cool."

Despite the pain and uncertainty and everything that Manny had been through in his short life, he found himself laughing again. Sydney joined him. The two of them laughed like two school friends who had just pulled off the greatest practical joke in the history of the universe.

"Ahhh, young love," a voice hissed from the shadows. "It's so sweet it hurts."

Manny whirled toward the voice, and froze. Literally. A sheathe of blue-tinged ice congealed around him, covering him from his neck to his toes. In less than two seconds he was trapped in a shimmering frozen shroud.

Sydney screamed. Manny was barely able to turn his head, but what he could see filled him with dismay.

Two figures stepped out of the shadows beneath the observation deck. One of them shone a brilliant azure blue, his head haloed by a flickering violet corona.

Deep Freeze.

The second figure clung to the shadows, like a bear unwilling to leave the warmth of its cave. Manny knew this was for good reason. The Corruptor was a creature of darkness; half-mutant/half-vampire, he was able to manipulate shadows the way a potter molds his clay. He possessed the ability to fill his victims' minds with the blackest despair. He'd once "corrupted" an entire church congregation, one Christmas Eve. By the time the police arrived, the church was in flames. Most of the congregation had been butchered at the hands of their fellow believers.

The Corruptor flowed across the observation deck like a black cloud, and wrapped his shadow/aura around Sydney.

"What a pretty polly," he whispered. "Filled with such delicious terrors. I don't know where to begin."

Sydney screamed again. At the same time, one of the Corruptor's black tendrils pierced Manny's skull.

"*Manny,*" Valiant said. "*Open the door.*"

"*I...can't,*" Manny thought. "*He's here, inside...he's inside my head.*"

"*Manny,*" Valiant said. "*You're frightened. Calm yourself. Focus...*"

"He's in my head!"

The Corruptor moaned with pleasure as he drank deep from the well of Manny's fear.

"Soooo good," he whispered. "These two are choice cuts."

"This is the girl?" Deep Freeze said. "She don't look like much."

He wore a tight blue form-fitting uniform, white gloves, and boots cut to resemble icicles. His face was obscured behind blue-tinted goggles.

"She's the secret to our victory, Carl," a voice said from above.

Manny's eyes rolled skyward.

Oh no.

Each of the five figures floating toward the observation deck was formidable enough to send the bravest hero scrambling for cover. Together, the Destructors possessed power enough to shake the planet.

Hell's Belle, a demoness, the daughter of an entity many believed to be Evil Incarnate. She was nearly seven feet tall, with skin the color of blood, and her head sporting the horns of a Brahma bull. In her left hand she gripped the Crimson Scepter, a magical trident smelted in the heart of a star. With it, Hell's Belle could incinerate a city block.

Titan: a mutant behemoth strong enough to crush boulders in his bare hands. His war club was the length of an SUV.

Professor Shiva: a man, once a teacher, who, after a centuries-long killing spree, transformed himself into the avatar of the Hindu god of destruction.

Nightslayer: American Cyberninja. Super fast, super strong. Completely psychotic.

But the man floating in the center of the newcomers was worse.

Immobilized by the Corruptor's power, Manny's terror deepened toward panic.

Not him. Not now.

John Slaughter.

Unlike many of his counterparts, Slaughter did not deign to wear the colorful uniform of a super villain. Instead he wore a simple black suit and tie, a large but tasteful silver skull belt buckle his only visible concession to fashion.

He was only a little above average height, but his rangy form was fitted out with the long muscles of a dancer, his every movement a study in lethal grace. He exuded an almost visible sexual magnetism, but his coffee-brown features were unremarkable, save for the air of unwavering confidence which emanated from them.

Manny shuddered. Slaughter's confidence was justified; a dark magician of staggering ability, his most infamous crime was the destruction of the English village of Wolking, during which he'd murdered nearly five thousand inhabitants. At the height of the murder wave, he'd resurrected the dead victims as flesh-eating ghouls and set them loose on the English countryside. By the time Valiant fought Slaughter to a standstill, nearly twenty-thousand innocents had perished.

The Wolking Massacre, as the event had come to be known, was part orchestrated chaos/part strategy, a supernatural energy exchange designed to increase Slaughter's magical might. It was successful: he was now arguably the most powerful metahuman on the planet, capable of abrogating the laws of physics with a snap of his fingers. He and the others had formed the meta-terrorist organization known as The Destructors.

Trapped in the alternity, immobilized in ice and dread, Valiant could only watch as Slaughter and the others settled onto the observation deck. Then a sharp stab of agony detonated in Manny's chest and his left arm went numb.

No!

Slaughter looked down at Manny and frowned.

"Where the hell did you come from? Munchkinland?"

Manny clutched at his chest. It felt as if something with claws was tearing him apart from the inside. His heart. It was his heart.

"Leave him alone!" Sidney cried.

Slaughter gestured, his fingers tracing a luminous web in the air, and the ice holding Manny vanished.

Manny fell to the floor of the observation deck.

Slaughter turned to the Corruptor. The fear manipulator had wrapped Sydney in a seething web of black tendrils.

"Let her go."

"No," the Corruptor snarled. "The girl is mine. You said I could play with her."

"*After* we destroy the alien," he said. "Until then, we need her. She's the bait."

The Corruptor shuddered, his dark energies writhing like the smoke from a burning corpse. "Liar," he hissed. "Big bad magic man, bossing everybody around. But it was my power that found her. *Me*. Not *you!*"

The Corruptor's black tentacles wrapped around Sydney's throat. The fear-eater clutched her to his breast even as his form swelled, gathering darkness to him, increasing his mass and height like a roiling mass of thunderheads. He vanished, swallowed up in a shrieking black whirlwind.

"She's mine!"

The Corruptor unleashed his "darkform" the ultimate expression of his madness and power—a giant black metamorph that could assume any form he chose. A black Tyrannosaurus rex roared out of the whirlwind and thundered toward Slaughter.

Hell's Belle, Nightslayer and Professor Shiva dove out of the way as the shadowmorph charged. Titan bellowed and leaped in front of Slaughter swinging his war club.

The shadowmorph rammed Titan head-on. The stunned behemoth flew over the side of the observation deck and plummeted out of view.

Slaughter cleared his throat, and the shadowmorph froze. The Corruptor screamed and dropped Sydney. John Slaughter chuckled.

"Ahhh, Vincent," he said. "You never understood your place in the Great Tapestry that is my will. I need your power. You, on the other hand, are, quite simply, expendable."

Slaughter raised his right fist. He relaxed his fingers and revealed a small star burning in the center of his palm. The star rose up, flew across the observation deck and attacked the shadowmorph, eating away at its darkness, burning it apart in a blinding shower of white sparks. The Corruptor's scream scaled upward into shrieks of pain. Slaughter opened his mouth and inhaled deeply. And all the darkness that was the Corruptor's power went into him.

A moment later, the Corruptor burst into flames. He fell, wailing, to the floor as Slaughter's power burned him to ash.

Everyone watched the smoking pile of ash as it swirled and eddied across the rooftop and out over the city. Finally, Slaughter broke the silence.

"Well that was fun."

He turned to Sydney, who lay crumpled in the spot where the Corruptor had dropped her.

"You're quite the social butterfly, young lady," he said. "I've expended a lot of magical energy searching for you. Now that I've found you, there's a question I've been dying to ask."

He leaned over, grabbed Sydney by the front of her t-shirt and hauled her off the ground.

"Where's Valiant?"

"Why?" Sidney shot back. "He steal your breath mints?"

Then she kicked him in the testicles.

Slaughter grunted, more in surprise than pain. He dropped Sydney and fell to one knee, clutching himself. Hell's Belle and the other Destructors laughed.

Sydney kneeled at Manny's side. She took his hand, leaned down and kissed him quickly on the forehead and whispered, "I still believe in you."

Then she took off toward the guard rail.

"Manny, open the door. Let me out."

"I can't, V," Manny said silently. *"Pain. Everything's fuzzy. Don't… remember…how."*

Sydney hit the fence and began to climb.

Hell's Belle reached up, snagged one of Sidney's legs between the prongs of her trident and plucked her off the security fence. John Slaughter got to his feet, his face contorted with a kind of demonic glee. No one was laughing now. There was a flash of light. Then his fist was filled with a long-bladed hunting knife.

From where he lay, Manny could only watch, paralyzed by the pain in his chest. He was having a heart attack. There was only one thing he could do.

It was time.

"Hold on, V," he said. *"I'm gonna shake things up."*

Sydney dangled in Hell's Belle's grip, hanging upside down eight feet above the observation deck. John Slaughter lifted the knife.

"Give her to me."

Manny Chose.

Lightning split the night sky. Power detonated across the observation deck and Hell's Belle was blasted across the roof. John Slaughter raised a defensive shield which diverted the power blast.

When the blinding light dimmed, a tall figure clad in radiant silver and gold stood in the center of the observation deck.

Valiant.

"Manny?"

But something was different.

The Valiant power had bonded with Manny Milagro during another moment of great danger. After a national news story about "Chicago's Miracle Boy," Manny had been invited to consult with a progeria specialist in California. During the return flight however, an engine malfunction threatened to bring down the plane with Manny, Miss Jackson and Karen Keen, his social worker, on board. As the passengers and crew prayed and wept around him, the bright door had opened. The Valiant force had spoken telepathically into Manny's mind.

Who would you save?

Everything, the screams, the flight attendants weeping in their jump seats, everything…froze.

The voice was clear, as if spoken by someone seated in the next chair. But Miss Jackson and Karen Keene were bent double in their seats, frozen in "crash positions."

"Who would you save?"

"What?" Manny said, looking around for the person who'd spoken. "What's happening?"

"If you had the power to save yourself, or the people you love, who would you save?"

Manny looked out the window. The green expanse of a large meadow spread out below him. In the distance, smoke from a tall factory hung, as if frozen solid, in the clear afternoon sunlight.

"Who would you save?"

Manny considered for a moment. Then he spoke.

"I guess I would save Miss Jackson and Miss Keane."

"Why?"

Manny shrugged. " 'Cause they took care of me when nobody else would."

"You have suffered. Pain and loss are your constant companions. But I sense no bitterness in you. Why?"

Manny shrugged again.

"That doctor told me I ain't got a lotta time left," he said. "That sucks. But there's other kids who've had worse stuff happen to 'em. Some kids don't have any family at all."

He looked over at Mrs. Jackson. The old woman had taken him in shortly after his diagnosis. She'd never hesitated in the face of Karen Keen's grim prognosis.

"Child needs a proper home like anybody else," she'd said. *"You like pancakes, son?"*

"Yes, ma'am!"

"Then you and me will do just fine."

Manny smiled, even as the smell of burning filled the cabin. "I'm still alive too," he'd said. "Figure I've been luckier than a lot of other people."

The voice was silent for a moment. Then it spoke.

"The Choice is made."

That was the first time he'd opened the shining door. Valiant had slowed the plane's fall by negating the pull of Earth's gravity upon it. He'd set them down safely in the open field and become an overnight sensation.

The Valiant force was, in reality, the personality and vast energies once wielded by an alien being of immense age; a member of a cosmic peace-keeping force that had, at one time, enforced the will of a mighty council of intergalactic lawgivers.

When the people of Earth saw Valiant soaring overhead, what they were really seeing was an amalgam, the blending of that ancient, alien force and the perfect adult, drawn from the imagination of a wounded child. Manny Milagro often dreamed of the one thing he could never, ever possess: a strong, healthy body unmarred by pain and sickness.

Because Manny Milagro would never live to adulthood.

Sometimes, when Miss Jackson could afford it, she brought him comic books. In his tiny room, he'd created a haven from doctors' offices and curious well-wishers, a cathedral decorated with images of modern-day gods and heroes; two-fisted, four-color avengers vying for space with prescription slips and medicine bottles. He'd made peace with the fact of his onrushing mortality.

But the Valiant force had given him a reason to fight.

Sometimes he would open the shining door, walk through it, and soar, unfettered by pain, untouched by time, through the divergent reality he called the "alternity." Indeed, it was Manny who had named the force with which he shared his life. Now that force was here.

And, somehow, using him as its unwitting harbinger, it had Chosen once again.

"Well well well," Slaughter said. "What have we here?"

Sydney was gone. The raven-haired amazon wearing Valiant's costume glared at Manny, her argent eyes round with terror and incomprehension.

"What did you do to me?" the shining woman said. "How can this be?"

The amazon clasped her hands to her temples, dropped to her knees and screamed, "Get out of my head!"

"*It's too much*," Valiant said. "*She is unfit.*"

"No," Manny said aloud. "She's the one."

Slaughter turned toward him then. He studied Manny, one eye squinted shut as if he were looking through a keyhole into a room filled with mysteries.

"It's *you*," he said. "*Now I understand.*"

Slaughter's eyes crackled with a golden flame, and he laughed.

"Imagine it. The World's Greatest Guardian hiding in the mind of a crippled, adolescent midget."

Slaughter stepped over the silver woman and grabbed Manny by the throat.

"I never needed the girl at all," he said. "Kill the hobbit and you kill the hero."

Slaughter squeezed tighter. The pain in Manny's chest doubled in intensity. Tears blurred his vision as the feral glow in Slaughter's eyes pulsed in time with his fluttering heart beat.

"Shall I tell you of my plan, Traveler? Since your attempt to pass on your considerable attributes has failed, you may be interested to know what I've planned for this stinkhole of a city after you're dead."

Manny struggled, but it was no use. Slaughter was too strong, the pain in his chest a drumbeat that drowned out the world. A cold wave of darkness began to envelop him. The golden light in Slaughter's eyes became a conflagration.

The Valiant force wailed, *"Manny!"*

" 'm...sorry," Manny whispered, as the cold closed over him. "Hurts."

Slaughter's face began to fade away, taking everything with it. Manny let himself fall into that other, darker void.

"Oh no, my alien friend," Slaughter said. "I've no intention of letting you slip away just yet."

A furious crimson flame pierced the dark void around Manny's mind. A sensation like a million angry wasps swarming over his skin exploded in every part of his body.

Pain.

White-hot agony, a searing cold that burned him to the core and flayed his every nerve ending. The shock drove the darkness from his mind...and brought him to his senses. Slaughter's face flooded back with razor clarity.

Manny was alive—in incredible agony—but alive.

"That's better," Slaughter said. "I like my victims conscious while I tear out their souls."

Slaughter turned to the others.

"Get ready, friends. The Darkness awaits."

Hell's Belle, Professor Shiva, and Deep Freeze formed a triangle, while Nightslayer stood watch over the silver amazon. She hadn't moved from the spot where she'd fallen.

"My friends and I are here to perform a Summoning," Slaughter said. "You see, Hell's Belle really does have royal blood flowing through those unholy veins of hers. Her father is a rather prickly fellow, who rules over a substantial piece of infernal real estate."

Hell's Belle raised the Crimson Scepter above her head. A blast of lightning struck the trident, igniting the demoness in a screeching corona of hellfire.

"Daddy's quite powerful," Slaughter said. "In the Great Scheme of Things, I'd say he falls just a tad short of...oh I don't know... let's say...*God.*"

Slaughter grinned. His eyes steamed, sending crimson whorls of power into the sky.

"However, Daddy's hoping to move up in the angelic ranks."

He pulled Manny in close enough to whisper.

"He's looking to move upmarket."

Manny tried to open the shining door, but he was still too weak, his mind clouded with pain. Slaughter's grip was cutting off the blood flow to his brain. He was dying, but unable to die.

"My friends and I will open the Way for our sponsor. At which time He shall step forth in all His Infernal Glory and burn this city to the ground."

Manny looked over at where Sydney, clad in the Valiant power, lay. She was staring at him, *through* him, her mouth agape, her eyes wide with wonder, as if she were listening to the strains of a distant choir.

"Fortunately, millions of innocents will die," Slaughter said. "And every death that happens in His name will add to His power, making Him that much stronger. There's only one being on Earth who stands a chance of stopping us. You."

Slaughter laughed and shook Manny like a rag doll.

"And you're not exactly 'you' anymore, are you?"

Manny wasn't paying attention. A new voice had entered his head.

"*Oh my god,*" Sidney said. "*It's so big in here.*"

"*Yeah,*" Manny said. "*Plenty of room for everybody.*"

"*There's a weird thing in here with me.*"

Manny smiled.

"*Don't mind him. He just cleans up the place.*"

"*Manny, in case you've forgotten, John Slaughter is about to destroy the world.*"

"*Trust me, V,*" Manny said. "*I believe in her too.*"

Back in three-dimensional space, Hell's Belle spun the glowing trident over her head, forming a luminous circle of power as she shouted words in a language unspoken on Earth for ten thousand years.

"Abis!" she cried. *"Abis e vort me perone dracis mal!"*

The observation deck trembled as a powerful gale struck the Lincoln Tower. Two thousand windows shattered as a concussion wave blasted the massive building. Every streetlight within a three mile radius exploded.

"That's my cue," Slaughter said. The light in his eyes grew blinding, as sharp as an acetylene torch. "Time to die, little hero."

Manny opened his eyes and smiled, but it was a cold smile, one filled with dark promises.

"Look over your shoulder, lugnuts."

Slaughter turned.

The silver amazon was holding Nightslayer over her head. The cyberninja dangled, unconscious, in her grip. Slaughter dropped Manny a moment before Sydney hurled Nightslayer across the roof. Nightslayer slammed into Slaughter and knocked him down.

"Kill her!" Hell's Belle roared.

She sent a livid blast of hellfire toward Sydney. Sydney raised her hands and a shimmering bulwark of power sprang up in front of her. The shield deflected the bolt of hellfire back at Hell's Belle, blasting her off her feet.

"Lookit that," Manny said. *"The kid's a natural."*

Deep Freeze hurled a blistering blast of arctic air, cold enough to freeze Sydney where she stood. Sydney countered with a shimmering orb of superheated air. The orb expanded, roaring like the scream of a fighter jet, and melted Deep Freeze's volley. Sydney expanded the orb even further, until it enveloped Deep Freeze in a swirling red whirlwind.

"Hot!" he howled. "Too hot!"

The amazon turned up the heat. Behind her, Professor Shiva unleashed his deathcry, a hypersonic scream that could disintegrate matter. The lethal sonic assault blasted the amazon off her feet and into the arms of Titan, who had just crawled up the side of the Tower. Titan caught the amazon by the hair and hurled her high into the sky.

"She doesn't know what she's doing," the Valiant force said.

"But I do."

"Your energies are flagging, Manuel. If you initiate the change now..."

"It was nice knowin' ya, V."

Manny Milagro raised his right hand to the sky.

And he opened the shining door for the last time.

He called the Power back to him, filled himself with its energies, swelling, expanding until only Valiant remained. There was a silver explosion, a silent detonation of cosmic power that shook the Tower to its foundations.

Sydney plummeted past the observation deck.

Valiant arced up and over the ledge, swan-diving through the night sky. A sonic boom shattered the night as he blasted through the sound barrier and swept past Sydney's limp form. Unconscious, she had reverted to her true identity.

He extended his power as they fell, siphoning off her momentum, carefully: too much power, too rapid a deceleration and her spine would snap like dry kindling. He let her fall, slowing her descent until they hovered a mere six inches off the ground. Only then did he take her in his arms. He was looking for a place to set her down when she opened her eyes.

"I messed up," she said.

"You did just fine," Valiant said. "How'd you do that?"

Sydney rolled her eyes. "Duhhh," she said. "I've only read like two *million* comic books."

Valiant smiled. They settled to the street amid a flock of reporters and curious bystanders.

Sydney laughed. "Isn't this where I came in?"

Valiant set her down as a horde of SWAT, emergency rescue workers, and police swarmed toward them.

High above their heads, red lightning ignited the darkness. A sound, like the tolling of a titanic bell, shook the earth.

"Take the girl!" Valiant shouted. "Get these people out of here!"

But it was too late. The world lurched beneath Valiant's feet and the smell of rotten flowers filled the air. There was a flash of bloody radiance. Then Valiant and Sydney were surrounded by a menagerie.

Pigs wearing Chicago Fire Department uniforms squealed and writhed on the ground, trapped by their clothing; S.W.A.T team members squawked and strutted, having been transformed into peacocks, police tactical units bucked and leaped, reconfigured into herds of panicked wildebeests.

"Hide," Valiant said.

Titan slammed into him with the force of two tons of TNT. The two of them rocketed across Grand Avenue; propelled by Titan's momentum, they bowled over a herd of confused wildebeests like ten pins, slammed into a support column of the "El train" and bent it nearly double. The affected section of track buckled, and sagged toward the street.

Titan headbutted Valiant with enough power to crush an onrushing semi. Valiant surged forward, drove his fist upward, into Titan's gut. Titan doubled over as the breath was driven from his lungs, and Valiant drove his knee into his jaw, snapping Titan's head back. Valiant pressed his attack, staggering the "Bloody Behemoth" with a hail of blows powerful enough to wreck mountains.

Titan fell to one knee, his face a ruin. Valiant tore open the local fabric of the universe and kicked Titan into the rupture a moment before the earth convulsed and threw him to the ground. The earthquake was localized, most of its force concentrated on the ground beneath Valiant's feet.

Professor Shiva and his Dance of Destruction.

The avatar of the ancient Hindu Destroyer whirled about in the center of Grand Avenue, a spinning blur of color and wild magic. As the unearthly music of the Devii groaned in tortured accompaniment, the Professor's every step brought ruin down upon the city.

Valiant leapt into the air, and was immediately brought down by the abandoned EL train as it slid off the damaged track. The train was coming apart in midair, its every fiber subject to the Professor's power. House-sized pieces of steel smashed Valiant to the street.

Then Hell's Belle fell on him from two thousand feet.

The explosion blasted a crater seven feet deep into the center of Grand Avenue. Several pigs ran through the intersection. A dozen wildebeests leaped away from the impact crater, from whence a searing red glow fired the night.

At the bottom of the crater, Hell's Belle gripped the Crimson Scepter with both fists. The burning, three-pronged fork of the trident was buried in Valiant's chest. Flames hot enough to melt steel turned the concrete floor of the crater into a molten lava pit.

"Burn!" the demoness thundered.

The Devil's Daughter hoisted the Far Traveler over her head, her eyes blazing as the inferno roared around them. With a triumphant howl, she blasted Valiant into the air. He rocketed upward on a whirling pillar of demon-fire, an unholy meteor shrieking toward the heavens. Valiant arced over the city and plunged into the Chicago River.

A moment later, the entire stretch of waterway churned, sending waves surging toward both side of the riverbank as a blinding blue light ignited beneath its surface.

Then the river froze.

Silence descended over the riverfront. In the distance, sirens wailed as the police cordoned off the conflict zone.

"Well done, Freeze," Slaughter said.

The Destructors walked across the ice toward the spot where Valiant had fallen.

"But it's not enough. I can sense his energies. He's still alive."

"No way," Deep Freeze said. "The water we're standing on is cold enough to..."

Freeze's last words were lost as he fell through the sudden hole in the ice beneath his feet. A howl of flame roared up from the shining space warp, followed by gout of molten lava. The lava poured over the lip of the warp portal, sending titanic gusts of steam into the air.

Professor Shiva grabbed Nightslayer around the neck, gripping him like a drowning man, his eyes bulging. "Can't breathe," he gasped. "Help...me!"

"What the hell's wrong with Doctor Dothead?" Nightslayer snarled.

Professor Shiva's eyes rolled back in his head and his lips turned blue. Then he fainted.

"It's the Traveler!" Hell's Belle shouted. "He's here!"

A moment later, The Dark Desdemona shot into the sky, smashed through the top two floors of the John Hancock Center and streaked into space.

John Slaughter stared after her retreating form for a moment. He waved his left hand and dismissed the clouds of boiling steam. They obeyed, falling as drops of heavy rain to the ice.

Nightslayer ratcheted himself around, his technorganic spine as flexible as a cobra, his cybernetic sensory array fully extended.

"Where is he?" he said. "My scanners can't pinpoint him."

"He's stalking us from a higher dimension," Slaughter said. "He opened up a portal to the interior of a volcano and dropped Deep Freeze into it. Right now Titan is in a temporary coma, dreaming in a tractless void as vast as our own universe. Valiant calls it the alternity."

The ice around them cracked, loudly. Nightslayer looked uncertainly at the frozen river beneath their feet.

"He increased the pressure of gravity on Shiva," Slaughter said. "Specifically on his respiratory system. I'd say the good Professor's lungs look like a couple of oversized walnuts right about now."

Behind them, a row of streetlamps uprooted themselves and sprang into the air, reshaping themselves even as they plummeted toward Slaughter. The streetlamps pounded themselves into the ice, surrounding the magician in an iron cage. He barely seemed to notice.

"He drained Hell's Belle of inertia and isolated her from the Earth's gravitic influence," he continued. "She attained escape velocity almost instantly. If she's still alive she's probably halfway to the moon by now."

Nightslayer looked doubtfully through the holes of his cowl. "If you can sense all that then why can't you find him?"

Slaughter laughed. "I don't have to find him, you idiot. He's standing right behind you."

Nightslayer dropped into a defensive posture and whirled to the attack. However, the sudden movement caused his boots to slip across the ice and he stumbled, struggling to regain his footing even as he reached for one of his explosive throwing stars. But the Nuclear-powered Ninja's feet shot out from under him and he fell, face-first, into Valiant's right fist.

The blow was felt as far away as New York.

Nightslayer flipped over backwards and vanished into the warp prison that Valiant had prepared for him.

The alien hero turned and faced his greatest enemy.

The two men regarded each other across the boiling hole in the ice.

"Excellent," Slaughter said, smiling. "Somewhere along the way you've learned what it really means to be human."

The dark magician's smile widened, his eyes shining in the dark like twin moons of madness. "You *cheated*."

"I prefer to think of it as pushin' the envelope," Valiant said. "I suppose you realize that those bars are composed of iron—enough to nullify your chaos magic."

Slaughter chuckled, seemingly unperturbed by his looming defeat. "Quite true," he said. "Even though I stole my powers from the King and Queen of Faerie, I'm still bound by their limitations. And as any idiot knows, iron and faeries don't mix."

Slaughter sighed and shrugged. "Checkmate."

Valiant lifted his right hand, preparing to send Slaughter into the same void in which he'd dismissed the rest of the Destructors.

"That won't be necessary, or even possible, I'm afraid," Slaughter said. "You see, I know something the rest of my colleagues didn't. You, my alien friend, are dying."

Valiant paused, the power he'd summoned flagging as his attention waned.

"You're insane," he said.

"You're right," Slaughter sang. "Nutty as a weasel stuck in a port-a-potty at the Super Bowl. But at least I'm still human. I was born in this dimension. I *belong* here."

Slaughter grabbed the bars of his cage and pressed himself against them. His skin burned where it met cold iron.

"But you? You're an anomaly."

Valiant staggered backward, his grasp on consciousness waning. The iron bars that formed Slaughter's makeshift prison began to shudder. He stumbled, and fell to his knees.

The iron bars of Slaughter's cage shuddered and crashed to the ice.

"Ah, yes," Slaughter said. "I imagine the strain was too much for your pet hobbit to handle. And without the mind of your host to anchor you on this plane, you're about as powerful as half-baked turkey meatloaf."

"*Manny!*"

"Everything about you offends me," Slaughter said. "You must be expunged, excised, like a tumor on the prostate gland of reality. You're an *abomination*. And me?"

Slaughter raised his hands. They began to glow with a blinding red light.

"I'm the scalpel that's going to cut you out."

He stepped forward and placed his blazing palms on Valiant's chest.

Valiant screamed.

The Far Traveler's youthful appearance eroded as the millennia through which he'd passed bore down upon him, draining him of power. Slaughter's laugh became a demon's howl of triumph. Valiant fell, writhing, onto his back, and Slaughter stepped on his throat.

"You may have disrupted the Summoning," he snarled. "But I'm still going to burn the city. However, while I'm at it, I'll tell every person I kill that the World's Greatest Hero died with his throat beneath my heel."

"Liar."

Slaughter turned to face the person who had just spoken her last foolish word.

Sydney.

Her eyes were a silver flame. Swirls of steam eddied around her, climbing upward in whirling gyres of argent power. The ice beneath her feet hissed as that power warped the space in which she hovered.

Slaughter launched a bolt of sheer magical chaos. It scorched the air as it flew, ringing like the trumpet of Judgment Day. The bolt struck the shield of cosmic power that surrounded Sydney. The concussion wave shattered the ice in a circle fifty square yards in diameter. The recoil blew Slaughter fifty feet into the air.

Sydney dove toward Valiant even as the magician righted himself and arrowed toward her, his eyes blazing, chaos magic raging in his fists. Valiant reached up with his right hand, nearly invisible now.

And Sydney grasped it.

Light.

Power hammered the ice upon which Sydney stood. A geyser of boiling water arced twenty feet into the air. But Sydney was gone.

Only Valiant remained.

Slaughter launched an assault from above, raining shards of the Corruptor's stolen darkness down upon the ice.

And Valiant went nova.

His halo expanded outward in a seething arc of cosmic energy, filling the night with the glow of a dozen suns. Light *suffused* him; it *exuded* from his every pore. In effect he *became* the light that dwells at the heart of every star, and for a moment, the city of Chicago was illuminated by radiance so brilliant it was visible from space.

Slaughter screamed as the Corruptor's power withered in the glare from that man-shaped star, screamed as the shadow battened onto his life force and began to feed. The Corruptor's power was itself a sentient being, one far stranger than even the creature that was the heart of that silent conflagration.

Wounded by Valiant's power and angered by the murder of its host, the resurrected shadowmorph reared, big as a small mountain, and smashed down upon the author of its misery; it ate John Slaughter whole before Valiant's power burned it to ash and memory.

Then the city went dark.

Sydney Carter skipped all the way home from Miss Jackson's house, her backpack bulging with all the books she'd borrowed from the college where her father taught medicine to young med students.

Turns out Miss Jackson had known about Manny being Valiant all along.

"You can't hide a big, beautiful man like that in a lonely old widow's house and not expect her to catch on," she'd chuckled over tea. Then, through tears, "I s'pose I always knew the day would come when my Manny would be leaving this world," she sighed. "I only wish I could have held him one more time."

And *that* was when Sydney had shown her the best surprise of all.

Now, Sydney was exhausted. Parts of her still hurt from last month's fight with the Destructors.

But she was happy.

The Dreams were gone. For the first time in a long time, she could put names, and even faces, to the voices in her head.

"*You're late for dinner,*" Valiant said from the alternity. "*Your parents will be worried.*"

"Chill out, Val," Sydney said.

"*Val?*"

"Yeah," Sydney said. "I like it. Even though you're not as hot as Val Kilmer."

"I've never been…hot," the Valiant force said. *"Although heat is a component of my electromagnetic capacities, my command over the construct's internal temperature has always been…"*

"Will you two quiet down?" a third voice said. *"I'm tryin' to relax in here."*

Of the two new tenants in Sydney's mind, that voice was her favorite. The one voice she'd feared she'd never hear again. And although Manny Milagro complained about his new permanent residence in the alternity at least ten million times a day, Sydney had to admit, his time spent as the Valiant's first host was invaluable to her now. Together, they'd saved at least seven hundred lives in the month since Manny's "death."

Sydney had provided exactly what the Valiant needed to stay on Earth—a young, healthy human anchor. She'd also provided what the Valiant could not—a comfortable place for Manny to call home.

The three of them were linked, bound together through the mind and body of an eleven-year-old girl. Sydney Carter, who was soft-spoken and short for her age, was also one of the most powerful beings on the planet.

At need she could summon the Valiant, and access all his powers. But she'd discovered new abilities, powers that Manny never even dreamed of, much less understood. She'd learned to "channel" Manny's consciousness, allowing him to speak through her whenever he wanted. She could even assume his appearance, *his normal appearance,* for a while.

That was the surprise she'd shown to a stunned Miss Jackson. Her ribs were still sore from where Manny's big-boned foster mother had hugged him to her ample bosom.

The power to manipulate the four fundamental forces of the universe covers a lot of territory, guys.

It was a landscape Sydney intended to master until she found the hope she sought. Her sister was lying in a hospital room right now, sick from radiation and the illness that hovered like a mournful spirit above their family. They *needed* the power she wielded.

And so did lots of other people.

But still…

The alien spaceships thundered over Grant Park and touched down near the Macarthur Band Shell, their massive engines incinerating the famous landmark, along with acres of trees and grass. The invaders, when they emerged, were massive, robotic creatures, some nearly fifty feet tall. Each was equipped with a terrifying array of city-smashing weaponry. A fact made painfully clear when the invaders opened fire on the innocent bystanders in the park.

"Well?" Manny said, over the screams.

"*Those are Tarkellian War Droids,*" the Valiant force said. "*They'll destroy this city and convert every living human into breeding stock for the Tarkel Horde. After that, they'll spread across the planet, destroying terrestrial civilization and enslaving the human race.*"

"So?" Manny snapped. "*What're we standin' around jibber-jabbin' for?*"

Sydney smiled. Then she closed her eyes.

And she opened the shining door.

A FATHER'S WORK

My wife has been brain dead since breakfast. That won't make killing her any easier. There's also the fear, the looming, corrosive dread that's been gnawing at my gut ever since the coming of the Takers.

Do it, Ben, she'd begged. *Kill me.*

They say that a good man loves his family more than he loves himself, that no sacrifice is too great to shield them from harm. But I was weak. I couldn't end my wife's suffering, no matter how much she begged. Finally, when she'd run out of tears, she called me a coward. I slammed the door in what was left of her face.

This is the price for my weakness.

I don't know how Melanie got the gun. She's been bedridden since the neighbors crippled her, nearly three months ago. Three months since the country went crazy. Three months since the Children's Plague made life in America a living nightmare. Three months since I held my oldest son, Cory, and told him how much, how desperately I love him. The Takers took that too.

Melanie shot herself sometime this morning, probably while Josh, my twelve-year-old and I, were out looking for a car to steal. We found one, an ancient yellow Ford Escort, sitting in Ed Modello's driveway of all places; ironic when you consider that it was the Modellos who attacked us the night the virus destroyed the neighborhood.

We were on our way home after a fairly benign charity fundraiser the night Melanie was maimed, mere feet from our driveway when a pale figure stumbled out of the shadows along Route 134.

"My God," Melanie said as we approached the waving figure. "That's Dennis Modello."

We stopped, of course. The Modellos were our nearest neighbors.

Their recently remodeled Colonial sat on the far side of the small highway that ran past our driveway. Our house sits a quarter of a mile back from the road, snugged deeply into the fifty-acre patch of woods that borders the Hudson Valley Nature Preserve. That was the main reason I'd pressed Melanie to buy the house: privacy.

Melanie often complained that the place felt too isolated, too removed from the other families in our neighborhood. I, on the other hand, loved the feeling of separation: seventeen acres of overlooked Westchester County real estate where I could pretend that we inhabited our own little corner of the universe; a sylvan glade where I could perfect my software and chase my children until we all collapsed, in an exhausted, laughing pile, to the lush green grass.

It wasn't until much later that my desire for privacy would save our lives, while damning my wife to a kind of living death.

"Dennis?" Melanie said as we climbed out of the car that night. "My God, Ben, he's covered with blood."

They were the last words Melanie would be able to say without having to use a pencil and paper. Dennis Modello looked like he'd been splashed with buckets of gore. His hair was encrusted with red and black clumps of matter. His dark gray eyes peered out at us from behind a crimson figure eight, a red domino mask inscribed in someone's blood.

"Dennis," I said. "What's happened?"

Dennis stared at Melanie the way a blind man recently gifted with sight might study his reflection in a clear lake, his head cocked, nostrils dilating as his breath hitched in and out of his lungs. That's one side effect of the Takers' virus, intermittent shortness of breath.

Dennis stood there trembling, his narrow chest heaving as he hyperventilated with a kind of moaning wheeze. His eyes were rolling around in their sockets, like those of a fright-maddened race horse. I was so stunned by the sight of him that I didn't see the butcher knife in his right hand.

I heard someone laughing inside the Modellos' house, a kind of wild roar that scaled upward into a shriek of pain.

"Dennis?" I repeated. "Where's your dad?"

Dennis raised the knife and charged at us.

None of us heard the black Porsche until it struck. Dennis' face bounced off the convertible's hood as the Porsche's momentum drove him up the windshield like Evel Knievel powering up a ramp. He flew twenty feet into the air and landed headfirst behind our car. The other sound I can't forget from that night is the *crack* Dennis Modello's neck made when he struck the highway. Or the terrible stillness that followed.

The driver of the Porsche, a teenaged girl, never even slowed down. She was still screaming as the convertible fishtailed, spun once and flipped over. It rolled twice and slid to a halt in the center of the Garrison's front lawn. A second later, the Porsche burst into flames.

Melanie was already moving toward the wreckage when David Modello leapt out of the darkness and stabbed her in the back. He was short enough to ride her all the way down, stabbing her again and again, the serrated blade in his fist pistoning up and down with a devil's speed as Melanie fell, screaming.

I grabbed David's collar to yank him off the mother of my children. He twisted in my grasp, like an animal with gum for a spine, and slashed the blade across my left forearm. I screamed as white-hot agony detonated behind my eyes.

David swung at me again, the blade of the hunting knife flashing red in the light from the burning Porsche. I half fell/half lunged backward. I barely avoided the slashing blade, and before he could cut me again I kicked him in the throat. The force of my blow snapped his head back and threw him into the drainage ditch that ran alongside the highway.

Melanie lay facedown in a spreading puddle of blood, spread-eagled across the center of the highway we'd traversed every day for the last nine years.

"Mel!" I cried. "Melanie!"

It was only then that I heard the gunfire. Police sirens blared from every direction, blocks distant, but drawing closer by the second. Somewhere, close by, a man was sobbing. His keening wail scaled upward and became a gobbling shriek. Then it was abruptly silenced.

I ran to the car, grabbed my cell phone, punched 911, and was rewarded by a busy signal. I stood there, screaming for help while I stupidly pressed *Redial* only to get the same busy signal. I must have done it twelve times. Finally, I picked Melanie up, put her into our car, and drove to the hospital. I remember wondering what I would tell my kids if she died.

Seventeen minutes later, I was turned away by a young soldier wearing desert camouflage and brandishing an M16.

"I need all you people to back away from this door," he shouted. "All civilian hospitals have been commandeered by order of the president."

Nearly three dozen vehicles sat idling in the emergency room parking lot. Their drivers had been stopped at the entrance by the boy soldier. The crowd screamed for medical assistance for themselves or their passengers. I was carrying Melanie in my arms. She'd regained consciousness by then. She was moaning in pain, and her blood was warm and flowing over my hands.

"What's happening?" I shouted.

The boy soldier shook his head. He was glaring at the gathering crowd with obvious discomfort. "Somethin' big, dude," he said. Oddly, he was smiling; his eyes fairly shone with a kind of glee. "Somethin' *real* big."

"I heard it's Al-Qaeda!" someone shouted. "The whole country's under attack!"

The screaming throng surged forward, as if moving with one mind, away from the idea that what was happening was some new type of terrorist attack. What was happening was too widespread, too *elemental* somehow.

The boy soldier lifted his rifle and aimed it at us.

"I told you people to back the fuck away!"

The crowd roared, and pressed closer. One woman, who was bleeding from a gash in her forehead, pushed her way up the steps and ran toward the emergency room entrance.

The boy soldier shot her in the back.

I turned and ran. By the time we reached the car, the boy soldier had switched to automatic.

"I told you people!" he howled. "I'm not responsible! I'm not responsible!"

He shot down at least seven civilians. He was laughing while he did it.

As I sped toward home, I turned on the radio. News of the

spreading violence was on every channel. The madness that had transformed David and Dennis Modello had turned its bloody eye upon my little corner of the universe. The Modellos were only the first of the infected.

They were ten years old.

The bedroom where Melanie made my decision for me still smells like blood and gunpowder. Somehow she managed to crawl out of bed and lock the bedroom door before she shot herself. She must have done that to make sure our five-year-old daughter, Zoë, didn't walk in to find mommy holding a gun under her chin.

But Melanie needn't have worried. Zoë was sleeping on the couch when Josh and I returned from our car hunt. She's been sleeping more and more lately, especially since we barricaded ourselves inside the house. She only woke up when I kicked in the bedroom door. Fortunately, I had the wherewithal to ask Josh to take her down to the garage on some phony errand. Zoë is bright, certainly brighter than her brothers were when they were her age.

My daughter's physical integrity, however, is another matter. She was inflicted with a plethora of minor respiratory ailments almost from birth: allergies, asthma…and reactive airway disorder, a restriction in the breathing passages that is fairly common in children born in smog-laden cities like Denver and Los Angeles.

Most children outgrow "baby asthma" after two or three years, but for Zoë, a minor respiratory concern grew into full-blown asthma. She's also allergic to nearly anything that moves, breathes, sheds, or molts. All of these qualities presented our family with considerable challenges in a normal world. In the world the Takers gave us, they've become potential nightmares.

Josh and Zoë are on the stairs now, still relatively safe behind the reinforced doors of the makeshift shelter we built after the power went out for good.

Melanie is a strong woman but a lousy shot. Somehow she missed the part of her brain that turns the lights on and off. I'm watching her eyes: they're open, rolling back and forth as if she were watching a ping pong match played in zero gravity. Occasionally, her limbs jerk and little gouts of blood overflow her lips, streaking her cheeks, making her smile appear ghoulishly wide.

That's right. She's smiling.

I have to stop crying. I've got to get hold of myself. I can hear the kids arguing on the other side of the door: Zoë wants to see mommy. Josh knows something's wrong. I can hear it in his voice. He's trying to be strong, for me and for Zoë, but the fear in his voice summons a storm of fresh terror from my gut. I'm more afraid right now than at any other time since the Modellos' attack.

Because I don't know what to do.

My kids deserve better.

We argued yesterday, Mel and I. She'd demanded that we leave her. She was too weak to be moved and she couldn't walk.

"I can find a wheelchair, Melanie," I insisted. "I'll carry you on my fucking back if I have to."

"wher wil we go, Ben?" she wrote. "case you forgoten, 'm paralized."

I'd refused even to consider abandoning her. We were relatively safe as long as we stayed indoors and didn't make too much noise. Being so far from the highway allowed us slightly more freedom than our neighbors. Most of them were slaughtered during the first weeks of the Plague.

We're hidden, set so deeply into the woods that unless you know what to look for you'd never see our house. Thanks to the Plague, the higher reasoning faculties of the infected children appear to degenerate at a catastrophically rapid rate, leaving behind only the meanest survival instincts and a blinding homicidal rage.

Most of the local infected kids meander aimlessly up and down the highway, at least until some living uninfected creature catches their attention.

But sometimes they surprise me.

The other day I watched a clique of infected teens break into Sunnydale, the retirement villa near the center of town. I'd broken into Chad and Jane Klauson's house looking for asthma medication for Zoë. She and little Emma Klauson share the same "asthma doctor." The girls had bonded over tales of scary allergic reactions and rampant coughing.

When I went inside I found Jane Klauson, Emma's mother. Someone had jammed a sharpened iron rod through her throat and pinned her to the coffee table. Her blood was still damp; she'd been killed recently. There was no sign of Emma.

I started for the bathroom. Then I heard the clique gathering in front of the house. After a frantic scramble for a hiding place, I ran up into the attic and pulled the ladder/door up behind me. From behind the attic window I watched the infected teens burst out of Sunnydale.

They were hurling several dirty white balls at each other, or simply kicking them up and down the street. I recognized some of them. I'd seen many of these same kids kicking soccer balls back and forth across the high school playing field.

I'll be damned, I thought. *They're playing dodgeball.*

I stared, unable to reconcile what I was seeing with what I knew to be true: that what the infected kids were doing seemed so normal, so...*human*. At the same time I knew that if they sensed my presence they'd storm the house and tear me apart. I was so disoriented that it took me a second to understand what I was really seeing—the "dirty white balls" were severed human heads.

After the teens had gone, I grabbed the one remaining bottle of Emma's medication I could find and went out the back door. *"your gona get kilt, Ben,"* Melanie wrote when I got back. *"braking into peopls' houses like that."*

"What choice did I have?" I shrugged. "Zoë needed the medicine."

The asthma attacks have been increasing in frequency since the advent of the Plague. In fact, all diseases have gained a foothold in the wake of the virus. Minor wounds fester and become gangrenous. The common cold has become a serious health threat.

Melanie smiled, with her eyes: Dennis Modello's knife had severed some of the nerves in her face. She would never really smile again. *"u're a good father, Ben,"* she wrote. Then...

"Promise...something."

I smiled.

Anything.

She put her face in her hands and wept for a moment. I tried to hold her, but she shrugged me away and wrote these words: *"don't let...children...suffer."*

They won't, Mel. I'll protect them with my life.

But now I know that's not what she meant.

"Dad? Is mom okay?"

Josh.

I pull my head out of the past and focus on the problem at hand. The mother of my children is lying on the floor with a hole in her head, grinning at a joke only she can appreciate.

"Daddy? I want to see mommy."

I can hear the fear in Zoë's voice, too, and the tightness in her chest. She'll be wheezing in a minute and I have less than two treatments left in the bottle I stole from the Klausons.

Pull it together, Ben.

But as I lean down and kiss my wife's forehead, my tears mingle with the blood on her face.

"Daddy," Zoë moans. "I'm scared."

I can't use the gun. The kids will hear it, and I'll be damned before I let them carry that weight. Instead I look around for something else I can use, something quiet, and my eyes settle on Melanie's favorite pillow. It smells like her shampoo, the one with the ridiculous name: Green Apple Rainsong, or something. I grab the pillow—

"I love you, Melanie Carson."

"Daddy, what are you doing?"

—And I put it over her face.

The infected victims are almost exclusively children between the ages of three and seventeen years of age.

They attack without warning, their victims the uninfected. In most cases that means parents, siblings, anyone unlucky enough to be in the same room when the virus takes over. The only warning signs are the harsh rasp of breath, what some have called a "walking death rattle," followed by a raging, sometimes fatal fever.

And the bleeding.

Some aspect of the virus causes bleeding from the eyes, nose, mouth and anus. Before the country went dark, scientists found more than a few similarities between the Plague and the Ebola virus, whose victims usually bleed to death before medical help can arrive.

In the case of the Children's Plague, however, the bleeding

stops shortly after infection. What's left behind *after* the blood, the screaming and the terror, is something that only the most devoted parent could love. I know.

My son, Cory, was infected three days after I murdered David Modello.

"Dad, they're coming. We've gotta *go*."

In my dream, Cory and I are standing in the Jensen's back yard. I've just smashed the window next to the back door when Darryl Jensen sticks a rifle through the hole in the glass and presses the barrel against my chest.

Cory screams, despite himself. He just turned sixteen yesterday.

Hell of a way to celebrate your sixteenth birthday, he'd joked. *Breaking into your dead neighbors' houses looking for food.*

"Get the hell off my property," Darryl snarls from the darkness of his kitchen. I can barely see him through the shattered glass, but I can feel the rifle barrel. It gouges the flesh above my left nipple with the force of an accusation. "No room at the inn, asshole."

"Darryl, it's me," I hiss. "Ben Morgan."

Behind me, Cory raises one of the shotguns I'd stolen from a sporting goods store the day before.

"Drop the gun, asshole," he says, too loudly.

He can hear them coming and he's scared. The infected children seem to possess sharpened senses, overdeveloped hearing and an acute hypersensitivity to movement. Contrary to popular mythology the infected don't eat the people they kill. Nevertheless, they employ the skills of the primordial hunter when running down their "prey."

"Easy, son," I say. And to Darryl, "Let us in...*please*."

"Get the hell away from here, man," Darryl snarls. "You'll bring those things over here."

"I said *drop the gun, motherfucker!*" Cory shouts.

Something shatters next door. One of them shrieks. A moment later, I hear glass breaking and more screams, but this time, the screams come with words, pleas for mercy, and a single gunshot.

"Jesus H. Christ," Darryl Jensen moans.

A chorus of triumphant shrieks rises as the infected root out whichever unfortunate and drag him or her from their hiding place. I think it's Lonnie and Laura, the lesbian couple recently arrived from Washington. The deeper of the two screaming voices sounds like Lonnie's, but I can't be certain. Beneath their howls, I can hear the women being torn apart.

"Darryl, they're right next door," I snarl. "You gotta let us in… *now*."

"You think I'm jokin'?" Darryl hisses, prodding me with the rifle.

Behind me, Cory jacks the shotgun—

Clatch

—and I grip the 9mm Glock automatic I lifted off a dead cop and point it at where I think Darryl's face must be. But another voice hisses from inside the house.

"You idiots are gonna give us all *away."*

The back door clicks open and Cory and I rush inside. Sabrina Jensen, Darryl's wife, carefully shuts the door behind us. Then, almost as an afterthought, she pulls down the shade.

"Thank you," I say.

Sabrina places one lacquered fingertip against her full lips and gestures toward the back door. I look up and my breath catches in my chest. A hunched, shadowy figure is standing on the other side of the broken window.

From where I'm crouching I can't make out its features, but I can see that it's big, over six feet tall. Most of the infected in this area are teenagers, and this one is big enough to qualify as a full-grown threat, with a thick neck and a linebacker's shoulders. I can hear it wheezing, snuffling, as if testing the night air.

The thing in the back yard looks back toward Jane and Lara's house, and, made arrogant by the darkness in which we squat, Darryl Jensen lifts his rifle to his shoulder.

Sabrina snatches the barrel down, her eyes wide with outrage at his stupidity, and I remember that she's one of the most strident parents in our local PTA. Her son, Zachary, sits next to Cory in sophomore homeroom.

Darryl lowers the rifle, and looks guiltily over at me, but I pretend I didn't see Sabrina's usurpation of his role as "kitchen defender."

A moment later, the hulking figure shuffles away.

"Cory, have you seen Zachary?" Sabrina whispers. "He disappeared last night."

"I haven't seen him," Cory says.

Sabrina's eyes shimmer in the moonlight and two tears streak the velvet softness of her coffee-brown cheeks.

"You must be looking for food or water, I guess," she said. "We've...we've got extra."

"Thank you," I insist, not knowing what else to say. "We didn't know..."

But she waves away my thanks and turns away to load up our backpacks while Darryl stares at the floor.

We leave, creeping through the woods while the neighborhood burns around us, until we reach our house.

And two minutes later, Cory's nose begins to bleed.

Cory let me tie him up before the virus took over. I thank God for that now. By the time it became obvious that he was making the transition, he would have been uncontrollable.

Melanie was still unconscious at that point, her torn throat swaddled in homemade bandages, her legs dead stumps. Dennis Modello's blade had damaged her spine, but without medical attention we would never know if the damage was temporary or not.

Cory's face had devolved into a blood-slicked grimace by then. He'd chewed his lips to rags trying to gnaw through the gag I'd improvised. His breathing was a muffled rasp in the stifling air of the garage. His eyes were red gashes.

I'd discovered a small cache of medical supplies in Sunnydale's supply room: syringes, a variety of first aid items, and morphine in pill form. I raided the nurses' station and found the directions on how to prepare the morphine for injection. I'd become proficient at administering the powerful analgesic to Melanie. Now I lifted a syringe filled with it.

Cory strained at the ropes, trying to get at me. Blood dripped out of the rag I'd stuffed in his mouth. I grabbed his hair and pulled his head back, locating the big vein under his chin. Then I jammed the needle in.

Whatever the Takers had filled Cory with, it was powerful. In his fury to escape, he ripped the fingernails of both hands down to bloody nubs. He fought the ropes so hard that his right clavicle snapped in two; the broken bone shard tore through the fabric of his *Pirates of the Caribbean* t-shirt. Two minutes after he'd finally passed out, his right arm dangled from his shoulder, swinging to and fro like a busted pendulum.

I picked up the other supplies I'd brought: rope, the Glock, and a sharp knife. Then we drove to a nearby park. The little yellow Ford ran out of gas halfway there. I quickly got out, grabbed Cory and the supplies, and walked the remaining six blocks, my senses alert for signs of attack.

The park was Cory's favorite local hangout. It overlooked the Hudson River; on clear summer days you could see for miles in both directions. Cory and I had fished those waters since his fifth birthday. I laid him gently on the riverbank. Then I cut the ropes away from his wrists and ankles.

"I love you, Cory," I whispered.

And because I couldn't kill my son, and I couldn't let him kill us, I simply held his hand. And I waited.

The sun had fallen below the horizon by the time I was certain he was waking up.

"Cory?"

He opened his eyes. They were filled with blood.

I left him, sensing that once he was fully awake my Cory would be gone. He would be whatever the Takers' virus wanted him to be.

I left him.

I was halfway home when I saw my first Taker.

As I passed through our gutted neighborhood, I noticed a strange light coming from the cul-de-sac, and a flurry of activity at the Jensens' house. I slipped through the woods, moving slowly, until I was within fifty yards of Darryl Jensen's front door.

A massive black object hung over the Jensens' house. It was huge—a hovering, oblong platform the size of a 747. The underbelly of the object was riddled with what looked like huge warts or tumors, each one filled with a brackish, yellow light. As I watched, one of those blisters ruptured, and a river of glowing excreta poured out onto the earth.

There was something moving in the light.

It was monstrous, something that looked like a worm or a

maggot, only as big as a grizzly bear. The pale thing had at least half-a-dozen tentacles. Each tentacle ended in four prehensile "fingers"; each finger sported two claws as long and sharp as new garden shears.

In the seething amber light from the hovering black platform, the worm seemed to flicker in and out of visibility, as if the fabric of reality recoiled from its presence. It shimmered, wraithlike, its pale skin shining as if lit by some internal luminescence. Then it faded into semi-visibility.

Twelve infected children were standing on the sidewalk in front of the Jensens' house. They stood motionless, as if unaware of the flickering abomination only a few feet away.

The titanic worm uttered a thunderous hiss, its resonance so powerful I could feel it through the soles of my feet. The infected children ignored the worm, their attention focused on something I couldn't see.

Something was moving on the Jensen's front lawn.

I crawled forward, scrabbling on my knees and elbows. I *had* to see.

Zachary Jensen had performed unspeakable atrocities upon his parents and his younger brother, Cameron. He sat surrounded by their gutted carcasses, his brow furrowed as if he'd just awoken from a confusing dream. Then he saw the pale thing shuddering on the sidewalk, and he screamed.

But this scream was different: *Zachary*, the Zachary I remembered from Cory's homeroom, was back. He knew what was happening to him. He was *aware*.

Zachary's scream galvanized the worm. It pounced on him, drove him face-first into the bloody grass. Zachary's screams were muffled as he disappeared beneath the worm's bulk. A reddish/yellow fluid flowed out of the worm's anterior end and covered Zachary in a gelatinous membrane. A cavity, similar to a whale's blow hole, opened in the top of the worm's head and extruded a long, fleshy tube.

The tube punctured the mucous membrane around Zachary, and a vile, sucking sound filled the air. The membrane was nearly opaque, but clear enough that I could see inside. Despite the fact that Zachary's mouth and lungs must have been filled with the worm's mucous, he was still screaming.

Then the worm began to move, undulating like a rolling wave of corrupt flesh atop the screaming boy as it fed.

It went on for nearly ten minutes.

Finally, the worm stopped. A moment later, Zachary, the *new* Zachary, pulled himself out from beneath the worm. The skin of his back had been shredded, reduced to raw meat where the worm's claws had gripped him. But if he was in any physical pain he didn't show it; his face had gone slack, his red eyes were empty once more.

Zachary and the other infected children turned and ran into the night. The light from the hovering black platform flickered and dimmed. With a sharp hiss, the platform turned and floated west, toward the river. I watched the yellow lights until they vanished somewhere over New Jersey.

The worm lay shuddering on the sidewalk, that earth-shaking hiss rumbling from somewhere deep within its body. It was solid now, fully visible, somehow more...*here*.

I ran all the way home.

I fear the future. I can't tell the kids what I've seen. What purpose would it serve? I'm not even sure I believe any of this is really happening.

But I fear the future.

We buried Melanie after lunch.

I believed we were safe. The infected seem most active at night. The children of the Plague own all of America's nights now.

"We're gathered here to say goodbye to Melanie," Josh began. "I mean...Mom."

He struggled with that part, his lips pressed into a thin white line. Zoë stared down into the grave we'd made, her eyes blank, her face unreadable. I took her small hand in mine and squeezed it. She didn't react in any way.

"I think God's an asshole," Josh continued. "He'd have to be to let all this shitty stuff happen. Cory and mom and...and Zachary and..."

Josh's voice broke, shattering beneath the weight of his rage. All the terror of the last three months was in his face. But he swiped fiercely at his cheeks with the back of one arm, frowning at the hole in the ground as if defying it to condemn his tears.

"But I know mom's in Heaven anyway," Josh continued. "I'm glad she's there, so she doesn't have to live like this."

Josh tossed one of Melanie's wild roses into the grave. We'd wrapped her in comforters and the tablecloth from the dining room, the one with the absurdly bright daisy pattern that I'd always hated. Those daisies stared back at me now, like yellow eyes cataracted by blood and clumps of grave dirt.

"Bye, Mommy," Zoë said, dropping her rose. She said nothing more, and hasn't spoken since.

Her eyes had the same faraway look I saw in my father's eyes when he came back from Vietnam, a look you only see in the eyes of people who've crossed a line most of them never even knew existed, the line that separates the Civilized from the Wild, the line that reassures us that everything will work out fine, that mommy loves daddy and everybody gets ice cream after dinner.

Zoë had crossed the Ice Cream Line. For her, there was no coming back.

The screaming startled me out of the grieving daze which had settled over us all.

"They're real close," Josh said.

I looked around, trying to determine the source of the screaming. It seemed to be coming from several directions at once: a large clique then.

I swept Zoë up in my arms while Josh grabbed the shovel and the guns. We'd barely secured the doors before the first clique stampeded into the back yard.

"Holy *shit*," Josh said with something like awe in his voice.

I stifled the cold surge of terror that clenched my gut, forced myself to do a rough head count. There were nearly fifty of them out there, stamping at the heat-baked earth, clawing at their faces like grieving widows. Their shrieks were the howls of the damned.

One redheaded boy with only one eye had been badly wounded. His left arm dangled by a strip of muscle and skin; his right foot dragged behind him like a family curse. He'd limped into the clearing, carried along by the momentum of the others. But his injuries were too great. He stumbled, and the others fell on him, tearing at him with nails and teeth. A moment later, several other children began to attack each other.

We froze, hidden behind the barricaded windows, stunned into a kind of dreadful wonder: so much violence, so much *wildness*, on our very doorstep.

Then I heard the automatic garage door rumbling open.

"What the Hell?" Josh said.

"Take Zoë to the safe room," I snapped.

"Dad, I want to help."

"GO!" I shouted. "Take your guns. Lock the door!"

Josh grabbed Zoë and ran upstairs. A moment later, I heard the door slam, and the sound of the heavy bureau sliding into place against the door. Even now, Josh would be throwing the locks and piling the objects we'd lugged up there onto the bureau: two televisions, an old microwave...

We'd practiced the routine enough times. He was strong enough, and adrenaline would help.

Downstairs, someone hit the basement door with something heavy. It sounded like a sledge hammer. The blows came, faster, with increasing force.

One of those things is in the house.

A moment later, the lights went out. The generator outside my bedroom window ground to a halt and choked itself off. I moved into the kitchen and grabbed the flashlight from the stove. Then I checked my Glock: it held a full clip, plus one in the chamber.

Something smashed open the back door.

I moved quickly down the back stairs, my heart racing, red starbursts exploding before my eyes.

Wait. Think.

Whoever had broken in had figured out how to open the garage door despite the fact that I'd activated the security locks. Somehow, the intruder had gleaned the access code. That meant looters, marauders looking for cash or food. Either way, he was about to be seriously disappointed.

I reached the first landing, the one that looked out over the laundry room, and stopped.

There could be more than one down here.

I couldn't let myself be ambushed, not with Josh and Zoë just a few feet above my head. They deserved better.

A quick sweep with the flashlight showed me an empty room. I stepped down into darkness. Whoever had broken in was either hiding in the garage…or…

A hand shot out from between the steps and grabbed my ankle. I tumbled headlong down the stairs. My forehead struck the last step and my back and heels smacked the concrete floor. The Glock bounced out of my fist and slid into the darkness.

I was hurt, each breath a red hot poker in my side. I couldn't breathe.

The intruder came out from beneath the stairs.

He was a grinning nightmare. The whites of his eyes were gone; effaced by burst blood vessels, they were nearly black. The skin of his face hung in shreds. He reeked of old blood and shit.

He was on me before I could scream, punching me, ripping at my face and throat. He grabbed me by the fabric of my denim shirt, yanked me in close and bit my left ear.

Pain exploded in the side of my head as his teeth ground into my flesh. I got my left arm up and elbowed him in the throat. He gagged, and released me. I slid backward, reaching for the Glock, but before I could reach it he grabbed me again and headbutted me with enough force to smash my nose and right cheekbone like rotten fruit. The back of my throat filled with blood.

The intruder grabbed me by the throat. His strength was the strength of madness. His breath was the reek of an abattoir, rasping… shrieking into my face, and even in my stupor, I recognized him.

"Cory!"

Josh was standing on the stairway down which I'd just fallen. He was pointing a gun at his brother.

Cory shrieked.

"Josh, wait!" I cried.

Cory moved. Fast. But Josh was faster. The first shot buzzed past my right ear and smacked into the concrete wall behind me. Josh didn't get a second chance. His second shot struck the floor near my elbow, then Cory grabbed him and pulled him down into the laundry room.

I got to one knee, my head spinning, my vision doubling, trebling. Three Corys seemed to be beating three Joshes to death right before my eyes. I wretched as an ocean of blood gushed down my throat.

I dove for the Glock, reached out my right hand, and grasped empty air.

He's killing him, Ben.

I reached again, grasped the gun, and brought it up.

Cory slammed Josh's head into the floor, once…twice…three times, changing its shape with each blow.

"Cory!" I screamed.

Josh lay unmoving beneath his brother, his ruptured skull leaking his life's blood, so dark it looked black in the wash of the flashlight beam. By that same wicked light, Cory looked up at me, his black eyes like tar pits in the gutted ruin of his face. He grinned, and opened his mouth.

"Daaaa…ddeeee."

Then he tore Josh's throat out with his bare hands.

And I shot him in the face.

Zoë and I are barricaded up in her room. The children are inside the house now; I can hear them breaking up the furniture. This is our Plan B. After Cory left, Josh and I made it damn near impossible to open the door from the other side. I suppose enough of them, working together, could do the job, but we'll be long gone before then.

Zoë's window looks out over the front entrance to our little green universe. Last year, I installed one of those roll-down ladders after a minor fire scare. When the time comes, Zoë and I can scramble onto the roof and take our chances with the survivors.

During the mad scramble to escape the things that came into the basement, drawn by all the gunfire, I ran out of ammunition. The only weapon left to me is the old log-splitter I store up here in case we have to chop our way out. It's little more than a weighted blade affixed to a long handle. It's awkward but it would make a devastating weapon, given enough room to swing and a pinch of good luck.

"Daaad-ddeeeee."

That's Josh.

Turns out he wasn't dead after all. The Takers' virus repaired his brain and knitted his skull back together. What he's using for blood right now is anybody's guess.

"I neeeeed yoooouu, daa-ddyyyy."

Josh wants to kill us in order to provide nourishment for the flickering monster on the lawn. That's right: one of the worms is waiting for us.

It doesn't matter. I'll do what I have to do.

Most of the children are dead or dying. The blood frenzy seems to have passed, for now. Maybe the Taker is satisfied with the suffering they've wrought. I've lost my wife, my two sons, and soon, the house we loved so much.

Maybe it's full.

At least I've still got Zoë. She's doodling in her favorite coloring book, safe from the things that killed our family, because of me. I protected her. I protected Cory, too, when I could, and when I couldn't protect him any more, I ended his suffering. Before we leave this house, I mean to do the same thing for Josh.

As I watch Zoë, I search my soul, and I tell myself that I've kept the promise I made to my wife.

I've done a father's work.

"Look, Daddy," Zoë whispers roughly, the hitch in her voice betraying the barest gasp. At first I'm happy. These are the only words she's spoken in over twenty-four hours.

Then I see the blood, and the eyes that turn red as I watch.

"My nose is bleeding."

I smile, hoping even now, to reassure her, as Josh hurls himself at the door with strength that can't reasonably be called "human."

"Daaa-ddddyyyyy!"

I understand finally, that a father's work is never done. I smile—

"Come to daddy, Zoë.

And I reach for the log splitter.

OUR KIND OF PEOPLE

"Don't you want to come in?" Ms. Wrong Number Who Gives A Fuck, purred. "I do one hell of a good Screaming Orgasm."

Marc Craft stared at the beautiful young woman with whom he'd just wasted four hours and stifled the urge to smash her perfect nose.

"I'd better not," he said.

"Why?" the waste said.

Because if I come inside I'll cut your head off.

Instead of throttling her, he smiled.

"I have to go," he said, injecting just the right note of sincerity, along with a hint of frustrated lust. "I have a deposition in the morning."

The blind date smiled, her full lips curving upward in a predatory sneer that was supposed to be sexy. She opened the door to her apartment.

"Just one drink," she pouted. "You know I've wanted to be with you from the moment we met."

She stepped in to him, into his space, and Marc kissed her. He poured himself into his performance. It was easy: the warmth of her lips, the taste of her tongue—merlot and fresh berries for dessert—made the kiss tolerable enough that he had to remind himself not to wring her neck.

The blind date had been set up by his father and Miss Wrong's father, an old family friend who also happened to be a prominent black judge. She was a former Miss Black New York, an accomplished young physician only recently arrived in Manhattan. She hailed from one of the better Caribbean families in her Upper Westchester County town.

The right kind of people, Marcellus, his mother had said on his voice-mail. *Our kind of people.*

And she couldn't disappear.

Miss Wrong's hands fluttered against his chest, pushing at him. When he finally released her, she staggered and almost fell, dropping her keys and the single red rose he'd brought her.

"What's wrong?"

Miss Wrong shook her head. She was staring at him the way a dog stares at a television program *about* dogs, attracted by the sights and sounds of something familiar, confused by the play of light and shadow.

"I'm…I'm sorry," she said. "I…I don't feel well."

"Are you sure?" he said. "Can I help you?"

"No," she said. "Some…some other time, maybe."

He stooped, grabbed her keys and the rose. She took the keys from him and stepped quickly into the darkness of her apartment.

"Are you sure I can't help…"

She slammed the door in his face.

Marc smiled. He turned and tossed the rose into the trashcan on his way out. He hit the sidewalk and headed south, barely able to keep from sprinting. If he hurried he just might make the 12:30 train back to Brooklyn.

The love of his life was waiting for him there.

He caught a cab back to Times Square and headed down into the subway station at 42nd Street. He had to wait for half an hour on the nearly deserted platform before the F train creaked into the station.

The only other riders on the platform were a pair of young lovers, too high to care about the lateness of the hour, and a New York City transit employee, a driver or maintenance man, Marc couldn't tell.

As the F train lurched to a halt, Marc reached under his jacket and touched the hilt of the hunting knife he carried with him every "Date Night." Reassured by its comforting bulk, he and the other riders boarded the empty car. It always amazed him, how, in a city as busy as New York, the subway seemed to clear out after midnight. At least on the weekends.

He chose a seat close to the front of the car, hoping to surprise his love when she arrived. He chuckled at the flutter of nervousness in his gut. He was always wrong when it came to anticipating her comings and goings. He never surprised her and he never outguessed her.

The doors hissed shut and the F train slid into the dark tunnel, bound for Brooklyn. Marc settled in, failing miserably to suppress his excitement at the thought of meeting his One True Love.

Tonight, he thought. *It's got to be tonight.*

Love is for fools and dreamers, Marcellus, his mother's voice reminded him. *People like us are bound by a greater responsibility.*

Over in the corner, the young lovers were having some difficulty. The boy was apparently ill, convulsing from whatever he'd ingested earlier. He lay moaning with his head in the girl's lap while she whispered into his ear. As Marc watched them, the boy fell forward and vomited on the floor.

"You folks alright?" the transit employee said.

"Fuck off," the girl snarled.

The transit employee shrugged and went back to his newspaper. Marc studied the big man for a moment, the thick forearms, the narrow waist just beginning to expand over his belt, the broad shoulders, and the heavily-knuckled fists.

The transit employee would be difficult in a hand-to-hand encounter. Marc would have to use stealth and cunning, sneak up on the bigger man and slice his throat before he could react.

Marc turned his focus toward the young couple.

The boy was tall enough, nearly as tall as Marc, who stood well over six-feet. But he was thin, too slight, with nothing like the kind of bulk Marc required.

And there was the problem of what to do with the girl.

She was staring at him, plainly interested. He knew he was a "catch," kept himself fit through proper diet and intensive exercise. He never stepped out of his apartment unless he looked his best.

Especially on "Date Night."

His father, however, had beaten him unconscious the one time he'd dared to bring a white girl home from college.

You are here to elevate the race, fool, the Admiral had said. *Your mother and I sacrificed to make sure you get exposed to the right kind of people.*

"Our kind of people," Marc said to no one.

The train pulled into the 34th Street station. The doors slid open. Marc leaned forward, his breath catching in his throat.

We've given you opportunities we never had, Marcellus. It's a parent's duty to make sure his children grow up ready to conquer the world.

A group of young men burst in through the doors. They shoved and jostled each other, noisily mock-fighting for seats on the empty car.

"Stupid ass faggots on this train," one of them said loudly. The others laughed. Marc knew they were talking about him but he didn't care. He was different from them, *better* than them. He had to be.

I don't hit you because I hate you, boy, his father's rage whispered. *I hit you to make you strong. You're to be a credit to the race, Marcellus.*

As the train rolled on into the darkness, Marc considered exactly how much of a credit he'd become. The child of upper middle-class African-American professionals, he'd grown up in a respectable neighborhood in Hartford, miles distant from the urban nightmares of places like Stamford and New York.

He'd graduated from Yale Law, landed a lucrative position as a young associate at a prominent Manhattan law firm. A year later, he'd bought a spacious apartment in Park Slope. Everything had gone according to his parents' plan. Their sole disappointment was his inability to settle down and find the perfect girl to become Mrs. Marcellus Craft.

The race must be perpetuated, elevated, the Admiral would say. *But not just with any kind of girl. She needs to be the right kind of people.*

One of the young men was coming toward him, chin jutting, head tilted at an angle meant to intimidate. He was big, ebony-skinned, and broad-shouldered with a scraggly beard and the eyes of a corpse. Behind him, the other young men cackled and egged him on.

Marc banished the voices, instinctively switched his perceptions to assess the threat presented by the bearded man. The hunting knife at his side dug into his ribcage and he shifted to ease the pressure.

"Yo, man," the bearded man said. "Why you wearin' them clothes like that? You some kind of entrepreneur or somethin'?"

Marc smiled. He was keenly aware of exactly how many of his teeth he was exposing, aware of his every verbal nuance, facial twitch, and eyelid flutter. He'd mastered the art of subtle intimidation at the negotiating table, facing adversaries who counted their worth in the billions.

He had murdered men more desperate than this one and sung along at a Broadway musical twenty minutes later.

"I'm talkin' to you, man," the bearded man snapped.

"I'm an attorney," Marc said.

"What kind?" the bearded man replied.

Marc made it a point to look the bearded man directly in the eye. It was a lesson he'd learned at the ends of the Admiral's fists. It was a lesson Marc had passed on to his victims before they died.

Look me in my eye when I speak to you, boy.

"Who wants to know?" he said to the bearded man.

The bearded man looked back over his shoulder at his friends. Something in his aggressive stance wavered; some reservoir of bravado ran dry. His tongue flicked out and licked at his upper lip.

"Do you read?"

The bearded man's brow furrowed. "What?"

"I'm going to kill someone tonight," Marc said. "You look just about the right size."

He reached into his jacket, produced the big hunting knife and showed it to the bearded man.

The train bumped over a rough spot on the track and slowed down, easing itself toward the 21st Street stop. Then the doors slid open and Marc's One True Love walked through the far entrance into the subway car.

"Oh shit!" one of the young black men snarled.

Marc stifled the urge to gut the bearded thug where he stood, staring at him like the idiot he obviously was. His Lady came on, pushing her cart through the gauntlet of gawping thugs. As she approached, the young men cursed and leapt out of their seats. They scrambled through the open doors and out onto the deserted platform.

The bearded man swore as Lady Love squeaked closer.

Yes, Marc agreed. *She is beautiful.*

Her skin was the color of a cadaver's sclera, her hair the color of ravens' wings, encrusted with filth. Dirty black spikes leaped out from her head like a shout of exaltation.

Her eyes were the color of summer skies, piercing in a face nearly black with blood and dirt. Her jaw had been paralyzed on one side by a stroke or birth defect. Her mouth hung open, her face fixed in a silent shriek.

She had covered herself in a one-piece jumper or snowsuit, stuffed at the sleeves and ankles with newspaper to keep herself warm down in the tunnels at night. The snowsuit was torn in too many places to count, the holes overflowing either with flesh or gray wads of newspaper.

Her feet, swollen from years of walking and neglect, had burst, black with gangrene, from the thick-soled cotton boots he'd stolen for her on their last date. Now, she plodded forward on bare, festering stumps. Things were moving beneath the rumpled skin of the snowsuit. Parts of it seemed to shift and shudder, as if the flesh beneath played host to multitudes of vermin. Behind her, a brown stream of liquid leaked down the backs of her legs and trickled out of the snowsuit, leaving twin trails of fetor in her wake.

Lady Love was pushing a grocery cart up the long aisle toward them. Something moved inside the cart. Marc stood to get a closer look at the gift she'd brought him.

It was a dog. A Golden Retriever.

Someone had broken the Retriever's back. A loop of intestine hung between its jaws. It lay, twisted and shivering atop Lady Love's ubiquitous wads of newspaper. Marc thought he saw tire marks across the dog's midsection but he couldn't be certain.

The Retriever's eyes rolled heavenward, bright with suffering, and focused on Marc. It whined and snapped at the loop of gut dangling from its mouth.

Marc didn't hear the doors open, didn't hear the bearded thug and the other people scramble out of the car. His focus never wavered from Lady Love's face. Tonight, he knew, she would favor him.

Confident, he extended his hand.

She accepted.

They found a spot on the tracks, well away from the glaring lights from the 14th Street stop. He hurried her along as quickly as she was able to move. They only had fourteen minutes before the next train.

If I died in her arms it would be worth it, Marc thought.

They lay down in filth, his heart racing as she reached for him, undid him, and tugged down his pants. He fumbled at the zipper of her snowsuit, his fingers clumsy with his excitement, and pulled it down, freeing her.

He stopped. The heat and smell that enveloped him were almost more than even he could bear. Parts of her body were moving in the darkness, sliding over his thighs, his groin, stroking, teasing him.

From somewhere far behind them, he heard the Golden Retriever whimpering in the shopping cart where they'd left it at the entrance to the tunnel.

What have you done, this time, boy?

Then his Lady grabbed him with hands and mouth and things he couldn't see, *wouldn't* see, things that caressed him wetly, pierced him, sank talons into his flesh, and hooked him to her.

He lost himself in blood and heat.

He lost himself in her.

Afterward, he lured a junkie down into the tunnel, ordered him to strip naked, and slit his throat. He dressed in the junkie's clothing while his Lady fed.

Then Lady Love screamed.

Marc ran to her, fell to his knees at her side. Her shrieks echoed up and down the tunnel, a dark cacophony of barks and growls that accompanied the suffering of the crippled Golden Retriever.

She squirmed there, a dark, toxic wonder, naked and vulnerable, her skin shining in the dim illumination. The parts of her that Marc would not let himself see hissed at him and tore her flesh like hate-starved lovers.

Lady Love lifted her head and shrieked. At the far end of the tunnel, the Golden Retriever howled.

Then something wriggled out from the dark thatch between her thighs. In the half-light from the platform, Marc could make out only a vague outline of the thing that twisted on the floor between his lover's knees. It mewled, and uttered a tiny, gurgling whine.

Then it slithered onto the Lady's stomach.

It was the deep-red color of heart's blood, about twelve inches long, a squirming tuber of bio-matter. It twisted and writhed like a snake trying to shed its skin.

The red thing lifted its front end and chattered at Marc, revealing a circular row of needle-sharp teeth. Then it opened its eyes and Marc Craft's tenuous grip on sanity blew away like trash in the wake of a speeding juggernaut.

A second tuber pulled itself up onto the Lady's stomach, then a third and a fourth. In moments, her lower half was crawling with more than a dozen squirming crimson larvae.

As if cued by an inaudible signal, the first larva, the one with the Admiral's eyes, began to crawl toward Marc. He tried to crawl away, but something like a tentacle extended out of the Lady's torso, wrapped itself around his neck and pulled him down, held his face close to her belly, close enough for the first larva to bite his cheek.

The bite sent a shock of agony through his nervous system and he screamed. Another larva tore his right ear off. Marc grabbed the tentacle that held him fast, tried to tear himself free. Lady Love barked and pulled him closer, groping at his face. Nails like black claws reached for the soft meat inside his mouth and tore it free.

We raised you up to produce something new, Marcellus. Your children will conquer the world. But they'll have to be the right kind of people. Our kind of people.

As his crimson offspring consumed his flesh, Marc Craft remembered his parents' advice. And as Lady Love tore his eyes from his head, two words occurred to him:

Mission accomplished.

THE GREENHOUSE

Henry Felt hated the Adventure Scouts of America. He hated selling crappy candy bars to complete strangers, who smiled at him like he was one of those poor "Urban" kids who had nothing better to do with their time than sell crappy candy bars to complete strangers. He hated Ed Crandall, his Scoutmaster, who smiled *way* too much and always smelled like fresh onions. As he marched up to the front door of Mister Murder's big old house, Henry decided that it was the smiling he hated most of all.

A confident smile and a firm handshake will carry you far in this world, Hank, Crandall always said. Henry hated it when people call him Hank, but Crandall never seemed to notice.

A confident smile says to the world: Here is a boy to be considered. *Here is a boy that matters.*

Henry didn't really believe that he "mattered." His father left the family before Henry was even born. His mother spent most of her free time in her bedroom with various "Uncles." By the time he'd turned five he'd lost count of how many "Uncles" he'd known. It was one of those "Uncles," a smiling cable TV installer, who'd hooked him into the Adventure Scouts. The smiling cable installer was Ed Crandall's brother-in-law. Henry's mother had called Crandall, and the next day, Henry's life, which was already pretty lousy, had slid down the toilet.

A confident smile lets everybody know, from teachers and preachers to CEOs and presidents of major corporations, this boy is gonna make something of himself someday. Yessir, this one's gonna be a worldbeater.

As Henry stomped up Mister Murdock's long walkway wearing his stupid Adventure Scouts uniform, he didn't feel like a worldbeater. No. He mostly felt like the biggest loser on the planet. As he raised his fist to knock on the front door, he mentally rehearsed his spiel.

Hi! My name is Henry Felt. I'm here today representing Adventure Scouts of America! Currently we're having our annual fundraiser to help promote ASA activities such as Arts and Crafts, Community Service, Back to Nature Weekends, and Fart Wrangling. Would you care to purchase some crappy chocolates so I can hurry home and kill myself?

The big oaken front door swung open before he could knock. Mister Murdock was standing there, staring down at him. The old mortician looked like he'd been sleeping in a dumpster. His gray hair, normally neat and parted on the right, now stood up in a big goofy afro. He was only wearing a stained undershirt and wrinkled black pants and dusty, battered old shoes.

Jesus, Henry thought. *He's not wearing any socks.*

All the kids in the neighborhood were accustomed to seeing Mister Murdock walking home from the Murdock Brothers Funeral Home. His family had owned and operated the place since the last ice age. It was one of the most successful funeral parlors on the South Side of Chicago. Henry always thought of Murdock Bros as, The Place Where Dead People Went to Freshen Up.

Mister Murdock was about six-feet-six inches tall, willow-thin, his limbs long and crooked as the legs of a great black spider. He was weird, but usually immaculate in his black undertaker's suit and tie and perfectly polished black shoes. Sometimes he looked at the neighborhood kids, who always paused when he passed. Sometimes he squinted down at them like a man trying to remind himself of some unpleasant but necessary business he'd forgotten. Sometimes he barely acknowledged their presence at all.

Everybody knew old Mister Murdock's story. How his wife had left him, boning out to no one really knew where. How he sometimes walked unseen through the guts of his big old house at odd hours, crying and singing weird songs in a language no one understood.

And everybody knew about how he'd murdered his own son and gotten away with it. That's why some kids called him "Mister Murder" behind his back. Everybody knew these things, or *thought* they did. Nevertheless, they accepted Mister Murdock as a weird, but harmless part of life on Everwood Street.

But now the tall mortician looked...*wrong* somehow. Henry couldn't put his finger on exactly what was out of place. Something didn't *feel* right, apart from the fact that the old man was only half dressed. There were little red spots on the front of his t-shirt, tiny round circles, like drops of blood.

Guess he could have cut himself shaving, Henry thought. Henry had seen one of his "Uncles" cut himself. The man had bled like a stuck hamster all over their bathroom, leaving little droplets of blood everywhere, just like the ones on Mister Murdock's scrawny chest. Henry thought that if he ever grew facial hair he would maintain a beard, just to keep from ever having to put a razor to his face. But he was twelve years old that spring, still years away from shaving.

Get on with it, Hank, a familiar voice chided. *Worldbeaters cut to the chase.*

Henry winced. He gritted his teeth and cleared his throat.

"Hi," he began. "My name is..."

"Henry," Mister Murdock interrupted. "You're that Felt woman's son. The one waits tables at the diner over on Seventy-Ninth Street."

Henry nodded. Sometimes his mother picked up extra cash over at the Greek place. It was funny, but he'd never imagined Mister Murdock eating at the place where his mother worked. He'd never imagined Mister Murdock *eating*. The man looked like a walking skeleton.

"Yessir," Henry continued. "Anyway, I'm here representing Adventure Scouts of..."

Mister Murdock lurched, as if suddenly prodded by someone standing behind him. His eyes widened like the eyes of a man who had just received a powerful electric shock.

"Will you help me, boy?" he gasped. "I need...help."

Henry winced again. He really didn't have the time or the patience to deal with the old fart and his problems.

"I don't know, Mister Murdock," he said. "I've got a lot of stops to make before dinner."

Murdock looked around him, as if he were trying to remember how he'd gotten there. His gaze travelled up over the lintel of his front door and down to the mailbox which was situated next to the doorbell.

"Murdock," he said. "That's right. My name is Lionel Murdock."

The old man glared down at Henry, as if he'd just discovered him crouching with a bag of dog turds in one hand and a lit match in the other.

"Who are you?" he snarled. "What do you want?"

Henry stared at the old man, uncertain of what to say.

"I...I..." he stammered.

When confronted with an opportunity, don't stand there mumbling like a moron. Stick out your chest and speak your piece. Worldbeaters know how to command the listener's attention.

"I'm here representing the *Adventure Scouts*," Henry said, forcefully. "Remember? I..."

"Come in," the old man snapped. "Let me get my wallet."

Without another word Mister Murdock turned and disappeared inside the big old house. Henry stood there for a moment, still uncertain. Something about the old man was...off.

Probably that old people's disease, he thought. *The one where you forget stuff.*

But still...

Fear didn't put Americans on the moon, boys, Ed Crandall would say. *Fear is for sissies. And what's the rule on sissies in the Adventure Scouts?*

No sissies allowed!

That last lesson had been reserved for Crandall's Scout troop only. After a series of class action lawsuits, Scoutmasters everywhere were forbidden from discriminating against any boy, "sissy" or not.

"Come in, Boyd," Mister Murdock shouted. "Need help with a problem. Then I can...purchase something."

Jesus.

Henry stepped over the dark threshold and into the house.

"My glasses," the old man said from the shadows under the stairway. "Left my glasses in the greenhouse. Blind now."

He turned and shuffled into the darkness.

"Follow me."

Henry followed him through the shadows of the old house. It was warm inside, warmer than seemed comfortable. Then again, Henry remembered that old people liked to keep warm. Something about brittle bones and cold weather. They walked through the house, moving past darkened rooms filled with shadowy shapes. In one of them, Henry thought he saw a collection of manikins lying on a bed. The manikins were all laid out in a row, fully clothed, their heads hairless, and shining, almost like dried skulls. But they didn't look like store manikins. To Henry, they looked more like something you'd find at one of those old novelty shops that sold practical joke items: Voodoo dolls and "shrunken heads."

"Practice," the old man grunted. "Needs more practice."

Henry nodded. By now he was more than ready to get out of the old house. Something about those life-sized manikins lying across the bed, their bald heads shining, their faces lost amid sprawled limbs and piles of clothing.

A Scout never backs away from a challenge, Hank. Challenges build character.

Finally, they came to a door that led into the kitchen. Mister Murdock shuffled across the kitchen, humming and muttering a strange, tuneless little song to himself. Every other word sounded like a half-moaned grunt, the sound of a man being kicked in the stomach, followed by a weird little chuckle.

As he looked around, Henry found himself remembering the stories he'd heard about Mister Murdock. How his wife had left him after the death of their son. How sometimes he spent nights in the funeral parlor, even when there were bodies there. Especially *young* bodies.

"Need my glasses to see two feet in front of my face these days," Mister Murdock said. "Getting old. Damn waste."

Henry remembered the worst story he'd heard about Mister Murdock, about his son Lloyd. How he'd come back from Vietnam all messed up on drugs. How he'd attacked Mrs. Murdock one day, nearly strangled her to death. Then Mister Murdock had walked in and found them, his only son trying to murder his wife. Mister Murdock had screamed at him, tried to pull him off of Mrs. Murdock, but Boyd, yes, *that* was his name, *Boyd*, had beaten Mister Murdock nearly unconscious. Mister Murdock had grabbed a big metal lantern and struck Boyd on the head, killing him instantly.

Mister Murdock had insisted on embalming Boyd himself. Afterward, Mrs. Murdock had gone back to Louisiana, where their family had come from way back in the '30s, or so the neighbors said. Henry shuddered. People in his neighborhood said strange things about people from Louisiana.

You stay away from those people, his mother would always warn him. *And no matter what happens: Never eat at that house.*

Why not, ma? he'd asked.

Because they're from New Orleans, and people from New Orleans consort with spirits.

Later, Mister Murdock had bought his brother's share of the family business. His brother, Ephraim, had retired, while Mister Murdock kept right on working, sleeping with the dead bodies sometimes, the neighbors said, walking around his house and crying to himself at three in the morning.

"In here," Mister Murdock said. "Home sweet home."

They were standing on a raised platform that looked out over a dark sunken area the size of a small dancehall. The place was enclosed in a ring of tall windows. Here and there were rows of potted plants and small trees that Henry recognized from his science classes: miniature banzai and eucalyptus trees. Some plants were arranged alongside cacti of varying shapes and sizes, some stood in the shadows of trees he'd never seen before. The smell of jasmine hung heavy in the warm air, high and sweet yet cloying, as if the air itself were too dense, too thick to be tamed by perfume. There were rows of yellow sunflowers, some as big as a dinner plate, rows of red, yellow, and white roses, wildflowers of every conceivable color. Here and there, Henry could smell the scent of citrus, perhaps from an orange tree somewhere in the vastness of the greenhouse. For a moment he was too stunned to react; so much color and fecundity buried in the recesses of Old Man's Murdock's musty old house. Who knew?

Overhead, the late-afternoon sunlight had faded away from the windowed ceiling. The floor of the greenhouse was slipping into darkness. One section of the floor, near the back of the greenhouse, was covered with a large tarp.

Mister Murdock stepped down into the rich dirt that lay everywhere and walked toward the far end of the greenhouse.

"Workin' out here last night," he grumbled. "Left muh glasses."

Henry followed him, fascinated by the riot of color and life all around him. It seemed that, as they walked deeper into the gloom of the greenhouse, he was entering an alien world, a magical land where maybe people *didn't* smile funny, and where Scoutmasters were whipped publicly. The stench of decay was barely noticeable at first. Then Mister Murdock stopped in front of the tarp. With a grunt, he stooped, lifted the tarp, and flung it aside.

The smell of decay grew more present, almost overwhelming.

"What's that smell?" Henry said.

"Fertilizer," the old man wheezed. "Look there," he said, pointing toward the tarp. Henry looked.

There was a hole in the dirt. From where Henry stood, the opening looked about ten feet wide and twice as long. He couldn't see the bottom.

"Dug it myself, back in Fifty-nine. Had to blast through Chicago bedrock to do it. Filled it in with rich red bayou Earth."

Henry wondered at the strange way the old man said "Oith," almost like a gangster from one of those old black-and-white movies.

Those people consort with sprits, Henry.

"Left muh glasses down there," the old man said.

Henry looked into the hole. For just one moment he thought he saw something buried in the darkness down there, a flash of white. And for one utterly ridiculous moment, Scoutmaster Ed's voice came to him as if he were standing at his side.

That's a skull, Hank, the voice said. *You're in deep doo-doo now.*

Suddenly, for no reason that Henry could think of, he was afraid. He stepped back from the hole, took a deep breath. Whatever was going to happen next, he definitely did not want to look down there again.

"I...I gotta go," he stammered. "My mom's waiting outside for me."

Mister Murdock just stared at him. His brows furrowed, as if he was concentrating fiercely on something Henry couldn't see. Then he chuckled.

"Liar."

Cold terror extended icy fingers along Henry's spine.

"What?"

"You're lyin,' boy," the old man said. "There's no one outside. Know how I know?"

Henry managed to nod and shake his head at the same time.

"I know because the *Green* told me so."

Mister Murdock lunged, faster than Henry would have believed possible, and grabbed him by the shoulders and pulled him in close, breathing heavily into his face, grinning.

"The *Green* tells me lots of things."

That was when Henry noticed his teeth. They were like stumps, fat little nubbins of something that looked like teeth but weren't. And they were green. Even worse, each nubbin seemed to pulse, to move independently of the others. Henry thought of a nature video he'd seen once, of tube worms living at the base of an undersea volcano, pale, blind creatures waving to no one in the darkness of the ocean's depths.

Worms living inside the old man's mouth.

Henry fought then. He kicked at the old man's kneecaps, his shins, tried to knee his crotch. The old man drew him in tighter, and Henry felt a sharp pain in his arms. When he looked down, he saw thorns, long black thorns where Mister Murdock's fingernails should have been. Thorns were growing out of the old man's arms, sinking into Henry's flesh, pinning him fast.

"Practice," the old man whispered.

"Please," Henry whispered. "That...hurts!"

The old man grinned his wide green grin. Then he spun Henry around to face the pit.

Something was crawling out of the hole. A nearly skeletal hand with black fingernails reached up and grabbed for purchase among the roots and sod at the edges of the hole, then another hand, pale, grayish brown, the color of sick, lifeless flesh followed by a long, bony arm draped in the tattered remnants of some kind of uniform.

"What...?" Henry whined. "What...? What...?"

Find your voice, boys. A worldbeater speaks with authority.

"What is that?" Henry cried. "*What is that thing?*"

Then a dead man's face stuck up out of the hole, its eyes as empty as the face of the moon, but *green,* as green as the first blush of spring across new grass. The uniform the dead man wore was green too, but old and tattered, the black shoes rotted through so that the toe bones clicked together as the thing climbed out of the hole. The thing that wore Boyd Murdock's body pulled itself to its feet and stood ramrod straight. Then it saluted.

"My Boyd," Mister Murdock said. "Brought him home after the government killed him. But the Old Gods demanded sacrifice. They demanded *blood.*"

Henry shook his head, kicking out with his feet, trying to free himself. But the thorns held him.

No...no...nononono...

"His mama was first. When she saw my gifting, saw how we could bring him back, she gave gladly of herself. But he needed more. She gave until she couldn't give any more. Then I put her down there with him. It takes blood to let my son walk like the man he should have been."

The thing in the uniform grinned, little more than a half-fleshed skull with green stubs where its teeth should have been.

"I'm old now," Murdock said. "Would have died long ago if not for him, his spirit...*eternity in the Green.* We looked after each other, didn't we, boy?"

"No more practice," the thing in the uniform hissed. "Ready."

"My time's up, boys," the old man said. "It took too long for Boyd to find his way back. His flesh is all worn out, and I'm too old."

Henry shook his head, screamed his throat raw, but the old man's hand covered his mouth, his thorns like pins, pierced his jaws, his cheeks, his throat, stifling him. The thing in the uniform staggered closer, its claws reaching for him, thorns extending like creeping vines.

"He's ready now," the old man hissed into Henry's ear. "Ready to claim the life the war stole from him. You'll do just fine. For a start."

The thing in the uniform lifted its hands, its finger bones clicking as it shambled forward and grabbed Henry. Its thorns tore though his Adventure Scouts uniform and sank into the flesh of his biceps.

Then it dragged him toward the pit.

And Henry Felt found his voice.

Scoutmaster Ed Crandall was still yelling at his wife when Henry walked up to their house. Henry could hear them arguing as he made his way up the walkway. They were loud enough to hear even without the *Green*'s help. But Henry didn't mind. Through their potted plants and flowers, through the mold on their walls and the tiny flora living in their intestines, he could hear them all: *people,* arguing and laughing and rutting and scheming their little schemes. In every house on Everwood Street there was plant-life, and so there was the *Green*. Henry Felt was seeing things from a different perspective now.

Sometimes a man's got to reconsider his options, boys, Scoutmaster Ed would say. *The world can change in the blink of an eye. Above all a worldbeater's gotta be flexible.*

The new Henry Felt was nothing if not flexible. The old man was dead now, consumed, his empty corpse a drying husk destroyed with all the others, nearly two dozen in all. Drifters, hustlers—people no one would miss. The old man had provided much for his only son, even in death. This new body was young and strong, the mind of its original owner still fresh enough to master with little effort. Everything the original had ever witnessed, everything it retained of its old life of bone and blood, was now a part of the *Green.*

It savored its most recent memories: the screams of the boy's mother, the stabbing thrust of its thorns as it overpowered her lover. The memory of their terror was sweet, their blood and flesh even sweeter. It had fed well.

But that was yesterday. Now it was hungry again, and the Old Gods demanded blood for their investment.

As it raised its fist to knock on Scoutmaster Ed's door, it rehearsed its spiel. And when Scoutmaster Ed flung open the door, demanding to know what the hell Hank was doing out at this hour, the new Henry Felt spoke right up.

"Hello," it said.

Yessir, this boy is gonna be a worldbeater.

And its smile was wide and bright and *green.*

JIMMY STICKS & THE OUTLAW CRITTER OF DOOM

Jimmy "Sticks" Bohannon broke the surface of Lake Michigan just after 9:00 PM. He staggered the last few steps toward shore, dragged himself up onto the pebble-strewn sandscape of Oak Street Beach, along Chicago's "Little Riviera," fell to his knees, and puked his guts out.

Beneath the fat Midwestern moon, Jimmy hawked up three gallons of lake water, a half-pound of sediment, six teeth, one shredded condom: X-tra large and ribbed for maximum enjoyment, and half a foot of his own intestines.

"Jee…sssus," Jimmy breathed. It was the first utterance of his dark new life. It was also remarkably similar to the last utterance of what he would soon come to think of as his "old life." "What's… happening…to…me?"

As if in answer to his query, a bright flare of—

PAIN

—something erupted in his head. It wasn't a physical pain so much as psychic distress, a remembrance of agonies too vast to fit into the decayed hard drive that was rebooting itself behind his eyes. See, Jimmy Sticks was beyond pain in the traditional sense, at least any kind of pain he'd ever understood.

Still—

HURTS

—*something* was gnawing at the insides of his skull like a rabid badger on PCP.

Jimmy reached up with one extremely long fingernail and poked at a spot between his eyes, the area from whence the ghost pain signal seemed to emanate the strongest.

His fingernail plunged, up to the second knuckle, into his forehead, through the ugly hole in the center of his skull and into the soft meat of his brain. To say that Jimmy was confused was like saying Dick Cheney had anger-management issues: insufficient and unsavory. Jimmy's forefinger hooked something hard, unyielding in that perforated jelly bowl of fish-gnawed graymeat goodness, hooked it and pulled. As the hard knot moved through his cracked brain-box, a flood of memories came with it.

I love you, Jimmy!

Miyoko! Leave her alone!

Somebody shoot this bitch before I puke.

A shock-surge of memory punched Jimmy in the lower 'taint. He tugged harder at the thing in his brain.

And Chink Bitch hits the water with a huge splash.

Hah-hah-hah!

Ouch! That's a Two from the French judge!

The hard knot fell out of Jimmy's head and hit the sand with a soft *plink*. Jimmy looked down: a bullet lay between his splayed finger bones like a smashed miniature beer can. The slug had pancaked, no doubt, after blasting through the failed bulwark of Jimmy's skull. Now it glittered, like a nugget of tainted starlight, upon the oblong shelf of stone atop which he knelt.

And Jimmy remembered it all.

He and Miyoko had gone out to dinner to celebrate their wedding anniversary: twelve years of happiness that a two-bit jazz drummer and a struggling graphic artist had little right to expect. They'd just exited Nolane's, Miyoko's favorite French-Asian-Cuban fusion place, and decided to take a moonlit stroll along the Lake.

As they strolled down Michigan Avenue, a black BMW loaded with glowing skull-masked teenagers approached, the occupants' howls accompanying electric piano and heavy bass guitar: a "techno" remix of the Doors' "Riders on the Storm" droned from the luxury sound system.

"Trick or treeeeeaat!" one of the luminous skulls shrieked, his laughter scaling up into a maniac wail as the BMW thundered past. Jimmy and Miyoko had laughed at the daffy bastards and made their way toward Grant Park, arms entwined against the crisp autumn deadwind blowing off the lake, as deeply in love as they would ever be in their short, happy life together.

They'd barely crossed Michigan Avenue when three men stepped out of the darkness, grabbed Miyoko, and put a hunting knife to Jimmy's throat.

"Well look at this," one of the men, a stocky blond, snarled. A large strawberry birthmark in the shape of an arrowhead covered the right side of his face. "Blackboy and his trusty chink sidekick out for an evening sabbatical."

The other two men were a study in contrasts. One, a hulking, heavily tattooed brute, sported a head like a mutated pink bowling ball. The smaller one affected a long brown ponytail, bad teeth, and a shitty mustache.

They laughed like the good beta males they undoubtedly were and took turns kicking the shit out of Jimmy. Then Arrowhead and Signor Mustache dragged Miyoko off into the darkness while Bowling Ball sat on Jimmy's chest and pounded his head against the pavement.

After a century in Hell, Arrowhead and Signor Mustache returned, dragging Miyoko, her clothing ripped and bloodied, by her hair.

"Gotta compliment you on your taste, my brothuh," Arrowhead sneered. "Crouchin' Tiger here's got a great rack."

"Yeah," Signor Mustache giggled, zipping up his fly.

"Nice shitcutter for a cum dumpster."

This comment elicited gales of laughter from the three thugs. Meanwhile, Jimmy tried to stand up. Unfortunately, his right leg was broken in three places.

"Hey, I like that jacket," Bowling Ball rumbled. "Looks like my size."

He'd stripped the black leather coat, a birthday present from Miyoko, from Jimmy's back. It slid with a hard, tearing sound, over his massive shoulders. Then he turned toward Signor Mustache. "Well?"

"Looks good," Signor Mustache said. 'Specially in the shoulders."

"Thanks."

"Hey, *faggots*," Arrowhead snarled. "If you're finished with the fashion show...let's do 'em and dump 'em. There's a Whopper with my name on it waitin' at Mickey Dee's."

Signor Mustache snickered, "They got the Whopper at Burger King, Lonnie."

"You wanna shut your shit-dribbler, Leon," Arrowhead snapped. "Or I'll shut it for ya."

They'd driven to the Michigan Avenue Bridge. At nearly three o'clock in the morning the Miracle Mile was free of potential rescuers. Bowling Ball and Signor Mustache propped the Bohannons against the railing. Then Arrowhead pulled a silver Smith & Wesson nine-millimeter automatic.

"Hold 'em still, you douchebags!"

Jimmy fought then. Bucking and rearing like a bull with its nuts in a bear trap, he'd managed to smash Bowling Ball's nose with the back of his head. Bowling Ball squealed like a girl scout who has discovered her favorite hamster floating facedown in the toilet.

"Owwww! Fuck!"

Then Signor Mustache kicked Jimmy in the balls. Arrowhead did something... *wet* to Miyoko, and that was when she gasped, and cried out in a surprised, *hurt* kind of way,

"I love you, Jimmy!"

"Miyoko!" he'd screamed. "Leave her alone!"

"Somebody shoot this bitch before I puke," Signor Mustache griped.

Arrowhead complied. The shot echoed out over the river, hiccupping between the Wrigley Building and her younger, uglier stepsister, the Chicago Tribune Building. Then they threw Miyoko's body off the bridge.

"And Chink Bitch hits the water with a huge splash!" Arrowhead crowed.

"Hah-hah-hah," Bowling Ball laughed, the sound somehow strangled and honking through his busted schnozz.

"That's a Two from the French judge!" This from Signor Mustache, he of the ponytail and punch-fucked facial grill.

"Kill you!" Jimmy snarled. "SweartoGodIllkillyouuu!"

Arrowhead laid the barrel of his nine-millimeter against Jimmy's forehead. "Look out, Leslie," he said to Bowling Ball. "I don't want to get Blackboy's brains on that fine leather coat."

Jimmy Bohannon had a moment to think: *Jesus, this is it.*

Then a bright red flash.

Then darkness.

Now, Jimmy Sticks looked up from the bullet that lay between his finger bones, and a howl of fury boiled up from his rotted guts.

And that was when he saw the possum.

The minute he laid eye on it—he only had one, as the other one had been eaten by a trout—he knew it was no ordinary possum. For starters, it was black. Jimmy had lived his entire life in the Midwest and never seen a pitch-black possum of the variety that regarded him from the branch of a nearby maple: gray, brown, and on one sad but memorable occasion hairless. But never black.

The black possum was bigger than your run-of-the-mill tree-rat, too; its rippling musculature suggested a capacity for branch clinging and telephone line-scampering that would have sent Satan's Own Monkey Brigade crying to their dens. But the three-inch-long claws on the ends of its paws, however, made it plain that line-scampering was the last thing the black possum was about. Its eyes were even weirder—lucid black pools, obsidian orbs that fairly throbbed with force. Dark gravity. Power.

"Vengeance," that force whispered. "Blood for blood."

"What...do...you...want?" Jimmy croaked, his voice a ragged rasp. "Where's...Mi...yo...ko?"

"I can give you peace," the force inside the possum whispered. "Would you have justice?"

"Miiyokooo..."

But Miyoko was dead. And, as far as Jimmy Bohannon knew, so was he. The men who had murdered them, however, were free to stalk the night, pouring ruin down upon the innocent like venereal thunderheads pregnant with gonorrhea rain. Jimmy could feel them out there. He could taste their laughter like acid smoke carried on a burning wind.

"Jus...tice..." Jimmy Sticks rasped. "For...Miyoo...ko."

The black possum spread its arms, and Jimmy saw the final difference. Gray sheets of skin unfurled from beneath its limbs; red-veined membranes stretched from the undersides of the possum's wrists to the sides of its tiny rear paws.

Wings, Jimmy Sticks thought. *It's got wings.*

The black possum reared up from its perch, its eyes blazing with that terrible force. Then it leaped into the air and flew into the night, gliding toward the dark sprawl of the South Side.

Jimmy Sticks lurched after it.

They'd seen the movie a dozen times.

He and Miyoko had rented it only a few weeks before their anniversary. It was one of his favorites: the one where mobsters killed Bruce Lee's kid and rape-murdered his innocent but hot young wife.

But Bruce Lee's kid had returned from the grave as an ass-kicking invulnerable super-wraith; a knife-wielding, shotgun-jacking, pistol-packin' kung-fu boogie bastard with a hard-on for Justice—all of this cinematic uber-bluster brought to you by a supernaturally sentient blackbird. Jimmy had memorized every line.

But the movie got it wrong. The creature that soared above him, carried aloft on leathern wings, was no crow, raven, or giant golden eagle, but it was a scary little motherfucker nonetheless. And powerful. Jimmy Sticks was dead, but he was alive, too. His bones showed through his mottled, rotten flesh; he would never star in any movie that didn't have "...of the Living Dead" featured prominently in its title.

But he was getting stronger.

As the possum banked over the rooftops of the sleeping city, Jimmy followed, his shoulder-length dreadlocks flying as he leaped across chasms that would have claimed the boldest crackheads. His waterlogged leather boots made barely a sound as they hit, darted forward, and sprang into space.

Nearly an hour later, the black possum touched down in an alley behind a bar just off Cicero. The back door of the bar was emblazoned with a huge shamrock. Perched above the shamrock was a rosy-cheeked leprechaun with a pot of gold under its ass. The name above the lintel read Dougal's Irish Pot. Despite the artist's best intentions, the leprechaun appeared to be taking the most expensive dump in the history of Irish alcoholism, the fabled "Pot" a receptacle for a shower of shimmering golden turds.

The air here tasted like one of Jimmy Bohannon's murderers: cheap tobacco and motor oil. It rang with the sound of the killer's laughter.

Homicidal rage rose up from what was left of Jimmy's balls. He growled, reached for the doorknob…and wrenched it out of its socket.

The dead man lifted the mangled brass doorknob up to his good eye and rasped appreciatively. Inhuman strength ran like electrical current through his bones. The ropes of decayed muscle that hung from his frame vibrated with black power that had nothing to do with his daddy's membership in the NAACP. Jimmy Sticks drew back his right foot to batter down the door.

The black possum hissed. Jimmy Sticks froze mid-kick. The creature hung by its tail from the arm of a nearby lamppost, its obsidian eyes radiating that weird force.

Patience

In a crackling burst of rodent telepathy, Jimmy Sticks understood. In his present state he'd cause a riot the moment he burst through the door. Even twenty drunken Irishmen were bound to notice the rotted corpse of a dead black jazz drummer backflipping across the bar. Miyoko's murderer might escape in the confusion.

Jimmy Sticks slithered beneath a parked SUV and fixed one dead white eye upon the front door of Dougal's Irish Pot, dreaming dead dreams of love and vengeance.

Miyoko.

Sometime before midnight, the front door of the bar swung open and eight partiers tumbled out, laughing, screaming with mock terror. One of the two women in the group wore a white wedding dress stained with red. A fake butcher's knife protruded from her ironing board-flat chest.

The other woman resembled a 1970's Midnight Shock Cinema queen—black Tina Turner fright wig, purple eye shadow, rouge, and lipstick, a skimpy black dress contrasting a peaches-and-cream complexion, and tits that jiggled like the ass-cheeks of a panicked white rhino.

One of the men wore a Chicago Cubs uniform with the name M.C. Gravy stenciled across the shoulders. M.C. Gravy carried a baseball bat casually over his right shoulder. Every once in a while, he would swing the bat in big, wavy circles around his head as if he were stepping up to the plate at Commiskey Park, not standing in front of a white-trash Irish juke joint in the middle of the night.

The biggest of the men stood nearly six-foot-seven, his identity hidden beneath a life-like George W. Bush mask. He was also wearing Jimmy Bohannon's black leather coat.

Miyoko's coat.

Jimmy Sticks wondered at the mask the big man wore. The women's clothing seemed unnatural, somehow out of synch with what he remembered from his pre-mortem existence. He struggled with that wrongness, frozen beneath the SUV, while his busted synapses sizzled like Puppy Chow on an old man's hot plate.

The black possum chattered into that meaty confusion.

Jimmy Sticks spasmed as the streetlamp in front of Dougal's Irish Pot flickered a Morse code flutterburst of illumination. The fog of fatality that enshrouded Jimmy's thoughts began to lift. Mental faculties that had gone slushy in the meat locker of Death's Diner of Damnation unlocked the doors, flipped on the lights and fired up the big gas grills.

It's…Halloween.

Halloween. Exactly one year since he and Miyoko were murdered. Three hundred and sixty-five days since he'd been dumped like a hot stool sample into the Chicago River. Hall-o'-friggin'-ween.

"Gooood," he snarled.

Jimmy Sticks shot out from under the SUV like black tar squirted from the depths of Lucifer's bowels. He didn't leap up onto the sidewalk beneath the flickering streetlamp so much as *congeal* there.

"Look at *this* asshole," M.C. Gravy sneered.

'George W. Bush' turned toward Jimmy Sticks. "Nice costume," he grunted appreciatively. "Little overkill on the melted face thing though."

Hey, I like that jacket. Looks like my size.

Jimmy Sticks whirled and punched 'George W. Bush' in the side of the head. 'George W. Bush' flew face-first though the plate glass window of the bakery that sat next door to Dougal's. The sounds of shattering glass and a tripped burglar alarm pierced the night.

Shock Cinema Slut screamed. M.C. Gravy and the third man, a big biker type with a long red beard, moved on Jimmy Sticks. The biker pulled a Bowie knife from the leather sheath strapped to his right thigh.

"I'm gonna cut you bad, asshole," he said.

At the same time, M.C. Gravy feinted to the left and swung his bat at Jimmy Sticks's head, or at least where Jimmy Sticks's head *should* have been. Jimmy Sticks had collapsed into a pile of liquefied bones and rotted flesh.

Shock Cinema Slut screamed again.

"Shut up, Tiffany!" M.C. Gravy snapped.

The biker and M.C. Gravy leaned curiously over the quivering bag of bone and muscle and rotted flesh.

"What the hell just happened?" Biker said. "What is that stuff?"

"Damned if I know," M.C. Gravy shrugged.

The two men leaned in closer, and the flesh, the bubbling meat-soup that was all that remained of Jimmy Bohannon's body, rose up like a living wave of putrefaction, smashed through the biker's front teeth, and shoved itself down his throat.

"Donnie!" M.C. Gravy yelled.

Shock Cinema Slut stopped screaming and bolted, her high heels clicking away into the distance. M.C. Gravy dropped the baseball bat and fled, the sight he would carry to his grave seared into the meat of his eyeballs: Donnie, choking and kicking on the sidewalk, as the flesh worm forced its way down his throat; his long red hair was braiding itself into dreadlocks, his skin turning first brown then black as pitch.

Donnie the Biker's boots thrummed against the concrete for nearly a minute. Then he lay still.

The Bloody Bride shimmied up to where Donnie lay, the handle of the fake butcher knife bouncing against her chest like a wayward hard-on.

"Donnie, honey?" the Bride whispered. "You okay?"

Donnie opened his eyes and sat up.

When she wasn't blowing strangers for money to buy meth, the Bloody Bride (whose real name was Sheila Dumbrowski) hawked mystery meat "nuggets" in the cafeteria of the Richard J. Daley Forensic Hospital For The Homicidally Incensed. Sheila knew what madness looked like.

As a permanent part-time food-service provider to Chicago's ambulatory fruit-basket community, she'd seen it in the eyes of many a fucked-up customer as they slobbered over their Thorazine fish sticks. But Donnie's eyes were the worst.

Because they weren't Donnie's eyes anymore.

The thing that had once been Sheila's boyfriend/pimp, but was now a horrible amalgam of Donnie and a dead percussionist, stood up. Donnie was six-foot-two on a short day. Now he *towered* over her, his face a black rictus of rage, cheekbones protruding from his ripped flesh like twin white tongue guards, his shattered chest heaving from the exertion of his transfiguration.

Sheila remained absolutely still beneath the burning eye of insanity. Her time spent in that luscious realm had inured her to the panic that might have crippled a weaker woman. Panic would only draw the madness to her. It would laugh as she fell, screaming, beneath Death's iron heel. It would pee its rubber underpants while she bled for real.

Instead, Sheila watched as Death bent over and scooped up M.C. Gravy's baseball bat.

'George W. Bush' came barreling out of the window of the bakery, his berserker's scream muffled by the rubber mask that hid his real face, the studded brass knuckles on his massive right fist promising to take Jimmy Sticks on a one-way ride to Torture Town. He ripped the mask off as he came.

Bowling Ball.

Jimmy Sticks turned and took a hard shot to the jaw.

Bones snapped, flesh ripped, and his newly acquired lower lip flew across the street and hit the windshield of an '87 Volkswagen Beetle. The lip hung there for a moment, clinging to the glass like a pink/black slug. Then it slid down the windshield on a tiny river of blood and spit.

Bowling Ball swung a brass-bound haymaker toward Jimmy Sticks's right cheek. There was a wet *splat* of metal-on-flesh-on-bone, and Jimmy Sticks's right eye flew out of its socket. Donnie's liberated eyeball dangled on his cheek, rolling and glaring at Bowling Ball like a witch's curse.

"You ain't so tough," Bowling Ball snarled, raising his fists. "In fact, you ain't nothin' at…"

And that was *all* he said, because Jimmy Sticks's right eye shot forward on its stalk and wrapped itself around his throat. Jimmy Sticks braced himself, took one step backward…and his elongated eyestalk swung Bowling Ball around in a wide, staggering circle and slammed him head-first into a nearby fire hydrant—

Bam. Bam. Bam.

—until his skull gave way with a rotten-melon *smush*. After that, Bowling Ball simmered right down. Sheila Dumbrowski took to her heels while Jimmy Sticks removed his leather jacket from Bowling Ball's shuddering shoulders and shrugged it on. Then he beat on Bowling Ball with the baseball bat until what was left looked like a giant smashed watermelon in a cheap Brooks Brothers knock-off.

Above them, the black possum chattered its dark litany of death and revenge.

Signor Mustache had just shot his ex-wife's dog when the smell of Death crept over the back fence.

"What the hell is that stink?" he said to the canine corpse at his feet. "You fart, you useless piece of crap?"

He kicked the dead Rottweiler and shot it again for free. He'd climbed Britney's back fence a few minutes earlier, violating a restraining order, hoping to throw a good scare into the bitch and maybe grab a shotgun handjob in the bargain. She'd recently remarried: some *schmoe* from Des Moines, for Christ's sake. But the *schmoe* had money and lots of it from what Signor Mustache (whose real name was Leon Van Sweringen) could gather. The house into which he was about to break had to run a cool mil. Maybe two.

Leon stepped over the perforated Rottweiler without a second thought. Any man who trusted the security of his property to a dog like that had to be a first rate numero uno Assholio Supremo. Leon preferred Akitas—Japanese hunting/guarding dogs. They weren't as solid as the Rotties, but they were mean little shits if you abused 'em right. Everybody knew that Rottweilers were *passé*.

Leon oozed toward the darkened mansion that sat at the front of the yard. It was an ancient colonial, recently remodeled, with four, maybe five bedrooms. He could smell fresh paint even from where he stood.

"*Well lah dee friggin' dah,*" he sneered.

Leon pulled on his ski mask and crept toward the back door. He'd brought along his favorite tools: files, knives, rope, rape kit, (with plenty of handi-wipes for afterwards) and, Preston, his favorite Walther P-38 automatic. He could just see his ex-wife's face as he forced her to watch him kick the crap out of the *schmoe*. Hell, maybe he'd kill 'em both. Leon was feeling generous tonight. The gleam of silver and chrome caught his eye. Leon looked over at the driveway and froze.

"Holeee… *shit*."

It was a Silver Shadow… a *Rolls Royce Silver Shadow*. The car sat, perched in the moonlight like a big-tittied blonde who has just won the Illinois lottery.

"The King of Kings," Leon whispered. He glanced around, eyeballing the shadows. For a moment he half-expected some Hollywood shit-slurp like Ryan Seacrest to jump out of the garage and yell, "Got ya!" When nothing of the sort happened, Leon nearly wept with joy.

"You gotta be greasin' me."

Entranced, Leon approached the Silver Shadow like a man in a dream, heedless of the shadow that dropped from the trees behind him. He had dreamed of this car since before he was old enough to realize he'd never be able to afford one. He touched the front fender gently, almost fearfully, like a high priest stroking the nipples of a menstruating war goddess. He brushed the skin of the hood, and ran his hands along its shining contours with something like lust in his eyes. He bent down, laid his cheek on the hood of the car. He might have raped it if he'd known how to get the gas cap off.

"Darling," Leon whispered.

It took him less than twenty seconds to jimmy the door, another thirty to take off his clothes and slide, naked and shivering, behind the driver's seat. The feel of the cool leather seat on his nude buttocks ranked among the finest experiences of his life. The sensation of the leather-wrapped steering wheel in his fists made him shiver, and the pink invader between his skinny thighs slithered into wakefulness.

"Oh, you hot little whore," Leon hissed, fingering the leather knobs on the steering wheel while grinding himself against the seat. "You like that? Huh, you beautiful bitch? Tell…daddy you… like…"

He might have finished himself off right there if the asshole in the stupid Halloween rig hadn't stepped into the moonlight.

"Hey, shithead," Leon said, Preston in his hand with a speed that was almost supernatural. "What the hell are you lookin' at?"

The big intruder didn't answer. He just stood there, half-illuminated by the autumn moon. Leon had to admit, the getup was good, even a little scary. He wondered how the intruder managed to make the phony eye hanging down from the mask's eye socket roll and glare at him.

"Nice costume, dickbreath," Leon said. "Very realistic. Now why don't you bugger off and leave a guy to enjoy the fruits of his labor?"

The asshole just stood there.

Now Leon was starting to get scared. And when Leon got scared, Leon got mad. The way the guy was just standing there, his head tilted as if he was listening to a distant voice Leon couldn't hear. And the way that goddamn dangling eyeball tracked his every movement…

That's just goddamn creepy is what that *is.*

"Hey, shithead," Leon growled. He got out of the car and pointed Preston at the shadowy figure. "What are you, deaf as well *and* queer? I said, clear out."

Then the big intruder stepped forward and Leon started to laugh.

"Les? Is that you?"

The guy in the mask cocked his head sideways again, as if listening to that distant voice.

"Jesus," Leon breathed. He stooped and grabbed his underpants off the driveway and shrugged them on. "I almost popped a cap in your stupid Irish ass," Leon chuckled. "If I hadn't recognized that jacket you lifted off that porch monkey last year I would'a drilled you good, ya stupid son-of-a-bitch. What're you doin' out here, brother?"

The big intruder moved forward, lurching like a cheap 1950's movie robot. Leon had a moment to register the smell coming from his old cellmate, Leslie. In the instant before the intruder grabbed him, he thought:

Wait…that ain't Leslie.

Instinct kicked in a moment later, and Leon lifted the P-38 and pulled the trigger an instant before the barrel punched through Jimmy Sticks's chest. The first shot bounced off Jimmy's ribcage and blasted part of his spine out through his upper back. Chunks of spinal column smacked the white backboard of the basketball hoop in the neighbor's driveway. The second and third shots went high and wide. One bullet struck a passing goose on the wing. The recently widowed goose fell out of the sky with a despondent squawk.

Back on the ground, Leon's gun hand was stuck in the hole it had punched through the intruder's chest. Leon tried to free the Walther but the trigger guard had snagged on one of Jimmy Sticks's ribs.

"Wait a minute, man," Leon cried. "Wait!"

Jimmy Sticks grabbed Leon's balls and ripped them off. Leon screamed. He took two staggering steps toward the Silver Shadow, clutching the gushing crater where his nuts had been, his eyes wide with horror.

"Why?" he whispered.

The dark figure lifted his manhood, dripping, into the moonlight.

"That's a...Two... from...the... French judge," Jimmy Sticks rasped.

Leon's eyes grew even wider.

"You!" he whispered. "But...we killed you. You and...and..."

"Mi...yo...koooo," Jimmy sticks moaned.

Then something flew out of the night and attacked Leon, a furry nightmare that moved like a whirlwind as it chattered and burrowed under his chin. The black thing ripped at his throat, tore up his face and clawed his eyes out. Leon opened his mouth to scream and the dreadful possum tore out his tongue. He fell, spewing, into the driver's seat of the Silver Shadow while the possum ravaged him like a streak of sentient black lightning, reducing him to a red ruin.

Jimmy Sticks shut the door. He watched as the Silver Shadow jumped and rocked back and forth on its wheels. He watched as the interior of the Rolls Royce turned red and various organs smacked against the windows. Then he opened the door and let the vicious little bastard out. He reached into the mess on the front seat and rooted around in what was left of Leon Van Swearingen. Two minutes later, he'd replaced the parts he'd lost to accelerating decomposition and Leon's bullet.

Meanwhile the black possum licked its paws.

One more, it said silently, its muzzle dripping red.

Then home.

Lonnie LaFleur was just about to skull-pop the rich bitch from Birney when the screaming started. Birney was a skid-mark suburb an hour west of Chicago, home to Big Eagle Country: the crown turd in the Seven Stars Amusement Parks crap-chain. The rich bitch and some of her rich-bitch girlfriends had staggered up to the Big Eagle Nosh Nest dressed, respectively, as a Sexy Witch, a Sexy Nurse, a Sexy Librarian and Pope Benedict the 16th. They'd demanded candied apples and popcorn.

Lonnie obliged them, filling their buckets while he eyed them over the counter. None of the girls was a day over sixteen, and in their tight costumes, "belly shirts" and "hot pants," every one of the little whores was asking for it and Lonnie told them so.

"You're disgusting," the Sexy Witch (the tall blonde with the nose job, of course) snapped. "My father is Charles Devereaux, you *freak*," she hissed as she whipped out her smartphone. "He owns this whole park, and you know what? I'm calling him right frickin' now."

"He's not even cute," the Sexy Nurse lisped through her braces. "What's with that goofy birthmark?"

"Yeah," Pope Benedict chirped. "Nice leprosy, shit-for-brains."

The rich girls laughed. Since he was about to get fired, Lonnie reached under the counter for his gun. Charles Devereaux was the billionaire CEO of Seven Stars USA, the corporation that fronted Big Eagle Country.

He was also a notorious ball-buster, and the star of the hit reality cable sex show, "Hey, America: Go F—k Yourself!" It was just Lonnie's luck that Devereaux was hosting his bitch daughter's sixteenth birthday/Halloween bash at the park tonight. Two hundred of Jennifer's closest sycophants, each and every one of them the demonspawn of some corporate asshole.

Lonnie drew a bead on the Sexy Librarian. The girls had all turned their backs on him, giggling as Jennifer relived her horror for Lonnie's boss. It was after midnight and this part of the park was empty. Lonnie figured he could off the three losers, abduct Jen at gunpoint, do her in his pickup, dump her body along I-95, and be at Burger King before they closed the breakfast menu.

"Oh, girrllls," he sang, his finger on the trigger.

That's when everyone started screaming.

After the forty-mile forced lunge up from Chicago, Jimmy Sticks looked like Hell. The energies that powered him were as puissant as ever; his eyes fairly burned with the fever of the animated damned. His remaining human parts, however, had been beaten to a gristly frazzle during his quest for vengeance. What shambled through the employee entrance to Big Eagle Country looked like motivated road kill on a hot summer day.

But the black possum had summoned reinforcements.

Seven bitter mariachi players from the "How America Won the West" show grumbled past Jimmy Sticks on their way to the employee parking lot. Most of them ignored the obviously fake zombie with the glowing red eyeball on his chest—it was Halloween after all—but a few of them fell to their knees and vomited. As bad as Jimmy Sticks looked, he smelled like a garlic-infused bowel movement on moldy onion loaf.

Only the bass player, Oscar Corvado, recognized the danger for what it was. Only Corvado saw the black monstrosity perched on the dead man's shoulder, and the roiling carpet of gray forms following in their wake. Corvado shrugged. Let the gringos in their stinking white funhole deal with *el muerto caminando*, the walking dead man. Then maybe they'd understand how the West was *really* won.

Jimmy Sticks cut a wide swath through dozens of stoned and/ or drunken teenagers while the black possum chittered into what was left of his right ear, drowning out the screams of upper middle-class teen horror. The heaving ocean of squealing gray bodies that surged behind him was growing hungrier by the moment. He took a hard left past the Heartland-America Chinese Railroad Workers Exhibit, staggered across Native-American Memorial Parade Way, and stopped just in time to see "Arrowhead" aiming his gun at the Sexy Librarian.

Jennifer Devereaux and her friends took one look at Jimmy Sticks and shrieked. His body was crawling with rats, some as big as their mothers' Shar Peis. The girls dropped their candied apples and bolted into the night, followed closely by nearly four hundred angry vermin. For her birthday present, Jen would receive seven different strains of rabies and one bitch of a yeast infection.

Lonnie LaFleur and Jimmy Sticks squared off. There were no dramatic speeches, no declarations from man or monster. In many ways, Lonnie was as much a predator as Jimmy Sticks. He instantly recognized the thing that had come to kill him.

"Mother...*fucker*," Lonnie whispered. Then he shot Jimmy Sticks in the face. His first shot shattered the creature's lower jaw and right cheek. His second shot tore a chunk out of Jimmy Sticks's throat. His third and fourth shots took out the nose and blew off the top of Jimmy Sticks's head.

Jimmy Sticks kept coming.

"Motherfucker," Lonnie chanted, squeezing off a shot with each breath. "Mother...fucker."

To Lonnie's credit, he stood his ground. His stance was firm and his aim steady. He didn't stop shooting until his gun was empty. Then Jimmy Sticks grabbed him, shoved his finger bones up Lonnie's nostrils, and *pulled*. Lonnie shrieked as the top half of his face came off like a wet meat mask. His lidless eyes rolled wildly in their bloody sockets.

"You..." he squealed. "Yooooooouuuuuuuu!"

Jimmy Sticks leaned down and spoke clearly into "Arrowhead's" exposed ear hole.

"My wife...her name...was Miyoko."

Then he lifted Lonnie up by the lapels of his Big Eagle Nosh Nest uniform and punched him in the nuts. His fist hammered those dangling pleasure-berries, and smashed them like overripe cherry tomatoes. Then his fist shattered Lonnie's pelvis and plunged deep into his intestines.

"Gah...gah..." Lonnie replied. "Gaaaaahhhhh!"

Jimmy Sticks yanked his arm out of Lonnie's guts and let gravity do the rest. There came a sound like a punching bag stuffed with manatee blubber suddenly letting go. Lonnie took three steps backwards and snagged his foot in the loop of gut dangling between his knees. Then he stumbled and sat down in a steaming pile of himself. The last thing Lonnie LeFleur saw was Jimmy Sticks feeding his face to the weird monkey sitting on his shoulder. Then the rats took him.

They chewed his liver and lungs; chewed their way up his ass and ate like rude relatives. They devoured his unruly penis.

Fortunately, Lonnie stayed conscious for the whole thing.

Until they got to his brain.

Dawn found Jimmy Sticks standing on the shelf of rock that looked out over Lake Michigan. He could feel her out there, waiting for him.

Come home, my love.

Miyoko's voice was in the waves. It whispered on the wind that tugged at his melting, borrowed flesh, as Jimmy Sticks looked up at the Black Possum.

Its obsidian eyes twinkled at him. Then it spread its underarm membranes and took off over the Lake. The dark figure glided into the dark, toward the mysteries of western Michigan.

It's time, my sweet.

Jimmy Sticks took seven steps toward the water and fell flat on his face. His skull struck a large outcropping of rock and ruptured, spilling his brains across the sand, but that didn't matter. By the time his cerebellum was gull chow he was in the spectral arms of his beloved, nestled together, their souls and memories entwined in eternal darkness.

He was home. With her.

And that didn't suck.

ACROSS THE BLACK PLAINS

Harlan Poole was beating the sorcery out of one of the twins when trouble hammered at his front door.

"Hieronymus Pike! I'm callin' you out!"

The old man's breath was a rasp in his chest. His good hand trembled, inches from his screaming son's backside, while red starbursts detonated behind his eyeballs.

You'll kill yourself yet, damned fool.

He'd caught the twain playing out in the old henhouse. Caven, the rowdy one, had somehow achieved an invisibility spell and gone ghost-stalking mild-mannered Hile. Poole had rushed out to the henhouse to find the twain fighting, seen and half-seen, both of them covered in blood and the dust of ancient chicken turds. Now here came a stranger, fouling the air with a name he'd hoped never to hear again.

He let Caven squirm off his lap and stood up, and the starbursts in his head redoubled their assault. He caught hold of the back of his chair and held on until the dizziness passed.

"I hate you," the ten-year-old screamed. "One day I'll learn the right words and make her hurt you bad!"

"Your mama's dead, boy."

"Liar!"

"Pike!" the rough voice barked. "Come out or we'll burn you out!"

Poole went to the window and looked out. Then he turned to Simene, his oldest.

"Take the boys out back. Keep 'em quiet."

Simene nodded in her customary way. Even after all these years it was impossible for Poole to look at the girl without seeing the woman for whom he'd earned damnation staring back. Long ago his love had ripped away his daughter's voice, and she had spoken no word since that night of bereaving.

"Simmie…if somethin' should happen to me…"

Simene nodded. At only fifteen winters old she was a dead shot with pistol or rifle. She could knock a nested screech owl off its perch at midnight from thirty yards. She was brown-skinned, lean and long-limbed like him, but with the ink-black hair and cat-tilt eyes of her mother's Crow people. And she was tough enough to take the piss out of any half-grown roughneck.

As Simene wrangled the boys into the back room, Poole tried to think of the things he should say, but his tongue lay fallow in his mouth. Instead, he gripped his revolver and checked its chambers.

Too old for gunfights.

He holstered his pistol and grabbed Ol' Gal from where she stood next to the front door. The semi-automatic Gatling mini-shotgun could fire sixteen rounds in an assfull'a 'ticks—more than enough firepower to make a reasonable defense.

Beneath the black leather glove he wore, the skin of his left hand writhed, mocking his presumptions.

"Kiss my ass," he growled.

Then he opened the door to the setting sun.

Two men sat mounted in front of his house. Each of them wore the drab brown or gray long coats most common among western Plainsmen. The tall, skinny one wore a battered brown fedora with the brim pulled low over one eye. The stouter of the two wore a faded gray bowler, its rim tipped back to reveal a boyish face and the eyes of a Plains hyena. Neither of them looked older than twenty-five winters.

"Hieronymous Pike?" Fedora asked.

"Who wants to know?"

Fedora's eyes went all squinty and he puffed out his chest. Poole saw that he was going to have to hurt this one before all was said and done.

"Would you be you the hired wand who turned the undead of Minapolis and sent them against Walker White Eyes?"

Poole worked his jaw, flicking his tongue at the bloody hole that had opened up on the inside of his right cheek that morning. Two of his teeth rocked back and forth like loose tombstones.

Comin' down with the damn 'fluinza.

If he was contagious he'd have to drag the kids to Doc Rosie's, over in Sacrifice, though only the Gods knew what he'd use for money.

"We're lookin' for the spellslinger who rode into Lansing and murdered the Dragon Brothers," Fedora continued. "The colored conjurer the Sioux call 'Satan's Fist.'"

"This here's my property," Poole said. "Ain't nothin' for you here. You boys should get on your way."

"I spy the black glove on your left hand, Mister Pike," the one in the bowler hat said, grinning. "Bit of a dead giveaway, don't you think?"

The fat sput's grin widened as he reached down, slowly, and parted the lapels of his threadbare travelling coat. Twin gun belts with pearl-handled heaters hung low across his hips.

"Enough formalities, duskie. I'm gonna ask you one last time: Are you Pike?"

Poole hawked and spat bloody sputum into the weeds.

"No."

Fedora swore, and raised his hands, his fingers waggling as they traced comet-tails of lethal enchantment across the naked air. The skinny roughneck was a low-level jinxer. The worst he could do was hex a grown man to sleep. Poole inhaled as that cold lash of stunning magic lit a sunburst of pleasure in his guts.

Been too long.

Then he stooped, grasped the handle of the iron slop bucket he kept next to the front door, and heaved it across the yard. There came the satisfying crunch of bone as the bucket shattered Fedora's nose, followed directly by his high-pitched wail.

"Oowww! By dose...!"

The skinny roughneck spewed like a gutted hog while he hopped up and down amidst the shining shards of his thwarted hex.

"The bastard boke by dose!"

Bowler grinned like a governor enjoying a new opera. He set one foot on the edge of the overturned bucket and lit a cigarette. In the match's glow, Poole saw the sigil tattooed on the right side of Bowler's face: a man-shaped, horned figure crouching inside the bottom half of a stylized dollar sign. It was a blood rune.

No, he thought. *It can't be…*

"My name is Desmond Molluck," Bowler chuckled. "My bleeding colleague here is Nix Taint. We came a long way to find you, Pike."

"You've got the wrong man."

"Bastard!" Taint wailed. "Lyin' black bastard!"

Molluck waved the dust and smoke out of his eyes.

"You deny the obvious, Mister Pike," he said. "Oh I may not be a famous wizard, but I know vigor when I see it. And the one who sent us hither told me Hieronymus Pike's got more grit than any darkworker on the Northern Plains, white, red, or dusk. It's that grit we've come seeking. Yes, even through the arrayed forces of Hell we've…"

A gunshot cut Molluck off. The slop bucket his foot was resting on flew ten yards and bounced off the north wall of the stable. Startled, he leaped backward, stumbled, and sat down hard on a pile of old horse-drop.

Simene half-leaned out of the kitchen window, her smoking Ladyhawk at the ready.

"I'm gonna give you boys one more chance to get off my land with your balls attached," Poole said. "We're just regular country folks out here. I don't do magic. Nor would I welcome magicians to partake of my company."

He spat for emphasis. The spittle that hit the weed patch was entirely red.

"Sorcery is Ket work, and those bastards have caused enough misery in the Cities. You tell whoever it was that sent you to look for his savior in Cheekaugwa or Deeters. He won't find him here."

"Even if that savior is poor as a damn church mouse?" Molluck grunted. "Seems a man in your position might be amenable to the retainer I bear. More money than most 'reglar country folks' see in a lifetime."

"I'm done jawin', mister," Poole said. "Next one doin' the talkin'll be my ol' Gatlin' here."

Nix Taint climbed atop his dull brown horse clutching his dribbling nose. "The bastard's crazy!"

Molluck stayed where he was.

"Fenris Nightslayer has made 'Rado Springs his own private Idaho."

The old man unsquinted. "What?"

"You tell Mister High and Mighty Hieronymus Pike that the Nightslayer has made the Springs a Hell no demon could stomach," Molluck said, speaking with another man's voice. "Tell him a Ket war party outta Denver is headin' his way. They mean to scourge the Plains, same way they scourged the Cities."

Molluck was under a speakspell, a *compulsed* voice. Poole swore under his breath. For only a powerful conjurer could have deployed such a charm.

"This rejoinder should cover the mess we made back in Okie City," Bowler continued. "With his sayso...I'm callin' my part in that mess bought and paid for."

"I *told* you," Poole snarled. "My name is Harlan Poole. I'm just a half-dead duskman with two shits worth of land and a nest-full of sick kids. I ain't no darkworker, mister. You tell Bart Bixby that."

For a moment, Molluck's college-boy façade cracked, revealing a flash of honest woe beneath.

"Sherriff Bixby's dead, Pike, tortured by the very Ket scum-licker that comes presently. Nix and me were his last contract."

From her window, Simene raised her rifle to her shoulder and thumbed back the hammer. It was only then that something in Molluck saw that something in the old trader meant business. He dusted himself off, bowed, and swung himself up into his saddle, pausing only to toss a leather satchel onto the ground at the old man's feet.

"For your troubles...Mister *Poole*."

The old man stood there until long after they'd disappeared into the hills. Only when he could hear no trace of Taint's curses did he look down at the pouch where it lay in the blood and dust.

"Bixby," he spat.

Hieronymus Pike swiped at the blood that dribbled down his chin and glared out at the dying sun as it slid, bloated and red, below the horizon.

"You backstabbin' son-of-a bitch."

It wasn't the money.

Although Pike needed Bixby's rejoinder more than he cared to admit, it wasn't the money that got him out of bed before dawn, three days after Molluck and Taint had gone. Nor was it the particular that his house had fallen into such disrepair even devil rats gave it a wide pass, or that the twain had both come down with the disease the locals called *scorbut*.

It wasn't any of these particulars that made him rise early, pack his old knapsack, two revolvers, his hunting rifle, and all the ammo he could carry. It wasn't love nor honor, nor even a thirst for revenge that dragged him out to the barn, shuddering in the teeth of a North Plains spring sunrise. 'Twasn't any one of those details, though they nettled him like sharp goads laid across the flesh of his spirit.

It was the hate.

And the smell of roasting flesh carried on the western wind.

The morning after Molluck and Taint's visit, Pike had looked through his spyglass toward the west and seen flashes of crimson lightning gutting the skies over New Des-Moines. The bastard Bixby had augured truly. The Nightslayer's forces were nearly upon them.

His old employer had also packed more gold inside that leather satchel than the neighbors would see in *ten* lifetimes. Pike recognized Bixby's rejoinder for what it was: a walking dead man's final bequest, and he used a portion of it to buy clothes and sturdy boots for the children. Then he loaded them into the wagon and headed into Sacrifice to see Doc Rosie.

The "colored hamlet" of Sacrifice had once been thought a beacon of cultural cooperation, a shining symbol of the New Midwest. Founded a hundred years earlier by a council made up of freed or runaway slaves fresh up from the postwar South, several of the local tribes and a handful of abolitionist whites, the town had grown faster than rabbit litters in the decades following the Great War. In the face of opposition from a few of the neighboring "English"-dominated towns, Sacrifice had even thrived, mostly due to its proximity to the *Misi-ziibi* River and its numerous trade routes to the rest of the nation its white forefathers had renamed "Greater Canaan."

But the invasion had revealed its dread face even to the proudest Cities of the young nation. Unable to save themselves, the Cities had abandoned their smaller rural counterparts. In less than five years, Sacrifice had become little more than a ghost town.

Doc Rosie was a Chinawoman out of what was left of Cheekawgua.

She was educated, and spoke English, *Chin*, and several of the tribal tongues and, like most of the locals, she was a professed New Quaker. But Pike didn't hold it against her.

"Got work," he told her.

Doc Rosie leaned forward, her sun-curdled face alit with curiosity. "What *kind* of work?"

"Out of *town* work," Pike said. Then he doubled over and coughed up a pat of fresh blood onto Doc Rosie's pitted wood floor.

"You're probably dying, Poole," she shouted. She was partially deaf and assumed everyone else was too. "That bloody tooth's the giveaway: scurvy! With congestive heart failure for dessert, I expect. And you can have that diagnosis free of charge."

"I'm fine, Rose," Pike said. "Just this damn 'fluinza. I'll be back in a few days. Two weeks at the outside."

Doc Rosie remained skeptical. She gave him three bottles of a tonic made from the needles of an arbor vitae tree.

"Go buy your colts some oranges, lemons, and a few vegetables from the hex-free market over in Darling. That's for the scurvy! It'll do 'em a power of good!"

"Thanks, Rose."

"I'll check on yer little ones while you're away, for a nominal fee," Doc Rosie hollered. "If you like we can go upstairs for a little medicinal intercourse, as I sideline in that particular area!"

Pike paid, since it couldn't hurt to have a real doc on the lookout. He declined the intercourse. For his heart belonged to a dead woman, and a jealous one at that. As he drove back to his spread, chocked with enough food, medicine and ammo to secure his house for a quarter-year, he felt like a provider again. Bixby's money made this feeling possible.

But it wasn't about the money. It was about hate. And so it came to pass that, early the next morning, Pike threw open his barn doors. For he was a man with a mission again, a dark purpose to fill his days with fire and his nights with dreams of the killing to come. For he could taste them now: the windblown taint of alien magicks so strong none of his generation could stand against them.

Pike moved past the dusty stalls, their occupants only ghosts, all save one, and he approached her with a kind of reverence. For he adored Gloria in Excelcis as much as a hard man could adore anything.

"And so you come, rider," the great black warhorse said in ritual greeting. "You smell of killing thoughts."

"So faster comes the End, bearer," Pike replied in kind. "I would beg your sayso."

She granted it. Pike brushed her coat until it shone like the last kiss of midnight. Then he unbraided her silver mane and brushed it free of knots, this their ancient ritual, the silent communion between warmounts and the darkworkers who rode them even unto Death's heartland.

"I would be free, rider," Gloria whispered. "I'm old. And I'm afraid."

"Aye, dearest," Pike said. "We can't hope to ride into the Ket's world and return unscarred."

"But I would be free of your *friendship*, rider. And your immortal hate."

"Agreed then," Pike sighed, though the words stung him. "After the killing's done, our run together will end."

Then he left her to conduct his final duty.

If company ever called on Pike—and company was rare after the Ket claimed most of the Great Cities—they never noticed the chained and padlocked trapdoor set in the floor of the old henhouse. If that company were canny (or unlucky) enough to break the lock and raise the door, they would find a rude wooden staircase leading down into the darkness.

For ten years the demoness had lain in that hallowed chamber, bound by shackles both magical and "dull." Occasionally it screamed jumbled incantations in the dead of night. Pike had lain awake those nights, fearing one of the children might gain the knowledge to pierce the barriers he'd set 'round the henhouse, only to discover the thing that waited below.

"And so you come, beloved," she whispered from the shadows at the rear of the chamber.

"You mean to consecrate our union after this handful of mortal years?"

The Lamia uttered its bass chuckle. Oil lamps flickered in each corner of the chamber, their colored flames dancing with the creature's exhalations. The smell of it turned Pike's guts, because it was *Sarah's* smell, only corrupted by the stink of demonic possession, like jasmine and honeysuckle gone rancid at the bottom of a charnel pit.

The Lamia's upper body was human, nude, save for a skein of bruises, her face a mockery of Sarah's long-faded beauty. Her hair had gone snow white and long enough to enshroud her human half. Her eyes were black pits behind that curtain of white, gaping shadows in a face sallow as Death's belly. Her lower half ended in the tail of a great red serpent.

"Sarah," Pike breathed. "Can you hear me?"

"Come to me, Hieronymus. How I've yearned for your touch, chained in this dungeon with only the memory of your rough affections. Touch me, my Hiro."

He had taken three steps before the agony in his left hand overcame the demon's allure; the ghost-pain in that murdered limb reminding him of his greatest folly.

How can you love one o' them damned things, Pike?

"Sarah…" Pike said. "If you can hear me…"

But, just like with Simmie, he didn't possess the words that could redeem them from his choices.

"I'll be back."

The sound of the Red Lamia's scorn followed Pike up the stairs and out of the chamber and back to the main house.

Two days later and a hundred miles west, he could hear her laughing still.

It was a bargain that brought about Pike's peculiar damnation. The things he'd done for Bart Bixby had made him a legend, but the love of a bad woman made him a man. He and Sarah had worked for Bixby as hired spellslingers—magical mercenaries who fought the bad fight whenever and wherever Bixby paid them to fight it. Then the Ket came to Earth. They were alien necromancers so powerful they could alter the roots of mortal life. In the first months of the invasion, the Ket had easily captured many of Pike's colleagues, killing them, or turning them to their cause. With their help, the invaders turned the Great Midwestern Cities into breeding grounds for their infernal experiments. Pike and his comrades had learned, all too quickly, that their magicks were impotent, powerless against sorcery so pregnant with harm its slightest utterance unleashed catastrophe. They'd fought on anyway.

And they'd failed.

"It's time," Gloria in Excelcis said. "They're coming."

Pike whispered calming cants to the black mare. Then he slid out of his saddle and dropped to the prairie dirt. His ankle turned with a jolt that sent pain shooting through his knees and up his spine. Pike swore hot enough to dry fresh apples.

"Noisy," Gloria in Excelcis snorted, not ungently. "You've grown old, rider."

"You ain't exactly a yearling, Lady."

They'd chosen to make their stand atop a windswept hill that looked out over the open prairie. Pike had set up camp a handful of miles from the mouth of Sarazin's Pass, the small range of low hills that formed a border between the easternmost edge of New Des-Moines and the Central Plains.

Pike limped back to the large open patch of rocky hilltop and doused his fire. Then he rechecked his guns, his spyglass, and the other things he would need. Despite the quickening of his heart he forced himself to move slowly, fearing that he'd forget something important.

In the darkening western sky, tendrils of black smoke writhed across the horizon. Bixby's warning had nearly come too late. A day later and the Ket might have taken his children in their beds.

"Your colts yet live, rider," Gloria nodded, sensing his thoughts. "While mine have returned to the Grass. I think my time to join them draws a'pace."

"You'll live," Pike muttered. " 'Pon my word and will."

An emerald flash drew his attention back to the entrance Plainsmen of old had blasted through Sarazin's Pass. Pike used his spyglass to get a closer look and offered a low whistle.

"Wolves."

"Aye," Gloria said. "And worse."

The shapes that gathered at the mouth of the Pass were *warwolves*—hybrids transformed by the Ket's magicks. A phalanx of them was pouring onto the open prairie.

"Stand ready, girl."

Less than two miles away, the pack leader of the wolves slid to a stop and rose up onto its hind paws. It was a big silverback, its gleaming coat spattered with fresh blood. In the light of the rising moon it shone like argent murder. The silverback threw back its head and roared. Then it began to run. Behind it, more than a hundred wolves followed.

Pike drew his hunting rifle, threw himself down on his belly, took careful aim, and squeezed off a shot. The first slug struck one of the trailing wolves. It fell and was torn apart by a handful of its packmates. The silverback roared, and came on.

"Ugly... *bastard...*"

The second shot struck the silverback in the throat, snapped its head back, and put it down.

Chaos swirled around the fallen leader as the lesser wolves snapped and clawed at each other in their confusion.

Then the alpha wolf leaped to its feet. The silverback sniffed the air, nostrils flaring, its senses seeking the direction from which the shot had come. It was only then that Pike realized his mistake: he'd packed unspelled ammunition—mere "dull" lead slugs.

"Son of a bitch."

Pike closed his eyes and uttered a canticle of Forbidding.

Nothing happened.

"Rider!" Gloria cried.

"I know."

A decade had passed since he'd last formed a Forbidding spell. Now he couldn't recall the proper configurations.

"Goddammit!"

The big silverback surged forward, its claws kicking up clots of blasted earth as it ran, eating up the yards in great pounding leaps.

"Rider! Remember yourself!"

And Pike remembered.

The words left his mouth like a shout of golden flame, a shimmering distortion that convulsed the air between them and the onrushing wolves, and coalesced into a shining golden barrier a quarter-mile wide. But an instant before the barrier solidified, the silverback poured on a greater speed and cleared it. A second later, dozens of the trailing wolves struck it head-on. Some split their skulls on the barrier. Others broke their necks. But more than half of them raced around the shimmering barricade and swarmed up into the foothills below Pike's camp.

Pike threw himself into his saddle and pulled his revolver, hoping the smaller wolves might be vulnerable to plain lead. The vanguard pelted up the hill, howling as they surrounded Pike and Gloria in a snarling circle of flashing fangs.

Gloria in Excelcis reared and slashed at the shadow shapes that tore at her legs and leaped up to claw at her belly. Her hooves, silver-shod and enchanted, smashed down like lightning, crushing wolf skulls or breaking the backs of the ones that got too close. She had slaughtered half-a-dozen wolves when the silverback arrowed in, its belly low to the ground, and leaped.

Pike spat a canticle of Fire. When it touched the silverback the spell exploded into a hundred separate flames. The detonation broke the alpha wolf and flung its burning corpse back among its brethren, and every wolf the flames touched took fire, adding fuel to the burning. As each flame fed, it birthed a stronger flame that, in its turn, burned yet more wolves. Pike's magic guided those flying fires, roasting his attackers as fast as they were replaced, while Gloria in Excelcis leaped and slew with every kick.

An eternal instant later, the hilltop was littered with dead and dying wolves.

"Goddamn," Pike gasped, when he could catch his breath. "Don't that *stink*."

"I like it," Gloria said. The warmare trembled, her sweat and blood-slicked sides heaving against Pike's thighs. "It reminds me of happier times."

Pike agreed. "That Ket bastard will have noticed all this hum-a-jum though."

"Aye, rider. He comes. By my mothers...his magicks..."

In the distance to the west, a red funnel cloud was eating its way across the dark horizon. It was growing larger as it turned, gaining speed and power from the destruction it left in its wake. A crimson glow blazed at the twister's center like a corrupted sun caged in a titan's belly.

Gloria in Excelcis stamped upon the bloody earth, her silver shoes ringing against smashed bones.

"He is fire and wrath and coldhearted murder," she cried. "And his power is too great, darling boy. Even for you."

Pike's senses confirmed the whirlwind's unnatural power. It was *wrong*; nature's fundamental laws perverted by alien sorcery.

"We'll just have to see about that," he muttered. "You ready, Lady?"

"No," Gloria nickered.

The black mare reared up. Her silver mane and hooves flashed, and with a ringing cry she broke the back of the last surviving wolf.

"Now I'm ready."

Sarah Pike it was, who discovered a reason to hope. For it was Sarah who revealed the source of the Umbrage, the magical essence of the Earth. It was Sarah who told Pike, Bixby, and the others about the ancient Powers that lurked in the guts of the world. Indeed, her own blood-sire was one of them—a demon of awesome potency.

Together, Pike and his newly pregnant wife descended into the earth beneath Okie City. Together they petitioned the Powers, suing for their aid against the aliens. The Powers agreed, asking, in return, for a single mortal soul. Pike offered his own, believing the price worth the redemption of the world, and was given a dreadful weapon: a talisman that granted its wielder a portion of the might the Powers possessed. But one of those Powers, the Red Lamia, had claimed Sarah's soul instead. Pike had barely pulled the twain from her womb when she ripped the tongue from their five-year-old daughter's mouth.

The Powers' bargain had schooled him in the ways and wiles of treachery. But Pike had still more to learn. For when they understood what he and Sarah had done, Bixby and his colleagues disavowed them, and banished them from their society.

"She ain't human," Bixby said, as he led them, at gunpoint, to the edge of Okie City. "How can you love one of them damned... *things*, Hieronymus?"

Pike had foregone the pleasures of explaining the contours of his heart to the man who'd betrayed him, and, drained of courage by the shadow looming over every horizon, neither man had the stomach to contest the other.

"Hope you like the table those Ket bastards are settin'," Pike had snarled.

"Damned fool," Bixby sighed, eyeing the two of them, as they rode into the darkness. "I suppose you'll find out soon enough."

Beaten by demons and betrayed by mortal men, Pike took his family and ran until he could run no more.

Then he built his house and changed his goddamned name.

"Rider! Attend!"

They were surrounded by a cadre of *dregs*, human captives melded with animal savagery and enough Ket blood to ignite a blasphemous regeneration. Pike shouted a canticle of Strength and repelled the beasts, blasting them back. But a huge creature, bred from grizzly bear, hyena, and human, rose up behind them. Sensing its presence...too late, Gloria in Excelcis wheeled around as the monster swung one massive paw and struck her across the throat. Their minds and hearts linked, Pike felt the blow as if it had snapped his own neck, felt her mind go dark as Gloria in Excelcis toppled backward and threw him to the ground. Pike's right ankle turned and gave out a sharp crack as he fell. He didn't even feel the pain.

"Gloria!"

The great mare disappeared beneath a swirling shriek of fangs and claws.

Pike's anguish ignited the air, scooping power from the well of his furious grieving, as all his promises to her fell to quivering meat. His rage became a susurration that blasted Gloria's murderers with killing magic, mass slaughter contained within the cadence of a dirge: a *deathwalla*. Elevated by grief and sorcery, Pike sang their deaths and their hearts exploded, their skulls burst with the futility of containing that awful threnody. He killed five, then twenty... then half-a-hundred more.

Agony rifled up his left side and stunned him with its fatal clarity. He saw the cants clearly now, pulsing before his inner eye with every lurch of his heart. He sent a succoring flame to seal the broken bone in his ankle. The pain of that healing nearly killed him, but he welcomed it, used the pain to sharpen his focus. With his good hand, he summoned lightnings and scourged his enemies with elemental fire. He became a burning man, raining death upon the heads of the damned until the air over the blackened hilltop rang like the trump of doomsday.

"*Gloria!*"

He'd been distracted by the past. Now his weakness had cost him the only being he could name "friend."

"You...damned...fool!"

Then a coiling tentacle of force flung Pike through the air and slammed him against the trunk of a burning copperwood tree. The impact hammered the breath from his chest, defused his lightnings, and the glowing chords of his spellsong shattered into luminous scraps. An unseen force held him in a crushing grip. He couldn't move, couldn't breathe.

"You killed my children."

The embers of Pike's doused campfire roared and became a bonfire. Fenris Nightslayer stepped out of the flames.

The Nightslayer's multi-jointed fingers twisted blacklight sigils across the night air, and tendrils the color of molten blood extended across the hilltop and wrapped themselves around Pike's throat.

"Pitiful."

The creature moved closer, its motion so subtle it might have been floating across the burning grass. Tall it stood, this overlord shrouded in black, clothed in the renunciation of light. It was a man-form nearly nine feet high, its arms long enough to drag its twelve fingers through the dirt.

"You are opaque to my senses," the Nightslayer whispered. "Some *extravagance*...imbues you, and occludes my perceptions."

The Nightslayer drifted closer. Pike gasped as the *yurt* around his throat tightened, and one glowing tendril sank into his head, invading him, mind and memory.

"I have seen such obstinacy before," the Nightslayer sighed. "You are a disciple of the insurgent Bix-bee."

Pike spat bloody defiance into the Nightslayer's face. The spittle hissed and boiled away to vapor.

"None of your peers revealed the source of this world's magicks," the creature said. "I questioned the fool Bix-bee. I peeled his eyeballs and let him watch while my truthseekers feasted on his brain. But he never revealed the trick of it."

Desperate, his consciousness flickering like a melted candle's final flame, Pike ignited the *lucid spark*, a survival spell that drew from his very life-force. With a curse, he spat hot death at his enemy, and a torrent of fire engulfed the Ket's body.

The Spark ignited the glowing tentacle that gripped Pike's throat. The limb squealed as it burned, and withdrew its tip from Pike's head. Pike dropped to the ground and fell to his knees.

Covered in flames, the Nightslayer raised one burning finger. Then Pike's soulfire shot skyward, leaving a fading spider's web of floating embers over the clearing. Beneath it, the overlord stood unharmed and wreathed in smoke, but its face was revealed beneath the charred tatters of its shroud. The unburnt half shone pale as swamp light on clean granite, its thick lips as black as pitch. A high-domed forehead gleamed, adorned by sharp black spines that ran from the bridge of its nose, over the dome of its head and down the back of its neck. Where eyes would have perched in a man's skull it possessed only slits of stitched flesh. A wet, ringed hole pulsed in place of a nose. To Pike's dying senses, the Ket seemed to radiate malice. Vast intellect. Boundless cruelty.

"I will not forgive such insolence," it said. "Perhaps you will yield the courtesies I seek."

"Let us behold this master of the Earth with our own eyes," Pike's passengers whispered.

No! Never again!

Fenris Nightslayer's flesh was healing with terrifying speed. But the pain in Pike's left arm flared star-bright, shuddering to the beat of his battered heart. And the voices of his failure were growing stronger.

"We have preserved you, Hieronymus Pike," they said. *"But we cannot confront the intruder as we are. Free us."*

"No!"

The overlord drifted closer, nearly whole now. The ringed hole in its face snuffled at the air.

"To whom do you speak, assassin?"

Pike growled the first note of a *deathwalla*. Weaponized by the canticle's power, the empty space around the overlord's head expanded and then contracted with killing force.

"Insufficient," the Ket said.

The overlord's face…unfolded. Its flesh split into separate limbs and parted like the legs of a great white spider. A flare of crimson light erupted from that opening, and with a deafening crack, the Nightslayer's magic broke the *walla's* power.

A bolt of agony struck faerie lights across Pike's sight. His left arm, his entire left side, convulsed. He was having a heart attack.

No, he cried. *Not yet. Not now!*

But Pike fell, twisted by a pain that pressed him into the dirt beneath the weight of worlds.

"Death comes, o' man," the Powers mocked. *"Even we may not sustain you beyond its borders."*

He'll kill my family

"Yes," the Powers agreed. *"He will afflict them to find every scrap of the power he seeks. They will know agonies beyond number."*

What do you want?

"Only one small sacrifice."

The overlord bent low and sniffed the air over Pike's body.

"The key lies within the brain, insurgent," it said. "Your suffering will provide the enlightenment I require."

The Nightslayer lifted Pike's chin, raised its right hand, and unsheathed razor-sharp claws...

Pike opened his eyes.

The overlord shrieked. In its hands, a blood-red spike nearly three feet long flashed. The Nightslayer raised that burning spear and stabbed it into the blasted earth where Pike lay.

But Pike was gone.

The overlord whirled, turning its blind head to and fro, seeking its prey. Behind it, Pike stepped out of the shadows and removed the glove from his left hand.

It was the color of an unhealed wound, half again the length of a normal hand. And it was covered with eyes, some of them bloody crimson, others sickly green, or yellow as a wildcat's dying piss. Pike raised that evil limb and thrust a battering ram of raw power at his enemy. The attack knocked the Nightslayer off its feet and sent it sprawling.

Pike strode forward, raising his bludgeon for a second blow, as the necromancer's face split open, filling the air with that ravenous bloodlight. That power stirred the night wind into a whirling red twister. Howling alien incantations, the Nightslayer flung the red whirlwind at Pike. The burning tempest tore the earth, tossing the bodies of the dead like storm-swept leaves. But Pike set his power against that blazing destruction. The scorching magicks clashed, spellslinger and necromancer wrestling to master the shrieking storm until, with a voice like thunder, Pike broke it into slivers. The detonation blasted the combatants apart.

Pike stood first.

The Nightslayer's face hung in tattered strips, its body, twisted and charred by the explosion. Even so, it was dragging itself toward the lip of the stony outcrop that overlooked the prairie. With a shrug, Pike ripped the Ket's arms from its body. Then he gripped it with his mind, and with a thousand unseen claws he pulled off its legs.

"Abomination!" the Nightslayer croaked.

Then Pike tore the invader's head from its shoulders.

Even dead, the Ket flung a few castrated lethalities while the thing that rode Pike's soul sampled the tang of those dying spells for a while. Then it smashed the Nightslayer's head beneath his boot heel, tore open its body, and rooted around until he held its pulsing heart in Pike's left hand. Muttering canticles of Transformation, the djinn ambled over to a convenient boulder and sat Pike's body down.

Then it ate until the prize was gone.

Simene was about to beat the twins when the front door swung open. She'd had two weeks of misery from the little bastards and was fed to the gullet with the whole sorry mess.

"Pa!" the twain cried, already halfway to the door.

But when they saw his face they froze. Their father had left them a sick man, his countless losses stamped across his soul, but the man who stood in the front parlor looked the picture of the gods' good news.

He also looked twenty years younger.

"Children," he said. "New blood."

Simene didn't remember his teeth being so long, nor so sharp. Or the way he held his left hand hidden behind his back.

"Pa?" Hile said. "You alright?"

"Oh, we're fine, son. We're just as right as rain."

Pike glanced toward the old henhouse, his head cocked, as if he were listening to a song sung by a long-lost friend.

"I understand her," he said. "Isn't that a fine thing? Guess you never really comprehend someone 'til you've walked in her *zapatos*."

"What're you jawin' about, pa?" Hile said.

"I *know*, son. I know what your mama needs."

From out back there came a sound, as of a great breaking in the bowels of the earth.

"Mama's hungry," the Pike-thing said. Then, turning to Simene, he said, "I think you'll do."

Horror filled Simene Pike like blood in a new bucket. She opened her mouth to warn the boys, but the rising screech of the thing in the henhouse, the thing that had been Forbidden, silenced her again. She pulled her pistol and leveled it at the kitchen door.

Pike spat cruel laughter. Then the gun flew out of Simene's grip, across the room and into his outstretched left hand. When Simene saw the hand that clutched her *pistola*, she screamed.

Pike pulled out his big hunting knife.

"Poppa's come home."

Then he fell to his knees, raised the knife, and stabbed its point into the great yellow eye that glared from the back of his left hand. Pike roared. And the thing from the henhouse smashed through the kitchen door.

Pike's children stood frozen, immobilized by the malign power of the creature that wore their mother's face. Its emerald gaze seemed to weigh them in turn, finally settling on Simene.

"Kiss me, daughter of Devils. I see your dreams...and know that you are damned."

And Simene took a step toward those waiting arms, reached out to her, finally, to kiss her mother, to touch her one...last...time...

A shot rang out and shattered the Lamia's *geas* and the Lamia's right eye burst open in a red gusher. The demoness recoiled, shrieking blasphemies.

"Simene!" a familiar voice thundered. "Recollect the cause of your silence!"

The voice dragged Simene's head around, crumbling the Lamia's glamour and clearing her mind. Hieronymus Pike stood there, his left hand raining black ichor across the floor. In his right hand he gripped his old Gatlin.

"Move, girl!"

Simene moved.

The last darkworker fired again, and the Lamia's right hand disintegrated. Then, moving faster than any mortal flesh, she fell upon him. Simene heard her father chanting in a language she knew only in dreams, as he was enveloped in the demon's coils. She heard the demonness howl her own murderous song, while the air around them caught fire. Then she grabbed her brothers and pushed them out the back door.

They were barely twenty yards away when the house exploded. Pike's children ran on as that song of love and death consumed the only life they'd ever known. They ran across empty fields, toward the light shining in Doc Rosie's window. While behind them, silence reclaimed the night, save for the crackle of burning wood.

And a deadly harmony that echoed across the Black Plains.

CHRISTMASTIME IN ZOMBIETOWN

'Twas the night before Christmas and gathered outside,
The creatures were stirring,
Leaving no place to hide.

Nimoy Green's Christmas list had grown long as his leg in the five years since the dead people first crawled out of their graves to attack regular people. It had changed over time, focusing more and more on items he needed, like food, fresh water or medicine for momma and daddy, instead of a better bike. The biggest changes had happened last Christmas, after Dad died, came back and hurt Mom.

Dear Santa, I know you're busy, but I REALLY want

1. A better shovel.

2. New hammer and nails. Lots.

3. Ammo. Lots

4. Transfixer Robot Lord with Red Requiem Lightblade & Mechadog.

This Christmas, his first without his momma, the list contained three new items, presents he suspected he couldn't live without. He'd always managed to scrounge up ammo from the abandoned houses around the neighborhood where he'd spent most of his ten years. He'd collected plenty of knives and even a few handguns. But now his ammo supply had dwindled. In some of the houses on his block the taps still worked, so water wasn't that much of a problem. Food though, had become what his mother called, "an issue."

He scribbled his list on the ragged strip of cloth he'd scavenged from the trunk of a car he'd found a few days earlier. The former occupants were gone, run off or eaten; Nimoy had no way of knowing and couldn't spend time trying to figure it out. The dried blood on the driver's and passenger's seats however, had given him the feeling that, whoever they were, they were probably motherfuckers by now. He hadn't seen another living soul in nearly six months, not since a parade of military vehicles had streamed past his house, on its way out of town, his mother had reasoned, headed for wherever real-life army-folks went now that the dead outnumbered the living.

Nimoy checked the spelling for mistakes, something he'd learned from his dad:

Be smart, son. Pay attention to the details. They can save your butt when the corners get tight.

Nimoy coughed to clear his throat. Then he folded the strip of once-white cloth into a rumpled square, smoothed it as best he could, and placed it atop the mantle. He made sure to put it in exactly the same spot his parents had every Christmas Eve of his life before the motherfuckers took over. The exertion made him dizzy, and so he waited for the dizziness and hunger pangs to subside. When he felt strong again, he made certain the old cloth sat in plain view on the mantle, unobstructed by the empty shotgun or a cord of firewood. Then he went to the window and looked out between the wooden slats.

The sun was up, the day unseasonably warm for a North Carolina winter. The street outside his house was quiet, but he needed to be sure before he opened the door. Nimoy pressed his face against one of the two-by-fours and marked a flurry of motion in the distance to the north. He could see three motherfuckers staggering around on the Graysons' front lawn.

His friend Nolan used to live there with his parents and twin sisters. He and Nolan had practiced their pitching and catching on the Graysons' lawn, since they both played for the Freehold Badgers Little League team. Mr. Grayson and Nolan had been taken out of their house one morning, two years ago now, dragged off their front porch by three burly soldiers. Even through the barricades, Nimoy and his parents could hear Mrs. Grayson screaming—something about Mister Grayson and Nolan being sick but not sick sick; not bitten or anything like that. But the burly soldiers, all wearing gas masks and hazmat suits, had thrown them into the back of their truck and taken off. Nimoy hadn't seen the Graysons since. Now their front lawn was alive with dead people.

Nimoy gathered the items he needed for that morning's field trip: his daddy's silver Glock 19, cleaned and ready to rock; his favorite hunting knife, the double-bladed one with the black rubber grip and red leather sheathe; and his hatchet. Then he inspected his red Radio Flyer wagon. He'd oiled the wheels the night before to make sure they'd move smoothly, quietly. Sheer force of habit made him check the Glock's magazine to make sure he had "one in the chamber." Then he shoved the gun into the waistband of his jeans, stuck the knife under his belt, and opened the front door. From somewhere close by he heard someone groan and the sound of shuffling footsteps. The groan sounded familiar, so he waited.

The groaner came out of the walkway between his house and the Jenkinses', next door, and Nimoy settled down. The groaner was a man, dressed in bloody farmer's overalls and definitely dead. Someone had torn most of the farmer's nose and lips off so that he seemed to smile, his face set in a permanent grin. When the white-haired motherfucker saw Nimoy standing in the doorway he groaned louder and started up the walkway.

Nimoy checked to make sure the dead farmer hadn't alerted the ones on the Graysons' lawn. The last living boy in Freehold North Carolina, Population: 1, looked both ways, scanning the rest of his block before he closed the front door. Then he pulled his hunting knife and went to give the dead farmer his present.

"Merry Christmas, motherfucker."

He only had to kill one of them on the way to the place where the Christmas trees grew. He'd gone to investigate a house that showed signs of recent habitation: its unbroken windows still barricaded with fresh two-by-fours and two fresh M.F.s sprawled in the street in front of the house. Last year, before TV went dark, the vice president told people to stack their dead on the curbs outside their residences for easy pickup and disposal by the militias.

That plan hadn't worked out so well, since folks who were squeamish about stacking their dead preferred to bury them in back yards or open fields. But the dead always came back home, and after a bajillion Carolinians were surprised in their beds by those same loved ones looking to take a chomp out of Granpa or Big Momma, the practice had ceased. The dead people on the curb had been recently deposited there. Maybe the people inside the house had ignored or missed the latest update. Nimoy took a moment to investigate the bodies: a young man, and a girl who looked about twelve. Both corpses had rectangular holes in the center of their foreheads. The holes, each about the circumference of a quarter, were dry and ringed by a thin crust of black blood. Nimoy knew that meant these two had died before someone was forced to put them down on the hoof.

Nimoy wheeled the wagon into the space between the houses to avoid any potential live marauders spotting it and coming in to investigate. He hadn't seen any marauders recently either but you could never be too careful. He went up to the front door and found it locked. Moving quietly, he went around to the back door and found it locked as well. Nimoy took off his fleece, shivering as a sudden cold wind raised goose bumps along his spine, and for once he was glad he'd chosen the heavy fleece to wear over his thermals and the red turtleneck his mother made him wear for special occasions. He wrapped the fleece around his right arm and used his elbow to break the window.

He waited for the sound of running feet or the ratchet of a shotgun, but the air inside the little house was stale and silent. Maybe the people inside had died there. He could see no sign of undead either. He smashed the rest of the glass and swept the windowsill clear as best he could. Then he crawled inside.

The place smelled...empty. To Nimoy, it felt as if it hadn't been lived in for a long time. Still, he didn't call out. In his short life he'd learned the value of keeping quiet. Instead, he pulled the Glock and made his way to the kitchen. But once he found it, he discovered only empty shelves and dust.

The last residents had left the back door relatively unblocked, using only a few boards and a two-by-four shot through two iron hooks on both sides.

Always leave a clear exit, Nim, his mother had warned. *You never want to hem yourself in.*

But maybe there were other things: medical supplies, ammo, or fresh water. He could always use more nails, too. He went through the living room, moving toward the stairway that led to the second floor. All the furniture had been destroyed, probably used for firewood or to fortify the barricades. Now only a few sticks and torn cushions remained.

He checked the second-floor rooms quickly, closing their doors as he made his way toward the bathroom at the far end of the long hallway. A part of him noticed the smell of death as he climbed the stairs, but he'd grown accustomed to the smell of dead things. Back when everything went crazy, in those first high, hot North Carolina summer days, that smell had been the world. But he was hungry. He'd stayed up late the night before, sharpening his hatchet and getting the house ready for the tree. He couldn't be blamed for not bolting the moment he registered the smell.

Someone had drawn the shades over the bathroom's single window. The bathroom was dim, as if the last residents had tried to shut themselves off from the morning light. Nimoy checked the shower stall: it was unoccupied. Then he went to the medicine cabinet. Inside it he found a few prescription bottles, a tube of antibiotic cream, a jar of something called shea butter, and an unopened box of Band-Aids. He pocketed those and shut the door of the medicine cabinet.

The person who looked back at him from the mirror over the sink bore little resemblance to the round-cheeked boy he'd been. Now he looked like one of those kids he remembered from those late-night commercials about starving kids in Africa, his cheekbones slicing like twin razors through too-thin skin.

Behind him, the water in the bathtub stirred. It was thick, more like soup than water—a rusty red so dark it was nearly black. In the gray light from the shaded window, he hadn't noticed that the tub was nearly full. As he shoved the items from the cabinet into his backpack, black water lapped over the sides of the tub. Startled by the noise, Nimoy turned, and his foot landed on something hard. He slid, lost his balance, and pain exploded in his ankle as it twisted and he fell. But he reached out and caught himself on the lip of the bathtub.

And something grabbed his wrist.

Something was rising out of the bathtub, a man or woman, Nimoy couldn't tell. Its features had been rubbed into obscurity by water and decomposition. But the motherfucker was fat, at least three hundred pounds. The thing rose higher out of the water, sloshing black fluids across the floor. Pendulous breasts bounced against its chest and the huge gut that jiggled, gray and wet. Nimoy tugged, tried to pull free and gain leverage on the slippery wet floor. He braced his foot against the side of the tub and pulled with all his strength, but the thing from the bathtub held him fast. It was using his resistance to pull itself out of the tub. Or pull him into that stinking black water. Nimoy only weighed ninety pounds, but the thing in the tub had to weigh three times that.

With his left hand he reached up and clawed at the thing's hand, battered that sliding flesh with his fist, knowing that the dead felt little pain, nor did they tire. Nimoy reached behind him, straining to grab the leg of the sink, but his fingers brushed against the leg and snagged empty air. Then his hand fell on something, a hard length of metal. Nimoy grasped it a second before the dead woman pulled him into the tub.

He straddled the thing even as it hugged him to its breast. But now he brought his weight down on the woman's chest, her long dreadlocks writhing in the water like black sea snakes. One of her eyes had been smashed shut. The other eye rolled like a dead white marble, seeing him, needing him. Her mouth opened and closed like a hooked fish gasping for air. Nimoy knew the thing in the tub didn't need to breathe, and she was going to pull him under the water and eat him. He braced his feet against the sides of the tub, pushed himself against the dead woman's chest, and freed his left arm. He gripped the thing he'd snagged—a crowbar—raised it over his head and rammed the sharp end through the dead woman's forehead.

The dead woman thrashed against the sides of the tub. Once, on a family camping trip to the Smoky Mountains, his dad had pinned a big copperhead. He'd held the snake down with the blade of a shovel as it whipped and coiled itself around the handle, until he'd finally decapitated it. Even so, the copperhead had writhed for nearly a full minute. Nimoy remembered that snake, and he pushed his weight against the crowbar, forced it deeper into the dead woman's head until he heard the sharp end strike the porcelain surface of the bathtub and the dead woman stopped moving.

She floated there like an obscene bath toy, her empty black eye still fixed on him, her mouth hinged open like the unguarded entrance to Hell. Nimoy could see specks of old blood in her teeth. The sneeze scared him so badly it took precious seconds to realize it came from him. He paused, waiting to hear the sounds of discovery from inside the house, but the only sound was his ragged breathing—the wet rattle that had grown worse over the last two days. He climbed out of the tub and sneezed again. This time he covered his mouth with both hands.

The dead motherfucker sank beneath the black water.

Nimoy found a man's clothes in one of the upstairs bedrooms and took off his Christmas turtleneck, his wet jeans, and underwear. He wrung them out and put them into a plastic grocery bag he'd found in the kitchen. As he was shoving his wet clothing into his backpack he realized something was wrong. His body was still covered by a clammy sheen of perspiration even though he'd re-killed the dead woman nearly thirty minutes earlier. Glancing out the kitchen window, he saw that the sun had moved farther into the west. His stomach announced that it was well past lunchtime. He sniffed at the sudden draining sensation in his nose and suppressed another fit of coughing.

His stomach growled even louder. It had been nearly two days since he'd eaten; his last meal was the dregs from a can of clam chowder he'd found a week ago. Since then he'd searched nearly all the houses in his neighborhood but found only empty shelves. He'd forced himself to ration the clam chowder, taking only two or three bites at each meal and drinking from his water supplies to fill his stomach. When the dead started coming back it seemed as if nearly everyone had hoarded bottled water. Sometimes he used his wagon to lug one or two of the huge bottles they used in offices like the one where his dad worked. But now the neighborhood taps were dying. And when all the bottles were gone, water would become "an issue."

"Gotta find some grub, son."

Nimoy whirled, the crowbar raised in a trembling hand.

"Hello? Anybody here?"

Outside, someone dragged a heavy sack across the tall grass. Footsteps. The sound was coming from the back yard.

Time to go, Nim.

Nimoy shook his head to clear the voices. He swiped at the droplets of sweat stinging his eyes, shouldered his backpack, and headed for the back door. He was about to crawl through the window when he froze.

The silver packet was lying behind the coffee maker, atop the counter farthest away from the kitchen door. He must have walked past it twice, once on his way upstairs and again when he came down. He scooped up the half-empty packet. The sound of ripping paper was like the crackle of thunder in the cold wind blowing through the open window. Inside the packet lay two chocolate chip cookies.

Nimoy tore into one of them. The flood of flavor that cascaded across his senses almost made him yell. Before the motherfuckers came back he'd preferred Oreos, but at that moment he thought the chocolate chip cookie the greatest invention of the vanished human race.

Eat slowly, Nim, Mom said. *Careful*.

"I know," he whispered. "Save some for dinner."

Nimoy rewrapped the surviving half of the first cookie, along with the second one, and shoved the packet into his backpack. He crawled through the window and stepped onto the porch. His stomach growled even louder, and he felt the cookie trying to back its way up the same way it had gone down. He swallowed chocolate and bile, took a deep breath, and held it until the nausea passed. He was shivering more now. As he slid the crowbar under the straps of his backpack so that it lay across his shoulders, his hands were shaking and he had to stifle another cough.

Then he went to get his wagon.

Nimoy remembered the Home & Garden Center as a bright place. His father had brought him here four years earlier to buy a small magnolia tree as a present for his parents' anniversary. His mother loved magnolias, and wept when they presented her with the tree. They'd planted it together in the garden she adored.

Now the Garden Center was empty, most of the plants long dead. The ones that were hardy enough to survive unattended for so long seemed to haunt the edges of the deserted aisles like forgotten Halloween decorations, their stripped limbs contorted like skeletal fingers.

The inside of the Garden Center had been ransacked, but the surviving trees and plants had been left mostly untouched. When the dead starting coming back, people had gotten too busy for landscaping. Nimoy had almost given up the search when he remembered the outdoor section. He made sure the aisles were empty, then ran through the open electric doors and into the "outdoor" aisles.

The "outdoor" section was really a long, covered shed about half the length of a football field. Large windows, some broken, let in the afternoon sunlight, painting the aisles and shelves and tall metal racks with a brightness that seemed otherworldly. In a shaft of that yellow light, Nimoy found a single holly tree standing alone near the back of the covered shed. It was only about four feet high, its remaining needles faded to a dull greenish brown. But to Nimoy, the little tree stood out like an emerald flame in the emptiness of the abandoned aisles.

It's too small, Peter.

It's fine, babe.

Last year's was bigger.

No way. What do you think, Nim?

"It's the best tree ever."

The cough that erupted from his lungs became a wet machinelike buzz in his chest. It hurt. But he remembered to cover his mouth.

"Keeps the germs away from other kids," he whispered, when the coughing subsided. "Keeps the dead people away."

Inside the Garden Center, something fell over with a loud crash. Nimoy wiped the sweat out of his eyes and checked the windows. A few stragglers stumbled across the rear parking lot, moving aimlessly, not in the focused way they did when they hunted the living. But the dead had a way of finding the living, either by scent or sound or some other sense no one could guess.

Nimoy stooped, reached through the branches of the holly tree, grasped the trunk, and pulled. Nothing happened. He pulled again. The exertion made his head spin and for a moment he thought he was going to pass out.

Focus, man. Figure it out.

But his head was pounding, his heart fluttering in his chest. He felt the skin of his forehead, found it damp and too warm. Outside, it sounded like more of the motherfuckers were gathering in the front parking lot. Nimoy's gaze flicked toward the rear entrance. He'd have to drag the wagon out through the rear exit, run like hell, and hope for the best.

Gotta go.

He got down on his hands and knees and looked under the holly tree, staring at the place where the trunk met the rich soil, trying to understand the problem. The last time his parents brought him here they'd bought a tree already cut and wrapped. The sullen teenager who'd sold it to them scratched the roof of their SUV when he and Nimoy's dad tied the tree to the luggage rack. His mother had argued with the manager about the damage and finally gotten him to agree to a partial refund.

But this tree was still stuck in the ground.

Somewhere inside the Garden Center, something big fell over with a sound like a dozen dropped cymbals. Nimoy heard what sounded like a dozen or more motherfuckers stumbling in through the main entrance. He stood, took two steps backward, and sat down, hard, on his rump. The sounds of breaking glass grew louder, closer.

Move, son. Can't lie down yet.

Nimoy balled up his right fist, brought it up to eye level, and punched himself in the nose. The bright burst of pain brought his vision back into focus and cleared away the fog: He needed something he could use to cut down the tree. He scanned the room, the rows of rifled display tables and empty racks, but found nothing he could use. He decided to use his hunting knife.

He knew he'd never cut through the trunk near the roots where it was nearly the circumference of a small soda can, so he chose a spot about halfway up, where the trunk was only about the thickness of a broom handle. Wiping the sweat from his eyes, he grabbed a branch and went to work.

He was forced to wait for the cover of darkness by the time he was done. A small pack of motherfuckers had surrounded the Garden Center and found their way into the outdoor section. Nimoy scrambled beneath one of the long tables, pulling himself along until he could tuck himself against the wall even as the dead burst into the outdoor aisles. He silenced his mind, consciously slowed his breathing, and envisioned himself shrinking, growing smaller and smaller, fading back into the shadows beneath the table. From there he watched as the aisles filled up with the dead, or at least their feet. Some wore work boots, others torn flip-flops or filthy sneakers, their laces clotted with blood. He watched as the light from the windows dwindled toward darkness.

"Come out, Nim. Daddy and I have been looking all over for you."

She was beautiful. Even after what happened with daddy in the back yard, Nimoy thought his mother, Sheila, was the most beautiful person he'd ever seen.

"C'mon out, babe. Everything's fine."

She was beautiful. Different from the way she looked after they killed Daddy, the night when she screamed at him to run and lock himself in the bedroom and not come out until she called for him. She was beautiful. And she'd come back. *All* of her.

"Don't cry, baby. Mama's here now."

She was here. Not in that other place. She was beautiful again. And she was reaching for him.

"I came to take you home, my beautiful boy."

He reached for her, where she knelt in the fading light, her hand reaching out to carry him away from this place once and for all. Her smile, her eyes...

No. That's not right.

...only her hand wasn't the hand he remembered.

Her eyes are wrong.

The nails were black, filthy with dirt and blood, torn, as if she'd clawed her way through three feet of...

"Come out, Nimoy. Mommy's here."

...clawed her way up from...

Mommy!

...*back* from the...

"You get out from there, boy! You get out from there right... NOW!"

He woke up so forcefully that the back of his head struck the bottom of the table. The space in front of his face was empty. Beyond it lay only darkness. And silence. For a moment, blind panic broke his control. How long had he been asleep? What time was it? Where were they?

His face was wet. His ribs hurt and he couldn't seem to draw enough breath. The tightness in his chest wouldn't let him breathe deeply. It felt as if something with claws was squatting inside his body and pushing him apart, swelling his ribcage...

I can't do it...can't do this anymore.

Something brushed against his foot. Nimoy scrabbled away from that contact, but the something brushed against him again, harder, more insistent. He kicked out with his left foot, felt it connect with the something, heard the something squeal. Then a rat ran past his face and disappeared through the open rear doors.

Nimoy poked his head out from beneath the table. The aisles in the shed were empty. A cough rumbled up from the depths of his chest, bringing with it a thick wad of phlegm. He slid from beneath the table, grabbed the two-foot length of holly tree from where he'd dropped it, and ran for the door. In the darkness he tripped headlong over his red wagon. He landed nosily, and knocked the wind out of himself. He lay there in the shadows for a moment, waiting for the motherfuckers to burst in and swarm him.

Maybe that wouldn't be so bad, he thought. *At least then I could sleep.*

When nothing came for him, he forced himself to get to his feet. When he saw the hatchet lying inside his wagon his heart sank. He'd brought the hatchet along to chop down the tree, forgotten it, and wasted precious time using his stupid knife.

Move. Now.

A handful of shadows shuffled along in the glare from the lone working arc sodium streetlamp that stood in the center of a circle of abandoned cars. Gripping the two-foot-long segment of tree, Nimoy imagined wings growing from the sides of his ankles. He made himself small and silent as a mouse.

Then he slipped out into the night.

The star that sat next to "The World's Only Half-Living Miniature Christmas Tree" glimmered atop his parents' coffee table. He'd been lucky to have enough dirt left over from burying his mom. The little holly tree stood interred inside a mop bucket filled with some of that same dirt.

Even with the throbbing pain in his chest, and the nearly constant coughing, Nimoy managed to pull himself up the ladder that led to the attic. He'd lain up there in the cool darkness, too tired to move, for a while. The attic was his Number 1 Fallback Position, in the event the dead ever breached the barricades. His father had assured them that if the dead ever breached the house they could retreat to the attic, pull the door up after them, and wait the motherfuckers out.

But the attic also held memories of Christmases past. Nimoy had been content to lie there for a while, amidst the insulation and suitcases, but finally he'd made himself locate the plastic crates that contained the decorations.

He had to struggle to get them down the ladder—a two-person job that kept his parents occupied for hours. Alone and nearly breathless, he had to make do with one box. But it was the one that held his favorite ornaments, tinsel, and the golden glass star his dad brought home from a business trip to Switzerland.

He draped the tinsel like a gilded boa, snaking it in and around the branches of the tree, making sure to cover them evenly. He hung the ornaments, tiny reindeer, chiming icicles, elves, and candy canes with care. There were no lights of course; no power without the generator—that had died last winter—and the gold star was too heavy for the top of the tree. Instead, Nimoy found a picture of his family. It had been taken during a trip to New York City, four years earlier. In the picture, he and his folks were smiling as they posed in front of the huge Christmas tree at Rockefeller Center. He carefully removed the photo from its frame and set it between the top branches of the tree.

Something's missing.

"Lights, son. What good is a Christmas tree without lights?"

Nimoy grabbed his emergency flashlight. He only had one other working flashlight: a penlight the size of a lipstick holder. If he used up the big flashlight's battery he'd be stuck with that.

"It's Christmas," he muttered. "What the Hell."

He set the flashlight down on the floor and used three paperback books to aim the beam at the tree. The light raced along the strands of tinsel, the bobbing glass ornaments, and candy canes, and the little tree came to life in a wash of silver and gold.

Nimoy yawned. His internal clock told him it was way past his bedtime, nearly midnight. The pain in his chest wouldn't let him do any more, so he made his palette close to the coffee table and lay down where he could see the tree. He hoped he could dream of Christmases past, instead of fat rats and heavy lungs and dead things in black bathtubs. He had nearly drifted off to sleep when he suddenly remembered the thing he'd found in the fat woman's kitchen.

With trembling hands, Nimoy reached into his backpack and pulled out the half-packet of chocolate chip cookies. He ate the half that he'd left for later, chewing it slowly. Then he turned to consider the last cookie.

There was no milk, no juice. He only had the half-empty bottle of stale water he'd scavenged the day before. He took a swig to wash the last dregs of the cookie away. Then he set the bottle next to the little tree. He opened the cookie wrapper, smoothed it as best he could, and laid the uneaten cookie on the packet. Then he placed it next to the water bottle. He checked his Glock and saw that it had one bullet left: "One in the chamber..."

For when there's no other way out.

He slid the gun under his pallet.

Then, looking at his Christmas tree, he lay down to sleep.

He woke up cold. His teeth were chattering so violently that his head seemed to vibrate with the smashing of boulders.

There was someone in the living room.

He could feel a presence, the way you could sometimes feel someone reaching to tickle the back of your neck just before their fingers brushed your skin. He tried to sit up, but his head and chest hurt so badly that he lay still, stunned by the pain. He turned his head at a sudden gust of wind, gritting his teeth to keep from crying out at the stiffness in his neck.

The front door was wide open.

Nimoy couldn't remember where he'd left his Glock...his hatchet. Panic filled his world and terror stole his shuddering breath. He froze.

"How did...? Did I...?"

"I had to get in," a deep voice said. "I thought—under the

circumstances—that the direct approach was best."

A man stepped out of the shadows behind the front door. He was of average height, thin, dressed in dirty, rust-colored woolen pants, the sleeves of gray thermal undershirt rolled up to reveal filthy elbows. Brown suspenders held up the heavy-looking pants, which seemed almost comically oversized. The intruder appeared to be wearing clothes meant for a much bigger man. His thinning hair and full beard were mostly gray and way too long. The beard reached nearly to his waistline. The stranger looked like the homeless guys Nimoy remembered his mother avoiding when they went shopping at Kroger, the ones who sometimes asked her for a couple bucks just to tide them over 'til their veterans' benefits came through.

The old man stepped into the living room, stood in front of the door with his thin frame backlit by moonlight. Behind him, another man was walking up the steps leading to the front porch. Nimoy recognized the second man. It was Mister Grayson, Nolan's dad, probably come to borrow his dad's chainsaw or set up a pitching practice for the boys.

Jack Grayson got taken away, Nim. Remember?

But Mister Grayson was staggering up the steps, reaching for the man in the baggy pants. Nimoy saw the bloody hole in his chest, the torn mess that had once been his throat. He tried to yell, to warn the old man, but his voice was a ragged croak.

"Door..." "How's that?" "Close...door..." "Oh of course! Silly of me."

The old man slammed the door just as Mister Grayson lunged for him. A second later, Nimoy heard Nolan's dad pounding at the door. The old man lowered the heavy two-by-four Nimoy's parents had installed across the door. Nimoy dragged himself up onto one elbow. He was too cold; the glow from the fireplace had faded to a pulsing glimmer. He felt the dampness of his pallet; his jeans and shirt clinging to his body like wet rags, and wondered if he'd peed himself.

"Not much time," the old man said.

"How did you...get in here?" Nimoy said.

The old man had moved into the room, studying the pictures on the wall like a visiting uncle as he inspected one of Nimoy's Little

League trophies and read the inscription like a collector evaluating an ancient artifact.

"I told you: through the front door," he said. "You had quite a fire going when I arrived." The old man sighed. "Once, I might have enjoyed the challenge. Now…it was all I could do to get through your little obstacle course."

Nimoy shook his head. He was confused. Something about the old man *disturbed* him, beyond the fact that he'd broken through the barricades. But Nimoy couldn't think. He could hear people moving around the house—footsteps, too many of them, thumping up the front stairs, their fists beating at the front door and the boards that covered the windows in the living room.

The old man sighed. "It's worse than even I imagined."

Nimoy slid himself across the floor to the nearest wall, a few feet to the right of the Christmas tree. Using the wall, he managed to raise himself into a reclining position. The exertion brought a fresh round of coughing. He leaned over and spat into a wad of paper towels he'd laid next to his pallet. The phlegm was thick, the color of split pea soup.

"Pneumonia," the old man sighed. "Very little time indeed."

Nimoy folded the paper towel and hid it beneath the edge of his pallet, ashamed that the old man might see it. At the same time, his right hand bumped against the cool grip of the Glock. Using his blanket to conceal his movements, he clutched the automatic pistol.

The old man pulled up a chair and sat down next to the Christmas tree.

"You and I have business to discuss, young man. I've come a long way—and at great personal expense—to meet you."

"What…what kind of business?"

The old man smiled. Something tugged at Nimoy's gut, a sense of loss so sharp he felt the threat of tears sting his eyes. He clenched his teeth despite the pain, forced the weakness back with curses. Beneath the blanket, he gripped his father's gun even tighter.

"Well," the old man continued. "Since you contacted me I imagine you know the nature of our transaction. It involves your letter."

"My…my letter?"

"Indeed, and a very detailed letter it was."

Nimoy tried to answer, but was seized by another spasm of coughing. When he could speak again it was barely above a whisper. "I didn't...write...any letter."

The old man furrowed his brow. "You are Master Nimoy Green, of twenty-two thirty-two Parkside Lane, Freehold, North Carolina?"

Nimoy nodded. He was hot. The room swam before him even as emerald flashes burst along the borders of his vision. He had no more energy for evasions.

"That's me."

"Good. It wouldn't do to be wrong about something this important. Now to our business." The old man reached behind his back and produced a large rust-colored knapsack. He set the sack on the floor between his boots. "I suppose you have your reasons for requesting these things. Indeed, when we learned of the changes taking place in the world, some of us despaired that..."

The front door made a sound Nimoy had never heard before—a loud crack, like the breaking of damp wood. Then a split raced from the top of the door nearly to its center. Outside, the thunder of hammering fists grew louder. The dead were breaking through.

The old man looked back at Nimoy, and saw the gun clutched in his trembling fingers.

"They're coming..." Nimoy said.

"Indeed. I suppose they must."

Nimoy tried to stand. He put one foot under his butt and tried to push himself up the wall. But he didn't have the strength. "They'll get in," he whispered, finally.

"Motherfuckers."

The old man winced. "Then we'd best be about our transaction."

"We gotta...go...back door..."

"As to your first request, I must admit that my resources are severely limited of late. Contrary to popular opinion I can't materialize objects out of thin air. To create the kind of plenty you wrote about one must build upon existing foundations. Nothing comes without cost in this universe, young Master Nimoy. Even for me. However..."

The old man stood. He walked over to the tiny Christmas tree, stooped and picked up the chocolate chip cookie from its place next to the tree. More than half of the cookie remained in its shiny packet.

"I've been on a strict regimen lately," the old man sighed. "Amidst so much suffering, indulgences like these are hard to justify. I will say, however, that the cookie was positively delicious." The old man brought the packet to Nimoy. "Thankfully, we can still share such bounty. Even in the most desperate times."

He knelt at Nimoy's side and put the cookie to the boy's lips. At first Nimoy resisted, remembering what his parents told him about accepting sweets from strangers.

"Easy now," the old man said. "Eat well. And *remember*."

But finally, Nimoy accepted the cookie. He chewed it slowly. And it seemed to him that with each bite, he *did* remember: his parents smiling in better times, Christmas mornings spent opening presents, the laughter of family and friends. With each bite, his mind and body grew stronger until, almost without transition, he found he was able to see clearly, his breathing eased, and strength flowed back into his limbs. By the time he swallowed the last morsel, he was able to sit up.

Outside, the groans of the dead had become one long multi-throated scream, the hunger cry of a starving army. Nimoy stood, a little wobbly, but he stood. The old man was standing by the stairway that led up to his parents' bedroom, although Nimoy didn't remember seeing him move.

"Excellent!" he said. Then he lifted his red knapsack.

"It's Christmas morning. Shall we begin?"

They were sitting on the section of the roof that stood above the back yard. Nimoy could see hundreds of the dead surrounding his back yard. They'd pushed down the barricades, stumbling over themselves to gain entry. Through the open window that led to his parents' bedroom he heard the dead stampeding through the lower portions of his house. In moments, he knew, they'd make their way upstairs. His parents hadn't bothered to barricade the upstairs bedrooms, hoping to be long gone by now.

"Why are we up here?" Nimoy asked. "We can't do anything."

The old man reached into his knapsack and pulled out a long, dark shape that glittered in the moonlight.

"Oh we can do many things, Master Nimoy, if we but cling to our courage. That's why I'm here. Your courage called to me like a bright beacon across stormy seas. Sadly, yours was the only call."

Nimoy accepted the object from the old man, and he felt its weight settle into his hands. It was a good weight, solid and well-balanced, as if it had been made just for him.

"She's just there, son," the old man said, pointing out over the yard. "By the fence."

Nimoy lifted the stock of the Sauer 202 Avantgarde Grande, the hunting rifle his father once owned. Peter Green had lost the rifle during the first weeks of the craziness. Back then Nimoy had been too small to lift it, but now, buoyed by the old man's gift, he easily raised the rifle to his shoulder. He placed his right eye against the telescopic sight and scanned the yard.

He saw her there, a shadow outlined in moonglow. She was still dressed in the clothes in which he'd buried her.

The body of Sheila Waldon-Green wandered along the fence, its hands outstretched in front of it like a woman lost in total darkness. When he resurrected, Nimoy's father attacked her face, tearing at her eyes, partially blinding her. It was Nimoy who shot Peter Green in the head. He'd saved his mother's life. Now she staggered forward, seeking home. Seeking him.

Mom.

"I can't."

A hand gripped his shoulder and squeezed it.

"Courage, son. Hold fast to the memory of her spirit...and consider the gift you may now provide."

And finally, the tears welled up from the place Nimoy had hidden them, a place so deep inside himself he'd forgotten the possibility of tears. Through everything since his father's return, his mother's burial, he'd never allowed himself to show that weakness, focusing on securing his stronghold, making himself small and silent. Now the tears came fat and hot. He lifted the rifle and sighted her once more, and in the last instant he might have sworn she looked up at him where he crouched. Did she see? Did she know? He cried...

"Bye, Mom."

...but he pulled the trigger.

Nimoy barely felt the recoil. Borne away by the crack of the rifle, the backward snap of her head, he barely heard the crash as two dozen dead broke through the bedroom door and tumbled into his parents' room. He hardly noticed the shatter of glass as they broke through the sliding bay windows and dropped onto the roof deck. Their numbers pressed some of the dead over the edge to plummet to the concrete below. But the rest staggered toward them.

Bye.

The old man stepped in front of Nimoy and opened his arms.

"Come along now!" he sang. "There's plenty for everyone!"

And they came. Pouring through the shattered windows like fat maggots evacuating a corpse, they came. Most of the dead went for the old man, grabbed at him, bit at his arms, his legs, his throat, digging for purchase at the flesh of his chest and abdomen. And as they scratched and tore and tugged and bit, the old man laughed.

"I know, dear ones," he roared. "I know!" And every corpse that attacked the old man grew incandescent, as if ignited from within. They staggered backward, their eyes and open mouths shining as that spectral light first infused, then ate them from their insides out. A few of them burst into parti-colored flames, flailing away from the old man and over the edges of the roof to plummet like a shower of bright-burning stars. And still more came up the stairs, through the windows and out onto the roof. But for every one that attacked the old man another bright red, green, or silver star was born, only to die moments later.

But three of them got past the old man. Nimoy lifted the rifle, too late, as a dead man with half his face ripped away knocked the rifle aside and grabbed him by the collar. And something, a massive, dark shape, struck the roof with the force of a detonation. Nimoy saw a flash of red and silver, the silhouette of something like horns. The shadow-shape leaped and bucked, whirling, too impossibly fast, to lash out at the invading dead with hooves and horns and bulk. It reared, pawing the air as it kicked at the skull of the half-faced man who grappled with Nimoy, and the half-faced man's head sailed out into the darkness. Then the shadow-creature wheeled and drove the last of the dead off the roof. The claw that gripped Nimoy's shirt spasmed once. Then it fell into golden fire and was gone.

In the silence, Nimoy faced the old man, who stood unharmed.

"But I don't...I can't..."

The old man chuckled. To Nimoy, it seemed that the trespasser had changed, somehow become...healthier. His gaunt frame had replenished itself, filled out his bright red pants enough to strain his suspenders. He smiled like a man who had just enjoyed the grandest celebration.

The old man laughed again, louder this time. But there was no ridicule in the laughter, only a kind of humor Nimoy didn't understand. But suddenly, he found himself smiling. Then he was laughing too.

"I think you understand a great deal, Master Nimoy," the old man said. "I think you understand well enough."

"But how did you do that?"

"Oh, I've danced across the rooftops of a billion hearts, my boy. I've slap-boxed with the great white bears that hunt the winter of the world and skinny-dipped in the chill darkness beneath Arctic glaciers. A few sad lovebites can't stop an old windbag like me."

The old man turned and looked out over the dead, hundreds of them, moving like animated scarecrows, toward Nimoy's back yard.

"You, on the other hand, are an entirely different story. Which brings us to your final gift."

Nimoy looked down at the red bag which lay crumpled at the old man's feet. In the distance, he could hear the screams of more dead drawing closer, and he understood that all his work, his parents' work, the time they'd spent fighting to secure his safety, had amounted to this: the dead would never stop coming. His defenses were gone. There was nowhere to go.

"The bag's empty," he whispered.

The old man's eyes twinkled.

"Yes. More of the...what did you call them?"

"Motherfuckers."

"Ah. Yes. More of them. They're on the move. The lure of the holiday season, I suppose. Unfortunately, as you say, my bag is empty. No lumps of coal for the bad ones and precious few diamonds for the good."

The old man placed his fingers between his lips and blew a loud, piercing whistle. A moment later, Nimoy heard the sound of hooves on the roof behind him. He whirled, raising the rifle, his finger finding the trigger as the shadow-shape that saved him from the half-faced man stepped out of the darkness. It was tall, deep-chested, its hooves shod with silver and gold.

"I'm afraid he's the last," the old man sighed. "With resources at an all-time low he was the only one with strength enough to get me here. And back."

The great beast dipped its antlers and nodded its head to nuzzle Nimoy's outstretched fingers.

"It's nearly dawn, Master Nimoy," the old man cried. "Our mission lies still before us. Shall we journey together?"

The old man laughed loudest then. He slapped his knee, and he howled as if the look on Nimoy's face was the funniest thing he'd ever seen.

And Nimoy understood everything.

Daily Reclamation Report: Southeastern Sector (S.W.N.C.) 4/2/16

Captain Joel Corcoran was tired. He'd been worn to the bone from two years of running street fights, low morale in his unit, lost personnel and general shittiness. It had been all he could do to keep his eyes open long enough to get the survivors back to basecamp. Now all he wanted was to get drunk and forget he'd ever heard the word "zombie."

Corcoran entered his report and logged off. He leaned back in his chair and rubbed at his aching eyes, soaking in the quiet from the momentary lull in the action. Then he remembered the impossible thing he'd found earlier that afternoon.

It was in the last house they'd searched. They'd found evidence of some kind of action in and around the house. Someone had made a stand, although how successfully and for how long, Corcoran couldn't have said. After securing the residence, he'd found the filthy strip of cloth tucked beneath a small pallet situated next to the sorriest looking Christmas tree anyone in his unit had ever seen. Now he took it out, unfolded it, and smoothed it across his desk.

"A *Christmas* list," Corcoran breathed. "Holy shit."

Written in a neat, tight little script, the list was dated from the year just ended:

Dear Santa, I know you're really busy. But I wish you can help me this Cristmas. I REALLY need some Food. Lots. And also a Sawyer 202 Avangarde hunting rifle to help my mom. And a Transfixer Robot Lord with Red Requiem Lightblade. But its ok if I don't get a Mechadog this year.

And, scrawled near the bottom of the page in what looked like blood, the last wish, so faint it was barely visible: *Home.*

Corcoran looked at that last word for a long time. They'd found no sign of a kid in that house: no corpses, walking or otherwise, only a badly breached perimeter and the vague smell of chocolate.

"Hope you made it, kid," Corcoran sighed. "Christ, I sure as Hell hope you made it."

With the screams of the dead echoing in the distance, Corcoran laughed, and swallowed the lump in his throat. Then he signed out and went to grab some sacktime.

But he never forgot that letter.

And he carried the robot with him 'til the day he died.

FOLDS

He was five years old and he was fat.

Not the kind of "baby fat" that haunts the cheek and thighbones of the average chubby American kid. Mohammed "Chun King" Jefferson weighed nearly a hundred and twenty pounds *after* we'd stripped him down to his adult diaper. And this was before he started in on the smorgasbord we'd offloaded onto *The Morrie Stapler Show* soundstage.

"I don't understand it, Morrie," the mother, a pretty young thing of Chinese-American ancestry, said. "He wasn't always like this. When he was born he was—"

The mother stopped herself in mid-sentence. She glanced over at her hog-sized chunk of offspring. Chun King was eating his way through enough junk food to poison a busload of Russian shotputters. He never even looked up.

"Jesus," I breathed. "Jerry, pull back and get me a low wide-shot of the kid and the food. Then go in fast."

Jerry Salazar, the operator on Camera Two swooped in on the junior behemoth from the right side of the studio. I swore as the image of Chun King Jefferson, messy of mouth and surrounded by mountains of processed carbohydrates, swelled to cinematic proportions.

The studio audience loved it.

As the Co-Executive Producer and Director for *Morrie* I'd signed off on booking the mother/son act. I'd made all the customary promises, referrals for counselors plus a videotaped copy of the show to play for their hillbilly relatives.

It was all standard bullshit, stated simply and without multi-syllables, to get everybody snuggly with the fact that we were asking these people to degrade themselves before a rabid national audience. I even shook hands with the mother before she signed the waivers.

Now, as the studio filled with "ooohs" and "aaahs," I patted myself on the bank account.

"Don't you move, Jerry," I hissed over the headsets.

"I mean, he's normal in other ways, Morrie," the mother said. "It's just— You know—"

"You're *worried* about your *child*, dammit," Morrie said.

"Uh oh," Cray Donavan, my associate-producer, mumbled.

"S.M. 3."

I nodded. "Somebody ate his *Prune Puffs* this morning."

Morrie Stapler had three "Sympathetic Modes" for when he wanted to torque the studio audience. S.M. 3 was the one he used when he wanted to appear understanding while maintaining his trademark, no-nonsense image. Morrie's "I feel your pain, but I'm also fairly sure you're responsible for it" brand of tough-love had knocked them for a loop back in Morristown, New Jersey, where Morrie had served his community as the Honorable *Mayor* Morrie for two infamous terms before taking the national airwaves by storm.

I hated Morrie Stapler. But God help me, I loved my job.

"Of course we all understand that, Sue," Morrie said.

"But I'm concerned about little Mohammed. Didn't it ever occur to you to take him to a doctor?"

"I've taken him to so many doctors," the mother said. "None of them can figure out what's wrong with him."

"He eats too damn much," one audience member quipped.

The audience went nuts.

"Camera Three, pull in pull in pull in!" I hissed.

As the mother's face lived large on monitor 3, I watched her eyes. She held her chin high while she waited for the laughter and the shouting to die down. She glared out over the audience, her eyes focused on some point far away from my studio.

The Fading Queen, I thought.

It was an old habit of mine, a holdover from the days when I wrote stories instead of copy: finding some remarkable trait in a person and bequeathing them a title to match that trait.

Susan Jefferson seemed, at least to me, to shine with the quiet dignity of a queen. Believe me, this quality set her apart from the scandal-hungry dunderheads that usually fill out our Friday afternoon audiences.

"I believe her," I said.

Cray Donavan cocked his head at me.

"What did you say?" he said.

I shrugged.

"I think she's really looking for help," I said.

"Yeah, right. Help," Donavan said, staring into the abyss. Onstage, Chun King was upending a family-sized bag of Extra-Cheezy GORDITOS into his yawning soup bucket.

"These idiots sell every scrap of human dignity for a few minutes on TV," Donovan said. "Just so they can be slobbered on like mini-celebrities when they get back to whatever hellish burg spawned them in the first place."

"I know," I said, the sound of my own philosophy banging into my ears. "But something about this one—"

Donavan was staring at me with the kind of suspicion I typically reserve for "reformed" sexual predators.

"Forget it," I said

Donavan shrugged and went back to studying the monitor.

But I was growing more and more unsettled by the thing that flickered in Susan Jefferson's eyes. Sincerity was something I was ill-equipped to cope with at that particular plateau in my career. To say that I'd become jaded in my dealings with the guests would be putting it mildly.

"Camera Four, give me a quick pass over the audience," I said. I needed to break the mood the Jeffersons' plight had woven around me. Toni Rinaldi, the operator on 4, panned her crane-mounted camera over the audience as ordered.

"Right there," I said. "B.B.W. on three looks good to go."

The image on monitor 4 changed as 3 pulled back. Rinaldi swooped down to snatch a tight close up of the tears on the B.B.W.'s face.

"That's alright, girlfriend," shrieked the Big Black Woman, when she realized a camera was looking in her direction. "You a good mother!"

"Yeah," I said, breathing easier.

"Much better."

"Am I the only one who's *hearing* this shit?"

Sarah Chang, my line-producer, glared at Morrie with an expression that would have turned him to stone if he were human.

"I'm talking about John and Jane Q Public, Sarah," Morrie said. "Way out in the cornfields and ghettos of Asshole America. In Asshole America, things are a little more 'black and white,' if you catch my drift."

"Morrie, that's..."

"Blacks, white trash, *maybe* a few Hispanics thrown in for variety, Sarah. *That's* who Asshole America wants to see in their living rooms. Look at our audience polls: *Asian doesn't fly in syndication.*"

"Morrie—" Chang said, white-knuckling her pen.

"Christ, Sarah, it was like watching a lost episode of *The Courtship of Eddie's Father.*"

Chang threw her pad down and stood up.

I was dying to get out of there. All I could think of was the look of damaged nobility that I'd seen in Susan Jefferson's eyes, and Morrie was making a complete jackass of himself.

"Morrie, that's the biggest load of corporate-media racist bullshit I've ever heard," Chang said.

"What the hell's wrong with you?" Morrie said.

Chang removed her glasses and shoved them into the pocket of her denim shirt.

"You, Morrie," Chang snapped. "You're a racist."

"I am not a racist!"

"Morrie, in case you hadn't noticed, *I'm Chinese.* You can't make racially chauvinistic statements like that *when I'm in the fucking room!* You're a Jew, for God's sake. I'd expect you to know better."

"Hey! Now hold on here, Sarah—"

"What have you got against Asians then, Morrie?"

"Oh, please, girlfriend," Morried snorted. "You're as 'Asian' as I am."

"Jesus Christ."

"Look at Marcus. He's black and you don't see him complaining."

Chang looked over at me.

"Yes, Marcus," she said. "How *do* you put up with Morrie's racist bullshit?"

Chang and I had spent many late nights fantasizing about ways to get Morrie off the show, but when you have a winning horse you don't jump off mid-race. Not if you want to stay afloat in television.

I repeated that to myself as I recalled the previous week's ratings: Top Ten, with all the right demographics. That meant a big Christmas bonus for me plus a decent piece of the syndication pie.

"Jesus," Chang said. "Try not to drool on the carpet, Marcus."

You never forget the sound a fist makes when it strikes flesh and bone. My father used his fists on my sister and me for years before he died of heart failure one Christmas Eve. The following Christmas morning was the happiest either one of us could remember in a long time.

But you never forget the sound.

I heard it as I was walking back to my car after the show: bone wrapped in meat punishing softer meat, followed by the muffled whimper of pain and the dull thud of a head repeatedly striking concrete.

Something in that cry held me rooted to the spot. The meat sound was repeated, and this time the cry of pain was loud enough for me to locate its source. It was coming from behind a rusted Nissan which sat idling a few feet to my left.

Leaning down, I could see two figures struggling on the concrete. I heard the terrible sound again, and before I knew what I was doing I had walked around to the other side of the Nissan.

The attacker knelt above the woman's chest, pinning her to the ground beneath his bulk. As I watched, he lifted a heavy arm and struck her across the face.

I was so stunned that I couldn't move.

But my mouth still functioned.

"Hey!" I shouted.

The attacker whirled, mid-blow, and the world lurched beneath my feet. It was Chun King Jefferson.

The fat toddler was sitting, not kneeling as I had thought before. He was sitting on his mother's chest.

As I watched, Chun King turned, wrapped his hands around

his mother's throat, and banged her head against the concrete, hard.

I grabbed him by the collar and hauled him off of her, revulsion making me rougher than I intended. I flung him away from her with such force that he hit the ground with a loud *thud*. He started to cry, a loud, squawking bark that was more roar than whimper.

"Don't hurt him!" the mother cried.

And for a fleeting instant, I was sure she was speaking to Chun King, not to me.

"He... He was attacking you," I stammered stupidly.

Then I knelt down by her side.

Susan Jefferson was sitting with her back against the passenger side front door of the little Nissan. She was holding her head in her hands and crying.

"Are you alright?" I asked.

"You think I'm stupid, like the rest of them," she said.

"Jesus," I said. "What the hell's going on?"

"I'm not stupid," she whispered. "I'm not like your other guests. Neither is Mohammed."

She got to her feet and retrieved her wailing six-year-old. He'd gone limp, allowing her to pick him up as if he hadn't just tried to fracture her skull a minute earlier. Remarkably, she was able to heft him into the back seat of their car. He was too big to fit into a standard car seat.

"Listen," I said. "I don't know what..."

"We need *help*," she interrupted. "I can't control what he eats now." She said this last part so quietly that I almost missed it. Once again I was struck by the quality of desperation that shone from her like a cry in the wilderness.

It's called sincerity, asshole, I thought. *You remember that, don't you?*

"You promised us some help," she said. "I'm at the end of my rope."

The flutter in my stomach that began when I saw her back at the studio kicked up a notch.

"Have you tried...ahhh...family counseling?" I volunteered.

It's the standard line used by all producers when confronted by a distraught guest. But this time I meant it. After what I'd seen I would have made the calls myself.

"I can refer you to someone..."

"We've done that," she said. "We've been to so many therapists, so many clinics…" She paused, as if searching for the correct words. Then she looked me in the eye.

"He won't stop eating."

Her eyes returned to the cement between her feet.

"And there are other things…"

She was interrupted by a wail from inside the car. Her eyes widened and she grasped her temples.

"Are you alright?" I asked.

She shook her head.

The windows of her car were all closed, but I could see Chun King sitting there staring out at us. His mouth was hinged open like a trapdoor, that high-pitched whine cycling up and out of him like the shriek of an air-raid siren.

"God," the mother said. "He's hungry."

"What?" I asked, disbelieving. "He *can't* be hungry. Not after all the…"

I was about to say *Not after all the garbage we let him hammer down his throat.*

"I have to go," the mother whispered. "If I don't get him something, he'll get…upset."

"Wait a minute," I said.

But if she heard me she gave no sign. Susan Jefferson turned and bolted for her car.

"Hey! Wait!" I yelled. "Mrs. Jefferson!"

As she reached for the driver's door, the mother stumbled. I caught her just as her knees buckled. During the taping I noticed that she was thin. We'd joked about it in the booth: *Skinny Mom Says: Help! My Child is Obese!!!* We'd seen it a million times on the *Morrie* show.

As my hands brushed the sides of her ribcage, I felt the jut of bone beneath her too-thin blouse. She felt as fragile as porcelain, as flimsy as a child's doll cobbled together from dried twigs. I gasped, animal reflex robbing me of social graces for a moment.

By now I could hear the kid screaming.

"I'm sorry," Susan whispered.

I heard the grief in her voice, the sheer exhaustion, as she threw open the door and flung herself into the car. I bent down and looked into the car. Chun King screamed louder. From where I stood his open mouth looked enormous, his features contorted in a grimace of need and...

Hate

The scream went on and on, seemingly without benefit of breath. He turned toward me, and when he did, his expression... *changed*. Then he lunged across the seat and smashed his fist into the window, inches from my face.

I fell backward and landed flat on my ass amid the tinkling chime of broken glass falling around me. The scream of burning rubber momentarily drowned out the boy's shrieks as the Nissan screeched away from where I sat. Stunned, I could only stare as the little car slammed over a speed bump, slewed onto the street, and shot away into the darkness.

I sat there, immobilized by the memory of the boy's eyes, the unmistakable message they bore, just before he smashed the window: *Stay away from us. Don't interfere. Danger.*

It took me a moment to convince my lungs to contract but I finally won the argument. As that first breath hitched in my chest, I put my face in my hands and wept.

I believe I knew even then that Chun King Jefferson was going to be the death of me.

The next morning, I broke two cardinal rules: I drove into my office on Saturday, sifted through the contact list for the last show, and located the Jeffersons' phone number.

I told myself that I was being ridiculous. This was a five-year-old boy after all. What real harm could he be capable of?

There are...other things.

I ignored the gooseflesh marching up and down my arms and dialed the number, unable to forget Susan Jefferson's eyes, her apparent inability to save herself.

Save herself from what, idiot? I thought.

"Hello?"

It was a kid's voice.

It's Chun King and he's going to kill you.

"Is... Is your mommy there?" I said, hating the sound of my own voice.

"I can't talk to you," the kid on the other end of the connection said. "I'll get in trouble."

"Can I talk to your mommy?" I said. "It's very important that I speak with her."

"She's gone."

Something cold unfurled itself in the pit of my stomach.

"I'll get in trouble," the kid repeated listlessly. There was something about the kid's voice, a buzzing asexual monotone, that set my teeth on edge. "I have to go now."

The line went dead.

I sat at my desk for a long time, looking at the contact list. I had the Jeffersons' address. I could have just driven out there.

Tell 'em they've won an all expenses paid trip to Hawaii courtesy of the show: "First place for *America's Most Fucked-Up Family!*"

Christ, any excuse would have been sufficient.

"You need a vacation, pal," I said finally.

I crumpled up the contact sheet and tossed it into the trash bin. Then I stood up, walked to my door, and turned out the lights.

"Too much time in the fucking freak show."

I went home.

"She claims that she spoke with you a few weeks ago," my assistant, Gina, said. "Something about her son's condition?"

Gina handed me the note and walled out of the director's booth. I'd spent the weeks since the incident in the parking lot trying not to think about Susan Jefferson. As time and toil pulled me further and further away from that strange episode, a welcome sense of normalcy had crept back into my life.

But I couldn't sleep.

I'd tried pills, prescription and otherwise, booze, sometimes both simultaneously. Whenever I neared the edges of sleep, however, the memory of her eyes was there to bar my way. I became adept at faking my way through the days. No one knew I was falling apart.

The show that day was called *"UFO PROSTITUTES! ARE YOU A HO' FOR E.T.?"* We were on a commercial break while the security guards broke up a fight between a woman who claimed to be "a willing sexual recruiter for the 'Venusians who secretly rule the Earth' and a teenaged girl who claimed she'd contracted

'Space Herpes' from her alien boyfriend, a stand-up individual with a spotty mustache named 'Prince Remulex.' " While the combatants were led off the set, I read the note:

Please help us. You promised.

I found the small house easily. It sat on a nondescript street near a decommissioned Air Force base two hours east of L.A. The house was in terrible disrepair. Two cars sat on cinderblocks in the barren front yard.

The front door was wide open.

A child stood in the darkened entry hall, just beyond the open door. A single bare light bulb burned over the child's head. In the ugly yellow light I could make out the same black curly hair I remembered, the same wide, up-tilted eyes and full lips.

Help me. He won't stop eating.

But it wasn't Chun King. It was a girl, taller, older by three or four years, and thinner by a thirty or forty pounds. Black bruises encircled her eyes. Her lips and chin were stained with something that looked like dried blood.

"My mommy's sick," the little girl said.

She stepped back, out of the light. I stepped over the threshold and out of the dry desert wind. The girl closed the door behind me.

The first thing I noticed was the heat.

It was too warm inside the little house. Tepid pulses of stale air gusted over me where I stood in the center of the hall. Despite the fact that it was at least eighty degrees outside, someone had turned up the thermostat.

The house was a mess. Empty fast-food cartons lay all over the floor. The sofa and lounge chair in the corner were covered with open containers of half-eaten TV dinners and empty potato chip bags.

"Where's your mommy?" I said.

"My mommy's sick."

The girl's eyes shone as she looked up at me. She was nearly as thin as the woman I'd met in the parking lot. Her light brown complexion had gone the sallow color of moldy cheese. Her skin glistened with a sheen of sweat that plastered her hair across her skull.

She turned and walked into the guts of the house.

I set my briefcase down on the floor and followed her into the kitchen. I wiped my sleeve along my forehead, trying to stop droplets of sweat from running down into my eyes. Moving through the house was like walking through a dry sauna.

Pots and pans covered with old food sat piled in the sink. An odor like rotten milk and old cat litter hung, so thick it was almost visible, in the warm air.

"She said you would come," the girl said as she led me into the rear of the house toward one of the back bedrooms. "She said you would keep your promise."

"What's happened?" I asked. "Does your mommy need a doctor? What's wrong?"

But as we turned the corner into the "master bedroom" I *saw* what was wrong inside that house.

Susan Jefferson was lying in bed, half propped up against the headboard. Her face was drawn, her cheeks hollowed out from deprivation. Her dull brown eyes stared out from deep black sockets.

Everyone has seen the Sad Children, the ones in faraway places like Ethiopia, El Salvador, or the Philippines...the children who lie dying in their own filth, too exhausted to brush away the flies that crawl across their too-wide eyes.

That's what she looked like, lying there on a filthy mattress in a two-bedroom house on the edge of the Mojave Desert.

It felt like the inside of a sweat lodge in that room, but she was too dehydrated to sweat. A filthy sheet half-covered her, her naked shoulders jutting like jagged coral reefs from beneath. One of her legs hung over the side of the bed, a broomstick with a small foot attached at the end, the toenails too long, more like claws.

"Oh my God," I said into the alien atmosphere of the small bedroom.

I took a step backward and something crunched beneath my foot. I looked down to see that I was standing in a half-empty box of ENGLEMAN'S FAT-FREE POWDERED DONUTS.

"What's wrong with her?" I stammered.

"He takes," the pale little girl whispered.

There was something moving under the sheet.

I thought it was a pile of dirty clothes. Piles of discarded clothing lay everywhere. Every open surface in the room was covered with half-eaten food and trash. I could smell the sour tang of stale nacho chips and rotten milk beneath the odor of sweat.

Whatever was under the sheet moved again.

"What the hell is that?" I said. The girl remained silent as she walked around to the side of the bed and stood at her mother's side. Susan Jefferson reached up and hooked her fingers into the front of the t-shirt the girl wore.

The girl's eyes never left mine as she reached down and removed the limp hand from her shoulder. Then she pulled back the sheet and showed me what was under it.

I stood rooted to the spot, unable to move, unable to think. Something obscene was crawling on top of Susan Jefferson, something from the pages of a Lovecraft story, or maybe one of Clive Barker's meaner nightmares.

Mohammed Jefferson lay there, bloated and enormous, like a leech that battens onto its prey and drains it of all vitality. He was wearing the remnants of an adult diaper that had long since burst from containing his bulk. Even now he wasn't much taller than the average twelve-year-old, but this only accentuated his inhuman girth.

As I watched, he suckled at his mother's shriveled breast as peacefully as a newborn baby.

Chun King's sister was watching me with eyes far too wise, a strange and distant smile dancing across her lips. When she spoke, it was with the passion of an apostle.

"It's my brother," she said. "Today's his birthday."

At the sound of her voice, the child-thing on the bed turned its eye upon me, pierced me with the malevolent gaze I remembered from before. There was a fire burning behind those eyes, a blistering *acuity* that scorched its way to the very core of who and what I was.

The thing gazed at me, mother's milk and blood soaking his chins, and I was frozen, staked there by the power of its will.

It spoke to me, or at least it tried to. What came out of the open wound where its mouth should have been was little more than a strangled sob, a wet groan that trickled like rotten honey into my inner ear.

"You're the first," the girl said. "Bring them to us."

The sister extended her left arm toward the creature. That was when I noticed the scars. The girl's arm was covered with scabs, some old, some more recent. It took me a second to recognize them for what they were.

Bite marks.

The thing on the bed reared up and fastened its teeth into the flesh of the girl's arm. A rivulet of blood dripped down onto the mattress, pattered across the mother's stomach as Chun King sucked and nibbled at the girl's flesh.

The sister remained still, her empty gaze taking in everything and nothing. At that moment, staring at some point on the wall above my head, she might have been any American kid watching her favorite Saturday morning cartoon show. Reaching down with her right hand, she retrieved a half-empty bag of GORDITOS from the bed and began to eat.

The room shifted beneath my feet as a flush crept up the back of my neck, enveloping my eyes and head like a hood. There was no pain, merely an unfamiliar sensation of warmth. The last thing I remember is the two of them watching me, their eyes burning into mine.

Then I blacked out.

I returned to work the very next day. No fictional dead relative, no weekend withdrawal required. On Monday morning I felt as right as rain.

I do my job now. I find them. The freaks and misfits and "Super Fat Babies," the cold-eyed pederasts and gender-flipped sex-fiends. I locate the lowest of the low and shove them out of the nest of anonymity and into the national spotlight of Morrie's modern-day freak show.

But I work for another boss, one who holds a lot more than my immediate financial future in his hands.

He's building an army, you see.

At first, when the sister mentioned the "others" I had no idea who she meant. But by the time I made it back to L.A. I had pretty well figured it out. The others: others like him.

He's wearing us down, understand? Destroying our sense of what is acceptable, what is sensible, and he's using the most powerful instrument of mass manipulation in the history of mankind to do it. Watch the television sometimes and you'll see what I mean. But I warn you, the game's afoot. His numbers are growing and the Nielsen's have never been higher. Yesterday's show was called "White Supremacist Meets Long-Lost Black Son On Death Row!"

Our overnights are through the roof.

He's bigger now. He's waiting in that little house on the edge of that vast American desert and he must weigh nearly four hundred pounds.

He's only seven years old.

I don't know how he got the way he is. Maybe he's a mutation, the result of an experiment gone awry. Or maybe he's an alien. The real deal, not one of the phonies we see on a monthly basis on my show.

I buried Susan Jefferson in a dusty field outside San Bernardino. I believe she was intentionally placed in my studio, on my stage, as a lure. Chun King needs big numbers. That means television. I believe that he used his mother as bait, to bring me into the fold.

The sister told me that their parents met while working in the nuclear waste processing plant out at the Air Force base. Maybe the answers to Chun King's origins lie in their radiation-riddled DNA. Their father, a black Air Force officer, was killed in an accident at the plant soon after Mohammed's birth. Such secrets will probably never be revealed.

That's the real tragedy. No one will ever learn how things like Chun King Jefferson and his sister came into being, though I have my theories.

He has power. With a thought, he can cause pain or pleasure. With a glance he can induce pulses of delight that make me forget the things he compels me to do. I've seen him drive a man mad with a whisper.

That night, standing before them in that darkened room, I felt that power. It thunders in my head even now, shatters whatever is left of my soul, and makes me *his* creature. I feel the touch of his pleasure moving along the nerves of my spine like invisible butterfly wings and know that I am damned, a modern-day Judas to the entire human species. And I am not alone.

All over the country there are others like him, more and more every day. They see my show, or others like it, and they come to me, across vast distances they come to me, and through me...to him.

And there are the folds: folds of soft tissue that cover his body, all dermal elasticity gone from the incessant stretching of his skin. There are *things* nestled in the folds of his flesh, things that come out at night to feed. They tell him where his people are.

The other day I interviewed a mother who videotaped herself murdering her seven children. When I asked her why she did it, she said, "Why, for the talk shows of course."

Oh yes, my friends. They're out there.

I'm writing all of this down as a way of earning a measure of peace. When I'm done I intend to drop it in the nearest mailbox. It's addressed to an old journalism professor of mine, a mentor. I think it will do the most good in his hands.

Chun King hates the human race that spawned him, the children that ridicule him on those rare occasions when he allows himself to be seen in public. He means to kill you all, or enslave you, and remake the world in his own image.

After I make my little mail drop I'll go to my apartment. I have a gun there, a syndication gift from Morrie. I'm going to drive out to the little house in the desert and put an end to it, one way or another.

The sister never leaves his side. In her own way she has become as grotesque as he, speaking his word and will, the Oracle of a dark new god.

Several former Guests have moved in with them. One of them is a trucker from Tucson who sleeps with his daughter and can kill with a touch. One man claims to be the reincarnation of Jesus Christ, complete with toxic stigmata, but if I can hide my thoughts long enough to get close to them, maybe I can use the gun.

I had to hurt myself in order to interrupt the flow of his power, the imposition of his will over my own. I'm free, for the moment. An hour ago, I called in a few favors around town. If my plan pays off, the pain will have been worth it. Maybe I can direct the spotlight to where it will do some good. If I can make enough noise before they kill me, the cameras will come. The cameras will always come.

If someone out there sees some part of the story, maybe enough real people will tumble to what's really happening.

As I close the envelope and seal it, I savor the irony. I think about Susan Jefferson's face, and her wide, wide eyes. And as I turn out the lights in my office for the last time, I laugh.

What the Hell.

Maybe my story will wind up on *The Morrie Stapler Show!*

SURVIVOR: MONSTER ISLAND 2025

Salvatore, the blind bus driver from Brooklyn, screamed while Queen Jombodrah ate his legs. Queen Jombodrah, the biggest mutant tarantula on Earth, swallowed. Then she fired a burst of her stun-webs at the bleeding green mountain behind her. Borgo the Brobdingnagian disappeared beneath ten tons of incandescent energy webbing.

Queen Jombodrah uttered her infamous "spider-shriek," snatched up the now-unconscious Sal, and waddled into the shadowy forests of Monster Island. Borgo's mangled, multi-tentacled corpse would last, preserved until the queen returned for dinner. Sal was lunch.

A lone pteronodon glided across the clearing.

A moment later, four tiny human figures climbed out of a hole in the trunk of the Prometheus tree that stood at the edge of the Northern Clearing. Mercedes, the blonde real estate agent and former Miss Boca Raton, spoke first.

"This…is…*bullcrap!*"

"Let's keep calm, guys," this from Geoffrey, the black Wall Street broker from Manhattan. "If we lose focus…"

"Lose focus?!?" Mercedes snarled. "Lose…freakin'…*focus*?"

Ken Obotu studied the other survivors.

Mercedes ran seven miles every day, and followed a daily calisthenics routine that would have ruptured Sylvester Stallone. Their first hour on the island, before the eyes of the other six original contestants and millions of couch potatoes watching at home, Mercedes had single-handedly torn the suckers off a giant leech that had battened onto their landing craft.

And later, while the other contestants were resting before dinner, Mercedes had slipped one of the poisonous suckers into the communal dinner pot, sending Eva, the personal trainer from

Holland, off-island for emergency medical treatment, and making everyone else too nauseous to compete in the "Challenge Round."

Everyone except Ken Obotu. He'd simply commanded his nervous system to convert the venom into a cocktail of harmless proteins. Mercedes had won millions of fans, ensuring her survival until the next episode.

"Sal just got eaten by a giant motherhumping *spider,* people," Mercedes raged. "I think we should *focus* on *that!*"

"Typical female response," Geoffrey drawled, eyeing the floating cameras. "Careful, Marissa. Whole world's watching."

The broker pointed languidly to the closest "game-cam," a glittering silver ball of 21st-century nano-optics that flitted above their heads. The game-cam zipped down from its standard operating height to capture the conflict.

"Wouldn't want the folks back at Hog Piss High to see a crack in the Amazon armor," Geoffrey crooned.

Mercedes shook her sweaty blonde ponytail.

"Screw…you," she said in her thick Florida twang. "And for the last time, it's Hoggsberg High School. *And my name is Mercedes, idiot.*"

"Whatever," Geoffrey sang.

Like Ken's host, Geoffrey was of mixed-African descent, lighter in skin color, with a build the news-vids had described as "pugnacious." Ken had considered forming an alliance with Geoffrey, who possessed the sheer ruthlessness required to win the ten-million-dollar prize.

But Geoffrey's ego was as monstrous as the island's mysterious inhabitants.

"You tricked Sal," Ken said.

"What?" Geoffrey replied.

"You led him into one of Queen Jombodrah's web traps. I saw you do it while the others ran for cover."

Geoffrey smirked and said, "Prove it, loser."

Shouldering his backpack, he sauntered over to the river to wash his hands. Ken followed him.

"You maintain an air of confidence," he said. "But a challenge to your ego, say, by a vastly more dominant personality would shatter the illusion like so much colored glass."

"Get away from me, you freak!" Geoffrey hissed.

Ken nodded and moved away. He'd made the right decision. On Monster Island, foolhardiness was tantamount to hanging a dinner bell around your neck and painting "Come and Get it!" across your backside.

"What do *you* think, Ken?"

Cindy Meinelschmidt, the narcoleptic redhead from Winona, Minnesota, trotted up to him. Small but fit, Cindy's freckled skin burned easily in the tropical sun. She was forced to cover herself in gallons of sunblock to keep from roasting to death. As a result, she always glistened, her skin a perpetual lobster-belly red.

"I think *you* should lead us up the trail," Ken said.

He listened to the stream of pheromones that wafted over him, propelled by Cindy's joy at his confirmation of her leadership skills. He also detected a vaguely acidic *undertrail* accompanying her normal emissions.

They'd enjoyed sexual congress last night, heedless of the game-cams and the roars of giants crashing through the dark. At the height of that experience, Ken had been barely able to control the tiny organic information packets that burst from his body to invade Cindy's reproductive pathways. It had taken all his focus to guide the packets, mentally selecting the most suitable ones while dead-ending the rest.

His efforts had not been wasted. Three months from now, Cindy would give birth to three fine offspring, a male and two females. They would look no different from the locals. In time, they would rule galaxies.

Ken released a burst of psycho-kinetically engineered pheromones to incite feelings of well-being in Cindy while bolstering her courage for the next challenge. Then, because he knew the folks back home were watching, he spread a plume of slightly different pheromones over the clearing.

A second later, Mercedes kicked Geoffrey in the balls and decked him with a hard uppercut to the chin.

While the game-cams bounced, Cindy's smile widened. She laid a hand on Ken's shoulder.

"I've never known anyone like you," she said.

Ken Obotu arched one eyebrow, a gesture he'd learned from

Geoffrey the night before.

"I know."

The island had been discovered twenty years earlier. It lay two hundred nautical miles off the west coast of Japan, at the farthest edge of a cluster of little-visited islands known locally as "The Dumps." Its official name was lost in the tsunami of publicity that followed in the wake of its discovery: an unexplored atoll the size of Manhattan, inhabited by carnivorous creatures the size of skyscrapers.

The first of the "Titanoids" to greet the news cameras was Vyperion, the gigantic, bat-winged rattlesnake.

As the *heli-vids* buzzed around its wedge-shaped, thirty-meter-wide head, trying to capture footage for the global info-net, Vyperion spat burning lances of hydrochloric venom at them, incinerating the heli-vids along with their human crews. Fifty-two brave broadcasters lost their lives that day.

Vyperion had tracked the twelve survivors to a large cave on the northern half of the island, and would have flensed them from the face of the jungle had the atoll's most terrifying resident not appeared at that moment.

"Thanodon Rex's lair is just over that rise," Ken said. "The producers stashed the Dragon's Horde there."

"We *know* that," Mercedes drawled. "How'd this jerkweed escape the vote-off?"

"Ken's a natural leader," Cindy snapped. "Unlike two other people I could name, he'd never betray a teammate."

Ken Obotu shrugged. As the others argued, the bundle of optic cells he'd left in near-Earth orbit high above the island issued a high-priority alert.

'We'd better hide," he said. "Something's coming."

"I don't hear anything," Geoffrey said.

A second later, the trees and shrubs around them burst into flames, and a second after *that,* Pyros the Fire Maggot slithered into the clearing.

"Quick!" Geoffrey shouted. "Into the lake!"

The survivors scuttled toward the glimmering northern shore of Lake Urquhart. Mercedes hit the water first, dove in, and struck out toward the center of the lake.

Along with her stress-related bouts with involuntary unconsciousness, Cindy Meinelschmidt had also acknowledged a powerful fear of water in her videotaped pre-interviews. But now, fortified by Ken's subtle enhancements, she dove in after Mercedes.

Geoffrey the broker, mere steps from salvation, screamed, and exploded in an oily gust of flame.

Ken Obotu recalled what he'd learned about the Maggot.

Pyros's territory lay over the Spinning Turtles, the mountain range that separated the northern and southern halves of Monster Island like the ridge down the back of a sleeping stegosaurus, but Pyros foraged for food on the northern side, which was far more lush with vegetation.

Pyros was the only herbivorous Titanoid known to science. The only reason it ever came this close to the lair of its mortal enemy was to dowse its legendary thirst at the largest freshwater source on the northern side.

Pyros was headed for the center of Lake Urquhart.

Ken Obotu scanned the rocky soil at his feet until he found what he sought. As one of the game-cams zipped toward him, he bent and selected a thin, flat rock about the length of his palm.

His primary mind shifted its perceptive mode and the world became a swirling kaleidoscope of energy matrices, bound together by ethereal lines of force. Facing the camera, he reached out with one of the many bio-electric enhancements he'd installed prior to his arrival and tickled one of those lines.

The game-cam zipped away to film a giant dung beetle pushing its boulder-sized burden up a grassy slope on the southern side. It would only be a matter of moments before the game-cam's onboard computers corrected the mistake and sent it back.

But a moment was all Ken needed.

"Ken!" Cindy cried, unaware that death by Maggot was mere seconds away. Pyros, though a staunch vegetarian, was notoriously territorial of its water supply. He'd been known to boil entire rivers down to the bedrock to destroy a single trespasser.

Ken Obotu studied the flat rock with that special dimension of perception. He sent a pulse of energy along the atomic pathways that held the rock together, agitating molecules, loosening their bonds.

Then he surrounded the rock with a thin shield of force. In three seconds, the flat rock was hot enough to burn through concrete.

On the far shore, Pyros reared up in a searing plume of wrath preparing to incinerate Cindy and Mercedes. Ken Obotu threw the rock. It flew three hundred yards, punched through the sound barrier, skipped seventeen times over the surface of the lake, and exploded, sending up clouds of steam.

Fire Maggots navigated using the glowing ring of sky-blue eyes at their anterior ends. The steam would confuse Pyros, but, more importantly, it would conceal Ken's movements from the game-cams.

As his companions faded from view, Ken turned and raced along the embankment toward the Maggot. Pyros ignited a square mile of lakefront real estate in its confusion. Ken dodged explosions, somersaulted over whirling tornadoes of fire, leapt high into the air, and landed on Pyros's head.

A dozen blue eyes the size of manhole covers swiveled to glare up at him. The air around him grew uncomfortably warm.

Ken opened his mouth and sang.

He'd learned the mating call of the Fire Maggots in preparation for this very moment. Using the formal tone/speech intended to address one of tremendous weight, a sign of high social standing among Maggots, Ken respectfully stimulated certain pleasure centers in the Maggot's brain, while implanting the suggestion that Pyros visit the cave of Infernis, the heaviest female Fire Maggot on Monster Island.

Convinced, Pyros shuddered, turned, and slithered back the way it had come. Ken pitied his companions. By tomorrow, this half of the island would be infested with twenty-foot-long, radioactive larvae.

But he would be out beyond the Pleiades by then.

They were a mile from Thanodon Rex's lair when an earsplitting hiss announced that someone was about to die.

"Sweet Jesus," Mercedes moaned. "That freakin' snake."

Vyperion.

Ken Obotu was communing with his optic cells, so intent upon perusing the latest audience surveys that he ignored his peril: ninety tons of mutated reptilian fury hurtling straight toward them.

"Over there!" Mercedes shrieked, pointing toward the Western sky.

"Where? Where?!?" Cindy cried, trying to look in all four directions at once.

Mercedes planted a foot in the small of Cindy's back and shoved. Cindy stumbled out of the forest and sprawled face-first into the clearing.

The Lord of Serpents struck the ground with the force of an earthquake.

Mercedes bolted toward a cave several yards to the east, while Cindy screamed and fainted. She dove toward the mouth of the cave, her face contorted by the naked lust for survival that had made her the "Number 1 Real Estate Superstar in Broward County."

Drawn by her erratic movements, Vyperion flew *over* the unconscious Cindy and impaled Mercedes on its fifteen-foot-long fangs, skewering the blonde Floridian like a Southern shish kebob. The Lord of the Naga regurgitated a cloud of toxic waste that flash-fried the former beauty queen alive, then swallowed her whole.

Cindy climbed woozily to her feet, her bare shoulders glimmering with X-tra-strength *Sun 'n Fun*. Vyperion half-flew, half-slithered toward her, encircled her in thirty-foot-high coils, its rattle hammering the air like rapid–fire dynamite charges. Cindy clapped her hands to her ears.

"It's just a stupid reality show!" she screamed. "It's not even in the top ten!"

Ken Obotu felt the Alpha-pod throbbing where it hung from his belt clip. No telepathic trick would deter Vyperion. If he died here, in this body, he would stay dead, at least until someone from the old neighborhood could come and back-engineer him, perhaps from whatever remained of him in Vyperion's droppings.

Ken grasped the Alpha pod and raised it above his head.

"Kyaputen…!"

But a sound like the death-cry of planets froze the words on his lips. The shattering roar was repeated. Ken's eardrums ruptured with a wet *pop!* and the world went silent.

Ken turned to face his prey. Even he was forced to admit Thanodon Rex was nightmare given flesh.

The Father of All Monsters stood nearly six hundred feet tall. His skin, which had withstood a direct hit from an ICBM, was a deep greenish gray. Thanodon was part dragon, part Tyrannosaur, and somehow, horribly...part human.

Cindy fainted again. Ken caught her and lay her down behind the trunk of a nearby Prometheus tree.

Pity, he thought.

Cindy would miss whatever happened next.

Vyperion launched itself at Thanodon, its fangs raining venom upon the earth. Thanodon smashed the Naga out of the sky and slammed it to the ground. From where he stood, Ken felt the earth tremble.

Vyperion drove its fangs into Thanodon's right forearm and began to chew. With a heave of his mountain-broad shoulders, Thanodon Rex slammed Vyperion's head against the northern peak of the Spinning Turtles until it let go.

A yellow flash ignited in Thanodon's eyes as he prepared to unleash his Omni-blast, the one power no living creature could resist. But the Serpent King whipped itself backward and spat death into the Death God's burning eyes.

Half-blinded, Thanodon dropped Vyperion.

The Lord of the Naga wrapped its tail around Thanodon's legs and snatched his feet out from under him. Thanodon toppled backward and crashed into the forest, crushing acres.

Vyperion reared high above the island, jaws agape, and unleashed a molten gout of hydrochloric venom. The burning fluid splashed Thanodon's face, scorched flesh, and exposed bone.

Thanodon Rex howled.

Ken Obotu moved. He'd come more than ten trillion miles and he wasn't about to let the trip go to waste. He raised the Alpha-pod above his head and shouted his mantra:

"Fushigi Kyaputen!"

A tremendous thunderclap shook the island as a flash of lightning blasted the spot where Ken stood. When the smoke cleared, he was gone. The shining silver figure that stood in his place bore little resemblance to the man who'd been selected as a finalist for the most popular reality game show on Earth: the dead man whose body Ken Obotu had "rebooted" three months ago.

Alpha Man performed a lightning *kata* to activate the weaponized *chakras* which formed the basis of his offensive capabilities. Cosmic power filled his limbs, expanded them until he was as large as the struggling giants before him. In a flash, the Alpha Pod became the deadliest weapon in the known multiverse: The Red Requiem Blade.

Alpha Man plunged the Blade through Vyperion's rattle, pinning it. Forged in the heart of a newborn star, the Requiem was sharp enough to carve a path to the planet's core. Ken Obotu summoned a fraction of its power to stun the Serpent into submission.

Vyperion spat a torrent of venom into Alpha Man's face.

Ken released the burning hilt of the Red Requiem and staggered backward, the living metal of his helmet screaming in agony, while Vyperion grasped the Requiem in its fangs and tore it from his body.

Ken tried to summon the Red Requiem to his side, but his armor's agony created too much psychic static. Its screams disrupted his connection to the Blade.

Vyperion struck. Alpha Man raised his right arm to block the Titanoid's attack, but Vyperion's jaws slammed shut and severed his arm at the shoulder.

A black burst of dark energy blew the opponents apart.

The servitor-class nano-organisms that inhabited the pocket dimension contained within Alpha Man's armor scrambled to staunch the energy bleed before it could ravage the planet. The servitors sealed the breach with a screech of molecular fire.

Alpha Man climbed to one knee, his defensive shields flickering. Vyperion's eyes were blackened pits. Its tongue lashed out, tasting, searching the air for its foe.

Alpha Man raised his left fist. And the skies over Monster Island turned black. A snarl of lightning gouged a crackling circle of elemental fire around Vyperion. Ken Obotu was loathe to destroy such a magnificent specimen. Monsters like Vyperion were rare in the universe.

Can't be helped, he thought, as the smell of barbecued reptile filled the air.

The force of Vyperion's takeoff blasted the surrounding forest into matchsticks. The King of the Naga rocketed through the air and stabbed its fangs into Alpha Man's chest.

Behind his silver faceplate, Ken's vision failed as neurotoxins flooded his nervous system. The nano-servitors in his blood refocused their energies against this new assault. His primary brain closed off access from his circulatory system, shutting the poison out. His limbs grew leaden as his reserve brain, the techno-organic cluster of cells in his right chest cavity, redirected energy reserves toward neutralizing the river of venom.

The lightning storm broke apart. Without Ken's mental influence it swept out to sea and disintegrated. The crimson light of the Red Requiem flickered and went out.

Is this death? he thought.

He wasn't certain. No one he knew had ever died permanently. Desperate, he peered into Vyperion's mind and attempted to shut it down.

eat. blood. crush. burn.

In response, Vyperion's fangs ground deeper into his throat, scouring his veins with molten lava.

Then, abruptly, the pain stopped.

Ken's vision grew sharper as both brains came back online. His blood cooled as the hydrochloric venom was converted and absorbed. His right shoulder began to throb. If he survived he would have a new arm by nightfall.

Alpha Man leapt to his feet.

A hundred yards away, Vyperion grappled with the Dragon God of Death. Thanodon Rex was dragging the Serpent into the churning waters of the Pacific Ocean.

Thanodon extended both arms, six-fingered hands splayed. Retractable claws, sixty-feet long and razor sharp burst from his flesh. The Dragon became a whirling blur. Chunks of snake meat the size of small houses rained down on Monster Island. Vyperion roared. A luminous eruption of hydrochloric venom lit the night like the wrath of Vulcan.

Ken Obotu summoned the Red Requiem Blade. It rose, singing, and flew to its master's hand. Half gutted, the Serpent reared, even as Alpha Man swung the Requiem in a shining scarlet arc. The Blade bit into Vyperion's neck and passed through. A moment later, Vyperion's head fell into the boiling sea.

Its body remained upright, its tail thrashing the waters. A moment later, twenty malformed buds burst from the bloody stump of Vyperion's neck. Each bud opened two carious green eyes and hissed.

Bloody Hell, Ken Obotu thought. *Twenty heads.*

Regenerated, Vyperion lunged.

And Thanodon Rex struck.

His eyes took fire from the storm, projected twin streamers of heat and force and flash-fried Vyperion with the full fury of the Omni-blast. A soundless detonation lifted Alpha Man off his feet and slapped him onto his back in the churning surf.

When his senses returned, Vyperion was gone. In its place a four-hundred-foot line of ash was the only evidence to suggest that the Serpent had ever existed.

Ken Obotu stared up at the King of all Monsters.

Thanodon stood, wounded but defiant, bright echoes of a terrible power flickering in the amber depths of its remaining eye—power that might destroy even Alpha Man.

Ken Obotu talked fast.

Thanodon Rex left the Earth an hour later.

It would take the transport nimbus five hours to reach the artificial wormhole that seethed on the far side of Earth's sun. Once inside the wormhole, Thanodon's voyage across the universe would be much quicker.

The air shimmered as Ken Obotu sloughed off the Alpha Man persona. As he shrank down to his borrowed six-foot frame, he realized that he would miss being human. He'd developed a fondness for eating and drinking, even sex.

But there were billions of planets out there, talent pools dotting the night sky. Few worlds, however, would host the kind of talent he'd discovered on Earth, talent that would make him the most successful Producer of Entertainments his race had ever spawned.

He'd gotten the Dragon to sign off: a three-millennia-deal that included broadcast rights to both local and neighboring universes, as well as any ancillary income from merchandizing, publishing rights to Thanodon's autobiography, both actual and telepathic, and a host of other perks. In exchange, Thanodon Rex desired only a warm cave to regenerate in and a good brawl once a month or so. Ken Obotu could scarcely believe his luck.

Thanodon Rex was a supernova, a hideously powerful star who also happened to possess nobility, even compassion, the perfect centerpiece for Ken Obotu's latest multi-reality-based Entertainment: *Monster Wars...Live!*

Cindy Meinelschmidt lay dreaming behind her burning Prometheus tree, her head filled with images of custard-filled bear claws and hot cocoa. Looking at her, Ken Obotu experienced a twinge of regret: he would never see the mother of his future children again.

We will care for her, they giggled from the depths of Cindy's womb. Ken nodded. He was a Producer, and there was a big multiverse out there awaiting his next Production.

All seven game-cams were circling now, fighting for the best close-up. Ken waved at the cameras, imagining the uproar sweeping the planet. Earth had officially made the Big Show. Humanity would never be "alone" again.

After a fond last look, Ken Obotu folded the contract bearing Thanodon's mark and shoved it into a pocket universe for safekeeping.

Then he smiled, and sprang into the sky.

THE LAST AMERICAN PRESIDENT

Dear Dairy,
Today in the Oval Office, the secretary of defense tried to swallow his own intestines. It was hard work. (They were slippery.) The slimy suckers just kept gushing out of Secretary Halvorsen's mouth and wrapping themselves around my national security advisor's throat like wet red boa constrictors.

Meanwhile Hally kept making these awful retching sounds. He begged and bounced and hollered like a man cho-hoodlin' down the crapper while trying not to shit himself. No doubt about it, Diarie: whatever the *Vox Mortis* had slipped into him wanted out in the worst kind of way.

Halvorsen shot up out of his chair (to gain more leverage on those guts I imagine) and accidentally elbowed the British prime minister in the nose. Prime Minister Bell backflipped out of his chair and slid under the War Table. It was a good thing too, because it was right about then that the pope turned into a saber-toothed tiger and bit Joan Collins's left arm off.

While the Papal saber-tooth was looking for a place to eat Vice President Collins, Gene Palmer, my National Security Advisor, turned blue and expired, throttled by the secretary of defense's chittlin's.

Outside, Hell was bending civilization over a log and making it squeal like a Christmas pig.

Something big, like *Godzilla* big, strode past the barricaded windows that overlooked Constitution Avenue. I think it was the Leader of the Vox, the one whose name (if spoken aloud) has the power to transmute your bones into ground glass.

Over across the mall, a female Vox was performing an act of double penetration on the Washington Monument. Christian decency forbids my describing it, Diarie. Let's just say that Congress outlawed such acts back in '02, *except* for those constrained by the bonds of holy heterosexual wedlock as defined by our Lord and Savior Jesus Christ Himself. Hell, we're gonna need the entire National Guard just to douche that sucker off.

As Hally's other organs began to chew their way out through his asshole, the Dalai Lama Number Who Gives A Rat's Ass got up and tried to help. He pushed his glasses up on his nose and grasped the spitting entrails that were boiling out of Halvorsen's mouth. But before the D.L. could offer anything more than an earnest tug, Vice President Collins reared up from behind the *Dirty Harry* pinball machine. The Papal saber-tooth hadn't left much of her: only an arm, her torso, most of her legs, and half of her face remained, but the people of the U.S.A. hadn't chosen J.C. as their V.P. for n-o-t-h... n-*u*-t-h...

Aw Hell, Dairy, I don't have to spell it out for you.

With the same pluck she'd displayed during her wonderful acting career, the vice president dragged herself across the room and tore the Dalai Lama's face off. The fact that J.C. was over eighty years old didn't slow her down. The fact that she was dead didn't stop her from ripping that peace-loving pacifist a new asshole. Literally.

Oh well, good riddance to bad rubbish I say. The D.L. was the biggest pain in the ass to my administration ever: always going on about "peace" and "compassion" and "democracy" and blah blah blah blah blah.

Speaking of pains in the ass, I can't believe what the female Vox did with the Monument after she'd pleasured herself. Christian decency forbids me to describe it, Dairy. Let's just say that when we made partial-birth abortions in the United States punishable by death we should have included "Extra-dimensional Iterations of the United States" as well. As of this writing, there's a smoking, fifty-foot-long Vox fetus skewered atop the monument. It's just hanging there squirming like a titanic black maggot.

Occasionally, the fetus extrudes its tentacles down to the ground to snatch up a mess of unwary soldiers and cram them into one of the terrible gaping maws that pucker what I'm taking to be its ass end. (I *call* it the ass-end because of the river of crap that comes pouring out of it every thirty seconds or so, enough to cover the monument with the foulest smelling matter I've seen since we started drilling the La Brea Tar Pits.)

Dr. Maisiella Fletchet, my Secretary of State, pulled her head out from under my desk and whipped a nine millimeter .357 Desert Eagle automatic out of the thigh holster she wore attached to her black leather corset.

As the dead vice president sprang toward me, the secretary of state opened up on her with that big black beautiful piece of hardware (the gun, not Maisy). What was left of the V.P. splattered like the Blue Ribbon Squealer at the NASCAR ANNUAL HOG-STOMP. (At which, incidentally, I had the great honor of throwing out last year's Black Piglet.)

Funny, I never thought about it, Diarie, but it seems like that was just about when the Troubles began.

That's when the Vox Mortis invaded Earth.

The Leader of the Vox, the one with the lethal name, was the first to step out of the great rip in space/time that appeared over Washington. He was the one who first informed the media about his damned race of devils, demons, witches, and whores.

They'd crossed over from another reality, he claimed, "from an Earth eons in advance of this one. One which cast the original cosmic shadow that spawned this pallid reflection."

Yeah. *Sure.*

They call themselves the *Vox Mortis*, the Voice of Death: a race of pirates and murderers, *parasites* who travel time and space feasting on the physical agonies and psychic misery of so-called "Lesser" Earths, depleting their resources, enslaving billions of intelligent beings to help expand their "Vast Empire."

A "vast empire?" Interdimensional travel by alien giants who stalk the spaceways torturing innocent people, impregnating unwilling women, eating children and butt-fucking Mother Nature 'til she rolls over and craps pink lemonade?

What kind of idiot do the Vox take me for?

I'll tell you what they *really* are, Diury.

Demons. Hellspawn. Evil.

I'm talking Big, Technicolor Evil with digital sound, Evil on the half-shell; Evil that could only be foisted on the world by that red-faced trickster who fell from our Creator God Jesus's Loving Grace a couple thousand years ago solely to cause wholesale planetary chaos.

That's right, Dairy: I'm talking about Jimmy Carter.

Just kiddin.' I had him executed years ago.

It's the End Times alright. I just happen to be the one whom the Lord hath chosen to witness His Final Judgment.

"Die, you incense-sniffing motherfucker!" Maisy screamed. Then she blew the saber-toothed pope's brains out. Maisy was a lapsed Catholic herself. Maybe that's why she was smiling when she pulled the trigger.

As Maisy did a victory dance atop the popecat's corpse, the barricades dropped off the doors. Then the doors swung open and a big red Indian walked into the room.

The Indian was wearing full ceremonial headdress, buckskins, and moccasins and leading a dinosaur on a leash.

The dinosaur was muzzled. The "Native American" (Hell, I still think of them as redskins even after what happened after the Vox stole Boston and replaced it with a city-sized open-air cannibal market) was not.

The Indian looked a lot healthier than most folks, seeing as how we'd outlawed exercise back in '01. I mean by 1989 the air and water were so bad that anyone without nose, lung, and rectal filters stood about as much chance of escaping a life-threatening disease as a crack whore working an AIDS camp at Chernobyl.

Hell, I wondered, *How'd we miss him?*

The dinosaur wasn't big. It stood only about eight-foot high. It was smooth, not scaly like the carnosaurs the Vox sicced on Texas when they first invaded. It sported a long, waving tail and a friendly, open expression. If it wasn't for all the blood and bits of rotted flesh encrusted around its jaws, I might have sworn it was smiling at me.

Oh, and it was purple.

"Freeze, scumbag," Maisy snarled, her Desert Eagle leveled and at the ready. The big Indian looked at the two of us for a moment. Then he spoke.

"I'm called Tom Hawk," he said. "I'm here to turn out the lights."

Maisy squinted and cocked her head like she hadn't heard him right. "What did you just say?" she said.

The purple dinosaur growled, a deep rumble that rolled up from its belly. Tom Hawk soothed it with some soft words and a snatch of song. For a moment, I thought I smelled wildflowers on the burning wind, a shimmer of spring that danced across the War Table and prickled my nostrils.

I sneezed, once. My son-of-a-bitchin' allergies were playing up on me again.

The smell only lasted for a moment, though. Soon enough the tang of incipient sunshine was replaced by the odor of frying flesh wafting in off the Potomac.

"I said I'm here to turn out the lights, sweetheart," Hawk said. "You assholes are done."

Maisy lifted one bushy eyebrow and hissed:

"Terrorist."

"Uh oh," I said.

Whatever was about to go down, it was gonna go down ugly. Maisy had a hard-on for towel-head reprobates, even though we'd never actually *met* one, and with his crazy, ethnic get-up and earthen pot complexion, Hawk looked enough like a Muslim fundamentalist to merit a high-velocity Teflon-jacketed Come-to-Allah.

Maisy lifted the Desert Eagle and pulled the trigger a nanosecond before Prime Minister Bell popped up from behind the War Table. Bell never saw it coming. A fist-sized chunk of the P.M.'s skull flew across the room and knocked my Ronald Reagan commemorative bust off its solid gold pedestal.

Maisy snarled and squeezed off another shot. The reinforced walls of the Oval Office rang as the cop-killer slug struck the barricade directly *behind* Tom Hawk. I ducked as it *spanged* off the brass menorah I was using as a toast rack, then Maisy screamed, clutched her throat, and dropped to the floor.

"Maisy!" I screamed. I fell to my knees and scooped her up in my arms. Blood was everywhere. "Goddamit!"

I'd already lost my parents, most of my friends, and my in-laws to the invasion. My wife Lonnie, only three days in her grave, had been torn apart and eaten by something that looked like a giant carnivorous hemorrhoid. I wasn't about to lose the best piece of tail I'd ever had to boot.

"Love you, pookie," Maisy rasped as black blood bubbled up

from between her luscious lips. "I'm...I'm..."

"Shhhh," I shushed. "You're gonna be alright."

The wound to her throat looked bad, but not mortal. I thought she stood a decent chance if I could get her to one of those emergency trauma centers.

Then Hawk freed the purple dinosaur.

The creature leapt up onto my War Table, iron talons gouging white tracks into its imported mahogany goodness.

Then it shrieked like one of Satan's harlots and sprang toward us.

I hauled my white ass outta there.

The purple dinosaur landed claws first on Maisy and began to stomp. As my honey pop screamed, the dinosaur bit and tore at her with those terrible flesh-clogged choppers. It gutted her the way I gutted Social Security back in '06. That goddamned thing did the Camel Walk all over my little chocolate bunny until there was nothing left but red sludge.

I snatched up Maisy's automatic, pointed it at the dinosaur, and fired five shots into its purple skull. The monster's head exploded. Then it fell face-first into the mess it had made of my sweet black hoochie mama.

I spun and leveled the Desert Eagle at the redskin.

"You ain't getting' me, Chief," I snarled. I had three bullets left and I wasn't aiming to waste 'em.

"I didn't come for you, *dickhead*," Hawk shot back. "I came to turn out the lights. You get to watch."

"Oh yeah?" I said. "Watch *this*, Mahatma."

I pulled the trigger three times. Maisy's gun made the Big Bang Bang and the Indian fell over like a dead redwood tree.

I let out a rebel yell and ran over to kick the corpse.

Hawk opened his eyes, sat up and spat out the three slugs. Then he grabbed me and dragged me toward the barricaded picture window.

"Wait!" I said. "Now you just wait one goddamn minute!"

Hawk rammed my head and shoulders through the thin wooden slats, breaking the window glass. Ice and ash filled up my lungs. It was the first time I'd breathed air outside the Office since the Ebola Wars destroyed Philadelphia. I gagged on a stench reminiscent of rotten eggs, burning flesh, and human waste.

Across the way, the Leader was painting the white dome of the Jefferson Memorial using an emptied-out tour bus filled with human entrails.

Dairy, I consider myself a tough man, a cowboy: rough and ready for terrorists, civil unrest, Affirmative Action, or any other evil thing that might arise. But when I saw the image the Leader had slathered across the Memorial, I felt my courage take off and skip naked across the Rose Garden of my mind.

The Indian whistled, a piercing blast of sound that ruptured my right eardrum, and the Leader of the Vox turned toward us. He smiled, his perfect teeth shining like a blaze of lightning, and gave Hawk a "thumbs-up."

The Indian didn't let me savor that vision of Hell for long, however, before he jerked me back inside. Then he punched me in the chest. I felt three ribs crack like wet twigs. While I gasped on the floor of the Oval Office, Hawk made me watch while he took a fire axe to my War Table.

"No!" I wheezed. I'd scored more tail on that table than Oprah Winfrey'd had hot dinners, but when Hawk was done, there wasn't nothing left but a ten-thousand-dollar pile of firewood.

"Time to go, *pookie*," he said.

"Take off your clothes."

The last thing he did was turn out the lights.

Then he threw me out of the Oval Office.

As I lay there butt-naked on the sidewalk with the world burning down around me, Hawk grabbed me by the hair, pulled me to my feet, and whispered one word into my ear.

"Run."

I ran.

Now, I sit here, Dairy, hiding inside this burned-out old bus station wearing a dead man's clothes, while the demons hunt me down. One of 'em almost got me the other day, a big black bastard of a thing that walked like a man and looked like a killer whale with a mouthful of steel teeth. I had to hide in the sewers to escape the fucker.

I couldn't hide down there for long, however. The Dead have taken over the sewers and they have an uncanny knack for tracking warm meat, especially at night.

I found the bus station this morning.

It was filled with regular dead people, folks slaughtered while trying to get out of the city. I could have told them, Diary, that no place is safe. Before the satellites and radio went offline I watched the Vox striding like God's own Justice through every major city on Earth, entire legions of the Damned shuffling in their wake. It's only a matter of time before they smoke me out.

The Leader of the Vox has set a bounty on me, you see?

"The human who brings me the head of the American president will earn power: territories vast and yielding to his every dark desire."

See, I'm the reason they're here, Diury.

The Vox were drawn by the anguish my friends and I "inflicted" upon humanity, or so they claim. Now the whole world wants to hack my head off in the worst frigging way.

I've secured myself a spot in the janitor's closet, all boarded up and locked in tight, but it's only a temporary solution. Five minutes ago the corpses in the bus station stood up and started screaming. I can hear them hunting for me even as I write these words.

But I've got a crazy idea.

I'm thinking if I play it right, maybe somebody with friends in low places will hook me up. Maybe somebody'll give me a job. Who knows? If I'm smart, I might just pull off the biggest comeback since Hitler invaded Manhattan. I've got the experience. Hell, *the Vox already admire my work.* And I think I can teach the Leader a thing or two about human suffering.

The screamers are right outside my closet now, Dairy. They're ripping down the barricades. It's showtime.

I'm ready, fuckers.

Bring it on.

About the Author

M ichael started writing back in the early Pleistocene when, as a young actor, he was injured in a freakish household accident. Unable to work (or walk) for twelve weeks, he took the unsolicited advice offered by a friend, who advised him that creative people needed outlets for their creativity. If he was to avoid madness, he needed to find something creative to focus his attention away from his lack of ambulatory options. He took the advice, and over the next twelve weeks, wrote his first fiction: a terrible screenplay no one will ever read. However, when he finished typing "The End", he found himself hooked. He'd created a story, without the need for agents, producers, directors or studio executives. He'd written something and never looked back. Since then he's written four novels: The Red Wake (Crossroad Press), Revenant Road (Darkfuse Press), Last God Standing (Angry Robot Books), and Who Wants to be the Prince of Darkness? (Angry Robot Books). His first short story collection, God Laughs When You Die, was published by Dybbuk Press, in 2003.

By day, he labors to bring other people's visions to life. He's appeared on Broadway, and co-starred in television shows like *China Beach, Spin City, Arli$$, Instant Mom,* as well as feature films like *Hamburger Hill, The Glass Shield, and The Peacemaker.* He's guest-starred on shows like *Law and Order, Criminal Minds, Gray's Anatomy, The Game, The Goodwife, and Warehouse 13.* He's been married for twenty-three years and have been fortunate enough to father four awesome kids—all of them voracious readers.

Curious about other Crossroad Press books?
Stop by our site:
http://store.crossroadpress.com
We offer quality writing
in digital, audio, and print formats.

Enter the code FIRSTBOOK
to get 20% off your first order from our store!
Stop by today!